FOURTEEN DAYS

A KAT BECKMAN NOVEL

K. J. KALIS

This is a work of fiction. Names, characters, places and incidents either are the products of the author's imagination or are used fictitiously. Any resemblance to actual persons, living or dead, or locales is entirely coincidental.

Copyright ©2020 K.J. Kalis
eISBN 978-1-7334480-3-1
ISBN 978-1-7334480-4-8
All rights reserved

Without limiting the rights under copyright reserved, no part of the publication may be reproduced, stored in or introduced into a retrieval system, or transmitted, in any form, or by any means (electronic, mechanical, photocopying, recording, or otherwise), without the written permission of both the copyright owner and the above publisher of the book.

The scanning, uploading and distribution of this book via the Internet or via any other means without the permission of the publisher is illegal and punishable by law. Please purchase only authorized electronic editions, and do not participate in or encourage electronic piracy of copyrighted materials. Your support of author's rights is appreciated.

❦ Created with Vellum

"If you truly believe in the value of life, you care about all of the weakest and most vulnerable members of society."

Joni Eareckson Tada

1

The chains from the swing creaked a little bit as Jack kicked his heels. He'd gotten heavier in the last few months after weeks of not wanting to eat or sleep. The psychologist he was seeing said that was normal after trauma.

It was a beautiful day. The sun was shining, and the first cool fall breeze had started to form. Kat pulled her jacket closer and looked to her right, "You okay there, Mom?"

Laura looked back at her. "You bet."

Laura had returned to perfect health after her bout with stomach cancer. None of the doctors knew if she had gotten sick on her own or if someone from Apex had triggered her cancer just to squeeze information out of Kat. Either way, the serum that they administered when the military had stormed the Apex building had worked. Laura was back to fighting strength.

Kat and Laura had become even closer over the months since the discovery that Apex was selling cures for cancer in return for information. Selling was a kind interpretation. It was closer to blackmail. Kat didn't know if anyone had gotten to the heart of the organization, but she did know that the man she thought she loved, Steve, had set her up for years, first as her boyfriend, then as her husband and then as Jack's dad. He was now sitting in a prison in Delaware waiting for his trial. Prosecutors had assured her that Steve wouldn't get out of jail during his natural life for his role in Apex. He was an accessory to murder. It was a federal case.

When it came to light that Steve had married Kat as part of a job assignment, Kat worried that she'd lose her relationship with Laura, Steve's mom. To other people, it might not make sense, but Kat didn't have any family of her own and didn't want to lose Laura. It didn't happen. Laura wanted a relationship with Jack, her five-year-old grandson. Laura was a bold woman and understood that although she had done her best with Steve, he had made choices that would now keep him away from his family. She didn't need to be a party to that.

A squeal from Jack interrupted Kat's thoughts. "No, don't do that!" A big caramel-colored dog with a long, thin tail nipped at his heels as he swung past. Woof was racing back and forth under the swing, trying to keep up with Jack. Woof had been the best part of resolving the Apex issue. Him and Van, of course.

Kat smiled, pushing strands of blond hair behind her ear. "Woof, be good," she said. The dog they had found at the Apex industrial park had been their constant companion since that night.

She felt a tap on her shoulder. Laura leaned in close and whispered, "Who's that?"

Laura had been staring across the street at a man who was standing next to his parked car watching them.

"I have no idea..."

A man in a tan coat was across the street from the park,

leaning on his car and clearly watching them. Kat glanced at him and eased her hand back to check that her pistol was in place. Before the issues they had with Apex, she only carried her gun into areas of Aldham that seemed dangerous. Now she carried every day and everywhere she could, legally, that is.

"Hey!" Kat heard a voice from behind them. It was Van. He was dressed in his normal outfit of jeans and an obnoxious t-shirt, although today he had pulled a stained sweatshirt on over it. He was carrying a tray of drinks and a bag with him. "Coffee, anyone?"

"Yes, please," Laura and Kat said in unison. Van handed Laura and Kat each a coffee. As he delivered Kat's he landed a quick kiss on her lips. Standing up, he yelled to Jack, "Hey buddy!"

"Hey, Van!" Jack said, still swinging.

"I've got hot cocoa and a doughnut over here for you."

Jack dragged his feet in the dirt and hopped off of the swing, "Did you bring anything for Woof? He's hungry too."

"Of course, I did. I got him a cookie."

Kat smiled. After the issues they had with Steve, she spent long nights crying and trying to understand how she had been duped into a marriage that was nothing more than a paid business arrangement for Steve. Van, who had only been her editor at the time, stayed with her, helping her to process what had happened and to tell the story of Apex and how they had been selling the cure for cancer by blackmailing people who had access to information, including them.

As Kat grieved the loss of her relationship and navigated the consequences of having given away secret government information, Van stayed with her. Their friendship grew. He spent more time at the house. Jack liked him and needed a father figure. Steve wouldn't be coming back. She had already finalized the divorce and Steve had given up his rights to Jack, growling to Kat the last time he saw her that he couldn't care less for them. Most divorces took a least a year. Steve was so uninterested in anything having to do with Kat and Jack that theirs filed in sixty days.

They took turns pulling treats out of the bag that Van brought. A chocolate chip muffin for Laura, a doughnut for Jack, a cookie for Woof and a raspberry scone for Kat. "Didn't you get anything?" Kat asked, taking a bite of her scone.

"Ate two doughnuts in the car on the way over," Van answered. He glanced toward the street "Who's that?" He nodded toward the man leaning against the car.

Only a couple of minutes had passed since Laura had first pointed him out to Kat. "I don't know, but he keeps staring at us." Kat turned away.

"He just did more than that," Van said. "He waved." Van put his coffee down next to Kat on the table. "I'm going to see what he wants. If you see me wave with my left hand, get them to the car and get out of here."

Kat watched as Van started walking across the field that separated their little group from the man across the street. She couldn't hear what Van said to the man, but they stood talking for a few minutes.

There was no wave.

After a few minutes of nodding, Kat saw Van start back across the field towards them, the man walking next to Van.

Kat was curious. What could the man want -- she didn't recognize him, at least not from that distance -- that made Van want to bring him over? Kat felt her skin prickle. She felt Laura's eyes on her. "You have to trust him," Laura's warm hand touch her own. Kat nodded. Laura was right. Ever since the night when Steve had been exposed, she felt like she was only able to trust people in small doses.

As the men got a little closer, Kat was able to make out more details. He was of average build, maybe a little less than average, with dark hair, glasses and a beard. He was wearing the tan coat buttoned up around him, the collar turned up, a pair of jeans and leather shoes laced up.

Van's voice broke through her suspicions, "Kat, this is Tim Morgan. Tim, this is Kat Beckman, Laura Beckman and Jack."

Behind Kat, she heard a growl. Woof had put himself between Jack and Tim. His lip curled. "Oh Woof," Jack said, "It's okay. Let's go play." Woof looked directly at Kat and she said, "Go play, Woof." With that, Woof and Jack ran back to the swings.

"I've got him," Laura said, getting up from the table and following Jack and Woof, "I'll let you all talk."

Kat, Van and Tim were left at the table. Kat willed herself to relax. Van gave her a nod, "Tim read your piece on Apex and wanted to talk to you about something. He needs some help."

Kat almost rolled her eyes. People who came to them with stories were generally coming with ideas that simply wouldn't fly. She started to say, "I don't know. I'm not really writing a lot right now..."

Van interrupted her. "Kat, I think you should hear him out."

Before Kat could answer, Tim stammered, "I'm so sorry, I didn't mean to alarm you. I called your office a bunch of times but didn't hear back. They said you like to go to the park. I was hoping to bump into you here."

"I haven't cleared my mailbox in a few weeks."

Tim held up his hands like he didn't want to offend her. He seemed nervous and edgy. Tim looked down. "Again, I'm sorry to interrupt your morning, but my daughter has been taken. I don't know where else to turn."

Van pushed him for more information, "Tell Kat what you told me."

"I'm sure you are going to tell me to go to the police. We've done that. They aren't getting anywhere." Tim flopped down on the picnic bench. "We just don't know what else to do. I was just about to hire a private investigator, but then my wife, Alana, saw your article on Apex and she thought maybe you could help."

"I'm not a private investigator, Tim," Kat said. "I'm not sure I can help." Kat felt her heart harden.

"The police aren't doing anything, Ms. Beckman."

"You can call me Kat."

"Thanks. There's been no ransom demand. No report from her or about her at all over the last two weeks. My wife and I are beside ourselves. We don't know where she is or what happened to her."

A bark interrupted their conversation. Woof was bowed down at Jack's feet, waiting for him to throw a ball. Kat watched for a minute as Jack tried to throw it as far as his little five-year-old arms could launch it. The ball sailed through the air. Woof pounced on it and brought it back to Jack.

"Is that your son?" Tim asked.

"Yes," Kat answered.

"Imagine how you'd feel if he disappeared and you had no idea where he was..."

Kat felt like she had been punched in the stomach. Anger welled up inside of her. Who was this man to insinuate that she had some responsibility in finding his daughter? Thousands of people went missing each year. Why was this her problem? "I'm sorry for your troubles," she said matter of factly, standing up off of the table. "I'm not sure this is something I can help with."

She walked off and headed for Jack and Laura. After what they had been through, she didn't need to be taking on other people's personal struggles. She was a journalist, she thought. Not a fixer.

Laura was pushing Jack on the swings. Woof had taken up a spot nearby and was chewing on some grass. "What did he want?" Laura asked.

"He said his daughter is missing. Thinks that I can help."

"Why would he think that?"

"He saw the article that I wrote on Apex."

The article that Kat had written on Apex's scheme had garnered her international attention. That was the last thing that Kat wanted. She knew that the story had to be published, but she didn't want to attract a lot of attention because of it."

"Do you know anything about his daughter?"

"Not much. Just that she was taken a few days ago." Kat took over pushing Jack. "I'm not worried about it. The police are involved."

All Kat could think of was Jack. Ever since that night that she and Van had broken into the Apex hideout in the industrial park, when Van was knocked unconscious and how she had to shoot Edgar to get him to release Jack, her family was all she really cared about.

She turned just enough to see that Van was still talking to Tim. Tim was motioning with his hands and shaking his head. It was clear that he was upset. Van had his phone out and was either recording him or taking notes. From where she was, she couldn't see which one. About a minute later, Van shook Tim's hand and turned to walk towards Kat. Tim stared in Kat's direction and raised his hand. Kat reluctantly waved back. She didn't want to encourage him.

"What was that about?" Kat asked as Van approached them. Van motioned her off to the side and Laura took over with Jack again.

"Tim's pretty distraught. He and his wife took their eleven-year-old daughter, Carlye, to a summer camp they found online about two hours from here."

"What happened?"

"They got her to camp and she called the first week like she was supposed to. A couple of weeks ago, she missed her call time and Tim's wife called the camp office the next morning. Apparently, Carlye was gone."

"How did the camp lose a sixth-grader? Did she run away?"

"That's what he and his wife are trying to figure out. No one seems to know anything."

"Maybe he should hire that P.I. after all," Kat said.

"Maybe..."

2

The way that Van's "maybe" hung in the air told Kat that he thought they should do something. One night, late, they had been sitting in the backyard huddled under a blanket after Jack had gone to sleep. Van had shared with Kat how he saw the work they did as more than just reporting the facts. He felt like they were really fighting for people who had nowhere else to go. By the look on his face, Kat that Van felt that way about Tim and his wife.

They didn't talk about Tim until later on that day, after Jack had curled up in his bed to take a nap. They had dropped Laura off at her house on the way home from the park with the promise to have Jack call her that evening.

While Jack was napping, Kat sat in the kitchen working on a story, her laptop open to research she needed to review. There were still loose ends to tie up on the Apex story. She had planned a series of follow up article releases once the lab got done processing the cancer cure serum.

Van sat next to her working on his own laptop. It started with Van bringing over food for her and Jack. He'd just sit with Kat in case she needed to talk. Sometimes she did, sometimes she didn't. After a while, he started bringing his laptop and just hanging out with them. He went to the office less and less and spent more time at the house with them.

Van suddenly stopped typing on his laptop. "Do you want to tell me why you don't want to know anything more about Tim's story?"

Kat sighed. She knew this was coming. "I would think the police have it handled."

Van raised his eyebrows. "I think that if Tim Morgan felt like they had it handled he wouldn't have come to track you down."

Kat closed her laptop and rested her arms on the table. "I know." The urge she felt to shut down was immense. She felt bad for Tim and his wife, but she didn't want to go near anyone else's tragedy. It was her way of coping. She didn't want to talk about it, but she knew that silence was a killer of relationships.

"Do you want to know what he said to me?" Van asked.

She knew he was probing. She loved that he was gentle in that way. "Okay, tell me what you know."

3

Carlye woke up. It was dark. She couldn't tell where she was. Fear gathered in her throat. It was so dark, a pitchy, inky blackness, that she couldn't see anything around her. She was leaning in the corner of what felt like a truck, occasionally feeling a bump. As her eyes adjusted, she realized that her wrist was handcuffed to a ring on the side of the truck wall. Tears began to fall down her cheeks. "Help," she whispered, knowing no one could hear her.

4

"When you walked away," Van said, "Tim got really animated. Not mad or anything. He just looked really desperate to get help."

Kat put her head down on her computer. She was listening but didn't want to. She'd had enough.

"Here's what he told me. Carlye is eleven. They sent her to a month-long summer camp called Camp Hope out in Bryson, so it's only about two hours away. She's supposed to start sixth grade this year."

"Why did they send her to camp?" Kat asked.

"I guess they wanted her to get a leg up on her academics and work on her social skills. Sounds like normal parent stuff. The parents had done what they thought was their due diligence. They checked the website, called the place, called references. They even drove out there ahead of time. Everything seemed fine until a couple of weeks ago. Carlye was supposed to call home on Sunday. She didn't. The camp takes their cell phones, so the Morgan's didn't have any way to reach her. They called the camp office on Monday morning and the counselors couldn't find her."

"I bet she's just a runaway," Kat said. She knew that Van was interested in this story, but the fight within herself to stay in her own bubble after what had happened was like being pulled by the most powerful force of gravity. It was willing her to stay safe.

Van scrolled down through his notes on his cell phone. "I asked the same question. Tim and his wife don't think so. She wasn't upset and they had told her if she didn't want to go or wanted to come home, she could. There are no markers that would make her want to run away -- no marriage problems, no big changes. Just that she's going into middle school."

Kat sat up, a sigh escaping her mouth. "So, why are you so interested in this case? Tons of kids run away every year. Why this one?"

Van's face hardened, "Because I don't think she ran away. I think she was taken."

5

The truck stopped. As the doors opened, Carlye pushed her small body back against the wall and made herself as small as she could.

A young man with wavy brown hair jumped up into the back of the truck. "How are you doing back here, Carlye?" he asked.

"Nathan, why am I here? Where am I?" Carlye felt relieved that she knew someone.

"I think it is best if you go back to sleep. We have a little time left on the road."

Carlye felt a pinch in her arm and saw the syringe as he was pulling it out. She started to say something, but the words wouldn't come out."

"Night, Carlye..." Nathan said, stepping back out of the truck and slamming the doors.

6

Getting the girls was easy enough and the pay was amazing. What happened to them afterward didn't concern Nathan too much. He was only worried about being able to pay for college. The money they paid him every summer, and sometimes over Christmas, was enough to cover all of his tuition and his expenses, plus have some extra for a little fun on the side. It was a good gig in Nathan's mind.

Nathan shifted around in his seat, pushing his jeans down a little farther on his legs. He rolled his neck and yawned. They still had about eight hours of driving left. After they made the delivery, he and Josh, who was driving the beat-up truck, would fly back first class. That's how it worked. The truck would get back to Bryson somehow. He never knew how that part of the process worked.

He leaned his head back in his seat. He was sure that the client would really love Carlye. She was young, with long blonde hair and intense brown eyes. While she had been out from the drugs, Nathan had taken a look under her shirt. He was sure that she would meet the approval of the client.

. . .

THE WHOLE PROCESS had started innocently enough. After his freshman year of college, Nathan had applied to work at Camp Hope for the summer to save money for his sophomore year. He figured the pay would be okay enough that with some loans he could continue to work on his engineering degree. After about a month at the camp, the director called him into her office. Isla McCall was a short, stocky redhead that he had stayed away from since he started at the camp. He had heard she was tough.

"Thanks for coming in," she said, sitting behind her desk. She shuffled through some papers and pulled out a couple of files. Nathan recognized them as camp applications. "I have a job for you to do. Our normal chaperone isn't available tonight and I have two girls that have been invited to attend a party. Can you take them for me?"

Nathan didn't see why not, so he nodded.

"Good. I'll text you the address. You'll need to leave here at 7:30. When you get to the party, all you need to do is to walk them in and introduce them to Mitch. He will be waiting for you."

"What time should I have the girls back?" Nathan asked.

"You don't need to bring them back. Mitch will take care of that."

"Okay."

That night, Nathan drove the two girls to the party. He met Mitch, a short stocky man with a thick gold chain around his neck, at the door. "Are you Mitch?" Nathan asked.

"Yup."

Nathan introduced the girls to Mitch. As he did, Mitch leaned over a little, "It's nice to meet you. Ready to have some fun?" The girls nodded. Mitch looked at Nathan, "Thanks. We are all set here. Isla told me to send you back to the camp." Mitch pulled out an envelope with cash in it. "Here's a little something as a thanks for getting the girls here."

Nathan stuck the envelope in his pocket, surprised but happy for the extra cash. "Thanks, man."

THE NEXT MORNING, Nathan looked around for the girls that he had handed off to Mitch but didn't see them. He went into the office. Isla was typing on her computer. "What's up, Nathan?"

"Just wanted to check in on the girls I dropped off. I didn't see them this morning?"

Isla didn't even look up from her computer. "Oh yes, I meant to tell you. They decided to go home."

Not wanting to pry, Nathan nodded and left.

7

"Why do you think she was taken? You don't think that Carlye ran away?" Kat asked, getting up from the table to put a pot of water on to boil.

Van talked as she filled the kettle with water and heard the clicking of the ignition on the gas stove. The flame jumped up around the burner and she set the pot on to heat. "I think," Van said, "that it's a little suspicious that the Director of Camp Hope has a background that is only two years old." Van pulled up a profile picture of Isla McCall, Camp Hope's director. "I didn't do an in-depth search, but her social profiles -- all of them -- are only a couple years old. I looked up some other basic information. As far as I can tell, it seems she's only been alive for a couple of years. If she's an adult, she grew up fast!" Van chuckled.

Van's strange sense of humor was one thing that Kat really loved about him. That and his love for sour cream and onion potato chips.

"So, what are you saying?" Kat asked, the kettle whistling. She put a bag of Lady Gray tea in the mug and poured the boiling water over top. While it wasn't the official English way of making tea, it was better than heating the water in the microwave.

"I'm saying," Van said, while Kat dunked her tea bag into the water, "that I think we need to take a look at this. If nothing else, it makes a good story on its own. But maybe we get lucky and we are able to help the Morgan's find Carlye. Wherever she is, she's got to be scared to death."

"If she's even still alive…"

8

After the first delivery to Mitch, Isla asked him to make a few more drop-offs. Every time, the process was the same. He'd put the girl or girls in the van, drive them to a party at an address where Mitch was waiting and then leave them there. And every time, the girls decided to go home right after the party. Nathan never saw them again.

Questions about what happened to the girls rattled in Nathan's mind, especially after his first summer, but with an extra twenty thousand dollars in his pocket, tax-free, he didn't ask too many questions. The following summer, he applied to work at Camp Hope again and was accepted. Isla McCall was still the camp director.

They had hardly made it through their first week of painting, games and tutoring when Isla called Nathan to her office.

"You remember Mitch, right?" Mitch was perched on the corner of Isla's desk, the same gold chain peeking out from the collar of his coral polo shirt, his hairy legs sticking out from a pair of khaki shorts.

"Yeah, of course. How are you, man?" Nathan reached forward and they shook hands.

Mitch nodded but didn't say anything.

Isla spoke next, "Mitch was wondering if you'd be willing to chaperone some of the girls again this summer? He's got to leave here shortly, so he can't take them."

"Sure," Nathan said, remembering that his bank account was almost at zero.

"Good." Isla looked down at her files. "There will be some opportunities on almost a weekly basis. We will have one tonight. Are you good with that?"

"Sure," Nathan nodded.

"Isla handed him a slip of paper. Deliver the Stockton twins to Mitch at this address at eight tonight. You'll have to leave here at seven." The look on her face told him that it was time to leave.

That night, he piled in the van with the Stockton twins, their wild curly hair bouncing with every pothole in the road and sang songs with them on their way to the party. It was the same as he remembered from the summer before, people hanging around eating food, drinking and Mitch by the door waiting for them. Mitch pressed an envelope in his hand before he left. "Drive safe," he said, closing the door behind him.

And so it went all that summer, Nathan delivering girls to Mitch and always getting an envelope for his troubles. A couple of the other camp counselors had asked him if he knew where the girls went. One particularly nosy counselor, Caroline, plopped down in front of him one morning while he was eating pancakes. "Hey, do you know what happened to Tara? I saw her yesterday and now I can't find her. I need to work with her on her math."

Still chewing, he said, "I don't know. Why don't you go ask Isla?"

Nathan saw Caroline carrying all of her gear out to her car just an hour later, her face red. It looked like she had been crying. Rumor was that she was fired for stealing. He never saw her again.

This year, things were a little different. He had the same meeting with Isla and Mitch, but they asked him to go with their driver to deliver girls a little farther out. "You'll be compensated for your time and travel," Isla said.

By this time, Nathan knew not to ask any questions. "Sure," he replied. Isla paired him with a new partner, named Josh. Josh was sullen with sunken dark eyes and long stringy hair. He would take the girls Isla told him to chaperone to a party and then he'd meet Josh out back at the truck for the twelve-hour drive into Colorado.

So far this summer, he'd turned a bunch of girls over to Jackson Maifer at his estate in the mountains.

Carlye was number five.

9

With a strained agreement between Kat and Van to at least meet with the parents, Van called Tim Morgan and set up a time to go to their house. Kat texted Laura to see if she could watch Jack while. Laura quickly agreed. Though they never talked about it, Laura seemed grateful that Kat had kept Laura in their life after what they had discovered about Steve.

It didn't take long to get Jack cleaned up and packed to go see Gramma. He had a backpack on and was waiting by the door by the time Kat and Van got ready. "Come on, slowpokes!" Jack said, pushing the door to the garage open. "Gramma's making lunch for me!"

Kat noticed that Jack's backpack was stuffed so full he could hardly zip it. "Whatcha got in there, buddy?"

Jack threw the backpack up on the backseat of Van's truck and crawled up after it. "I've got all my trucks and my books."

"That's a lot of stuff to take to Gramma's." Kat smiled. Jack had recovered well after his kidnapping, or at least that's what the psychologist had told her. It had been a tumultuous combination of hours of heartache and inspiration. Kids were so resilient, she thought. She hoped Carlye was as resilient as Jack.

TIM AND ALANA MORGAN lived in a nice, two-story home about twenty minutes from Kat's house. Like many of the streets in Aldham, it was a pleasant place to raise a family. Kat noticed that the house, red brick with white shutters, was well taken care of. The shrubs were trimmed, the grass mowed and even a floral wreath on the door. It spoke of a couple who took raising their kids seriously.

"We must be in the right place," Van said, turning the truck into the driveway. "That looks like Tim's car."

Kat wrinkled her nose. She didn't mean to, but Van must have seen it. She felt his warm hand on hers. "Thanks for doing this for me." She tried to receive his comment graciously, but the mix of anger and fear that was swirling inside of her was hard to ignore.

They got out of the car and made their way up to the front door. It opened before they even had a chance to knock. "Thanks for coming," Tim had on jeans and a polo shirt. Kat could see the circles under his eyes from behind his glasses. She tried to imagine what their life had been like over the last few weeks. The realization that Carlye wasn't where they had left her. Knowing that she was out in the world, but they didn't know where. The questions from the police that they probably couldn't answer.

And the guilt...

Tim's voice interrupted Kat's thoughts. "Alana is in the kitchen. She made some coffee."

Kat and Van followed Tim into the kitchen. The house was as well-kept on the inside as it was on the outside. As they walked from the entrance to the kitchen, down a short hallway to the back of the house, Kat could smell something baking.

There was a table with family photos on it. Kat stopped to look. Tim pointed, "That's Carlye," he said.

Carlye was a beautiful girl with pale skin and intense brown eyes. Her long blonde hair hung in a sheet around her face.

Kat noticed that in some of the pictures she was wearing a medal around her neck. "Does Carlye do sports?"

Tim nodded, "Gymnastics. She's really good on the balance beam."

Kat heard his voice crack. She put a hand on his shoulder. "I'm sorry. This has to be so hard."

Tim nodded, "And this is our son, Michael." He pointed to another picture. "He's nine. He's been hiding in his bedroom since we lost Carlye."

Kat didn't know what to say. Though she had come into the Morgan's house skeptical, seeing Tim's pain made their loss more than real. She felt her own eyes filling with tears. She pushed them aside. Now was not the time for emotion.

"I want you to meet Alana," Tim said, walking towards the kitchen.

Van was already sipping a mug of coffee and was standing at the end of an island. On it were plates, coffee and muffins.

Tim's wife moved towards Kat, "I'm Alana," she said, reaching to shake Kat's hand, "Thank you so much for coming."

Kat knew where Carlye had gotten her intense brown eyes. Alana had them as well. She was a petite woman with brunette hair. She was dressed in jeans and a sweater, her pale face glowing white above the collar. "Can I get you some coffee?" she asked, "Or a muffin? I just made them."

"That sounds lovely."

Alana poured a mug of hot coffee for Kat and set it near her, pointing to the cream and sugar. She put a muffin on a plate and handed it to Kat with a napkin.

"Maybe we should go sit down, honey?" Tim asked.

"Yes, yes. I'm sorry. Where are my manners..." Alana answered, leading them down two steps into a sitting area.

Kat and Van took up seats next to each other on a couch, Tim and Alana sitting on either side in upholstered chairs. While Kat was putting her coffee down, Van started, "Would you like to tell us what happened and how you think we can help?"

As Tim started talking, Kat wondered how many times they had told this same story over the last few weeks. It had to be wrenching. "Carlye is a great athlete, but she doesn't always relate to kids as well as we'd like her to. She likes to keep to herself, so we thought if we sent her to camp over the summer, it might help her make friends."

Kat noticed that Alana had pulled a tissue out of the box next to the chair she was sitting in and was dabbing her eyes, "I'm sorry," she said, noticing that Kat was looking at her. "This is just so hard."

"It's okay, just tell us what happened," Kat said.

Tim nodded at Alana. She spoke in a voice that was barely above a whisper, "Carlye has always been quiet and intense. I was like that as a child. We noticed that she didn't have a lot of friends. That was okay. We just wanted to prepare her for middle school as best we could. She's going into the sixth grade..." Alana's voice trailed off as a fresh round of tears poured down her cheeks. "I'm sorry. I don't know if I should be saying 'she is going' or 'she would have been going.'"

Kat glanced over at Tim. He was watching his wife. He spoke while she gathered herself. "Carlye will be going into the sixth grade," he said firmly. "We found Camp Hope online. It looked great. Alana and I even drove out there to take a look one day when the kids were in school. We checked their references and met with the staff."

"Who is the camp director?" Van asked, opening his notebook.

"Her name is Isla McCall."

"And she's the one that you've dealt with?"

"Yes."

Van nodded, "Good to know. Please continue."

"We took her there. She was there for half of the camp session. Each one is a month. She called every Sunday night. They took their phones away so they could concentrate on making friends and their studies without having screens in front of them every minute. We thought that was a good thing..."

Kat watched Tim. He took off his glasses and rubbed his eyes. He looked even more tired without his glasses off than with them on. She always wondered how nurses and doctors did it. Her own therapist had spent hours with Kat as she relived the accident that had given her PTSD while she was an embedded journalist in Afghanistan. It was a sensitive durability she just didn't have.

Kat looked at the floor and felt herself biting her lip. "I'm sure that you did this out of love for Carlye. When did you miss a call from her?"

Alana took a deep breath, "It's been two weeks. She should have called, but she didn't."

Van looked at Tim, "What did you do then?"

"We called the camp the next morning. We thought maybe she was just having fun and forgot to call us. That would have been okay. They said they'd check and have her call. About an hour later, the camp director called us and said they didn't know where she was."

"That was Isla McCall?"

"Yes. So, we called the Aldham police and the camp called the Bryson police. They put out an Amber alert right away, but she was gone."

"What has happened since?" Van asked, tapping the end of

his pen on his notebook. Kat knew that he tapped like that when he was trying to figure out the next step.

Alana stood up, a sudden rage in her eyes, "Nothing. Absolutely nothing." She walked off.

Tim looked at Kat and Van and put his glasses back on. "I'm sorry. We are trying to hold it together, but it is hard sometimes. We go from being angry to sad to scared to death. Mostly scared, I'd say. The police were camped out here for the first couple of days, but since there was no ransom demand, they decided to continue the investigation from their headquarters. Alana is taking this really hard."

"There's been no ransom demand? No communication at all?"

Tim shook his head no.

Kat caught a slight wrinkle form on Van's brow. "Why did you come to find us?"

As soon as the question came out of Van's mouth, Alana came back. "I'm sorry about that. Would anyone like more coffee?"

Kat gave Alana a smile, "We are fine, thank you."

As Alana settled back in her chair, Tim answered Van's question, "We were just about to hire a PI when we ran across the work that you did in breaking the Apex story a while back. We were hoping that you could help find Carlye. You seem to have ways of getting information."

A question formed in Kat's mind, "You aren't confident in the police?"

Tim looked at her, "Off the record?"

"Of course."

He nodded to Alana. "We really appreciate what they are trying to do, but there hasn't been much progress. They brought home her things from the camp, but they seem to be pretty sure that she ran away."

"Do you feel like she did?"

Alana's sobbing caught Kat's attention, "She would never run away. We love her so much. None of it makes sense."

Kat saw Tim look straight at her and Van, "Will you at least take a look? She's only eleven. I can't imagine how scared she is." There was a pause. "She's our daughter and she's out there somewhere..."

10

Carlye started to wake up from the last dose of drugs. The darkness and motion told her she was still in the back of the truck. She felt a wave of violent nausea come over her. She turned her head to the side and threw up. The smell was overpowering. With her wrist handcuffed to the side of the truck, she couldn't get away from it. She tried to scoot a few inches to the side, looking for a cleaner space to sit. As she did, she noticed wetness between her legs. She had urinated all over herself. When she didn't know. She started to cry.

The truck stopped and the back door opened up.

"Oh man, she pissed herself," Nathan said, jumping up into the truck. "You didn't need to do that, Carlye."

"Please Nathan," Carlye whimpered, "I'll be good. Just please let me go back to camp."

11

Kat and Van stayed with the Morgan's for a few more minutes. Tim and Alana shared the names of the detectives that were working on the case. They never saw Carlye's brother Michael.

On the way home, Kat felt Van grab her hand tightly. She sighed, knowing what was coming.

"What do you think?" Van asked.

Kat knew that he was really asking if she would work on the project with him, but she decided to answer a different question. She needed a minute to think. "I think they are going through hell. That poor family."

"That's not what I was asking."

Kat pulled her hand away from Van's. "I know. I'm just not sure what to say."

Van glanced at her. "What do you mean?"

"There is a lot of hurt in this one. No matter how it comes out, the Morgan's are in for a long road. If someone can find Carlye, who knows what kind of shape she might be in. That's if she is alive. If she's not, the Morgan's have closure, but grief."

"That's a pretty clinical assessment." She saw Van frown.

Kat decided to change the topic. "You didn't tell them about Isla's mysterious background."

"No. I'm not sure what to make of it, to be honest. Maybe she changed her name for some reason? Witness protection?"

Kat chewed her lip, "From campers? Probably not. So, what's our next step?"

"Does that mean you'll help the Morgan's?"

Kat stopped to think for a moment. Was she really willing to go into a situation that had

nothing but hurt no matter how it turned out? She stared out the window as the streets passed by. A young family was walking past a coffee shop. She saw the kids stop and point. Kat hoped for their sake that nothing ever happened to them like had happened to Jack and the Morgan's. She didn't want to go down the rabbit hole of the Morgan's pain, but not helping would be worse. She turned back to Van, who had been silent. "We should visit with the detectives, I think…"

"Sounds good."

12

The truck had finally stopped and the back gate had opened. The bright sunshine pouring in nearly blinded Carlye. Nathan jumped up into the truck, unlocked the single handcuff that had kept Carlye lashed to the truck and pulled her out from the corner, dragging her, his hand pinching her arm.

Carlye couldn't remember where she had been or how many days it was since they left camp. All she remembered was being carried and waking up long enough to swallow some water and a little food before the pinch in her arm came again.

Carlye blinked a couple of times. It looked like she was standing at the back entrance of a home. It wasn't a home like she was used to. There had to be at least three stories above looming above her. There were dense woods on both sides of the house and they seemed to be on a slope, as if they were in the mountains. Carlye had never been to the mountains before. Her stomach clenched. She didn't know if there were mountains close to her house. She didn't think so.

The driveway sloped down into a garage that was on the backside of the house. Carlye could see cars parked in the garage. There had to be at least ten of them. From behind the cars, two women walked out of the garage. Carlye had to squint in the bright sunlight. Her heart was racing. She didn't know where she was. She had never known terror like this before. Just as the women approached, she retched again. This time only bile came out and dripped onto her shirt.

"Nathan, I told you not to give the young ones so much!" The older woman said.

"Sorry Dora, she just kept waking up."

Carlye looked at Dora, trying not to throw up again. She was tall and very thin, wearing a red dress and matching red heels. Her hair was pulled back into a bun, like the ones that she used for gymnastics. She had bright pink lipstick on her lips.

Carlye looked at the ground as soon as she saw the woman turn her way. "Carlye, we are glad you are here. We've been waiting for you. Lily, show Carlye to the shower and to her room. She stinks."

With that, Carlye saw Dora turn and walk away. She looked at Nathan and then at the girl that Dora had called Lily. "Nathan, where am I?"

"Oh Carlye, you will like it here. Only our most special campers get to come here."

Carlye felt confused and scared. "Please, will you call my parents for me? Tell them where I am?"

Nathan smoothed the back of her hair, "Of course, sugar."

Carlye heard him laugh as he walked away and got back into the truck.

"We've gotta go," Lily said to Carlye, tugging on Carlye's hand. Carlye watched Nathan get back in the truck and start it up. "We don't want to get in trouble." Carlye felt Lily pull on her arm more firmly.

They walked quickly heading toward the garage. Carlye had to trot to keep up with Dora and Lily. As she followed, there were cars there that Carlye had never seen before in person -- only in the books that her brother Michael had in his room. She didn't know what they were, but they were nothing like the cars that her family drove.

Dora went through a door. Carlye followed Lily to an elevator at the back of the garage. Lily pushed the button and the doors opened. Lily pushed the button for three. Once the doors closed, Carlye looked at Lily. She was clearly older than her. Maybe sixteen or so. She looked a lot like Betsy, one of her favorite babysitters. Lily had on a yellow dress and bright pink lipstick, just like the other woman. "When can I call my mom?" Carlye asked. "I don't know where I am."

"Shhhhh," Lily said. "We can't talk now." Carlye saw her glance up at the corner of the elevator, near the ceiling. "They are watching us."

Carlye felt like she was choking. She couldn't breathe. As the elevator stopped, she felt Lily pull on her arm again. When they stepped out of the elevator, they were in a small hallway. There was a door with a pine tree painted on it in deep green tones. The other doors were plain.

"See that pine tree?" Lily whispered. Carlye nodded. "Don't ever go through that door unless someone comes to get you, okay?" Carlye nodded again. They walked down the hall to the third door. "You have your own private room for now," Lily said. When she opened the door, there were two twin beds in the room with matching yellow bedspreads. The room smelled like disinfectant cleaner. On one of the beds was a blue dress and a few changes of clothes that were folded neatly near the pillow. "That's for you." Lily pointed to a door, "That's the bathroom. Go take a shower. Leave your clothes in there and put the blue dress on. Don't put on anything you have now. I'll be back in a few minutes."

Lily left the room. Carlye heard the door click quietly as it closed. She went over to the bed and looked at the dress. It was plain, with just a ruffle at the bottom of the skirt. She picked it up and took it into the bathroom, turning on the water. There was already shampoo and soap for her and a set of towels. A toothbrush, toothpaste, a comb and a tube of lipstick was on the sink.

Carlye didn't know what to do. She thought it she just took a shower like they'd ask, they'd let her call her parents. She peeled the vomit and urine-soaked clothes off of her and left them on the floor in the corner. She stepped into the shower and felt the hot water cover her skin. As she washed her hair, she stifled back tears. She thought that going to camp would be okay. She was even excited to get invited to go on a special trip with Nathan. He was cute.

A FEW DAYS BEFORE, Nathan told Carlye they had a special field trip planned for her and another girl named Holly. They needed to be ready at seven o'clock. The camp van pulled up in front of the lodge at exactly seven and the girls got into the van, excited.

"What are we going to do, Nathan?" Holly asked.

"We are going to stop at a party."

Carlye looked at Holly and smiled. Holly was fourteen and had a mass of black curls and mocha skin. Carlye had gotten to like Holly. Her laugh was contagious.

About an hour later, the van had pulled in front of a house. Nathan stopped the van and said, "Here we are! Time to go to the party." With that, the girls followed him in. Carlye had expected there to be kids at the party. Maybe kids from other camps. There weren't. As her eyes darted around the room, she saw several men smoking cigarettes and playing cards. There was a woman putting down a tray of food.

"I want you to meet my friend, Mitch," Nathan said.

Mitch leaned over and said, "Hello, ladies. I'm glad you could join us." His breath smelled like old beer. "You must be Carlye." Carlye nodded. "And you must be Holly."

"Yes," Holly replied. "Hey look, they have tacos. Can I get some food? I'm starved!"

Mitch nodded. "You go do that. Carlye, I have something I'd like to show you. Do you like horses?"

"Yes, of course!"

"Come with me." With that, Nathan and Carlye followed Mitch out of the house toward the backyard. Carlye was just about to ask about the horses when she felt a pinch in her arm. "Ow. What was that?" She started to feel dizzy. Before she blacked out, the only thing she saw was Nathan and Mitch smiling at her.

THE MEMORIES BROUGHT a new wave of nausea to Carlye. She threw up again, rinsed the bile down the drain and turned the water off, wrapping a towel around her body. She dried off and put on the blue dress. It fit her, but she didn't like it. She was used to leggings and t-shirts.

She sat down on the bed and almost started to cry again when she heard a soft knock. Lily came into the room without asking. "Are you ready?" she asked. "You didn't put on the lipstick. I left it for you. Didn't you see it?"

"I saw it, but my mom won't let me wear lipstick. Where are my panties?"

"Don't worry about those. Let's just get your lipstick on."

Carlye thought it was strange that Lily was so worried about lipstick. She saw Lily go into the bathroom and quickly retrieve it. "You always have to have this on when you leave your room. Don't forget." Lily handed Carlye the tube and showed her how to put it on. "And, you have to wear your shoes. Don't forget your shoes, ever."

As Lily bent over to help Carlye with the shoes, Carlye saw a black bruise on Lily's arm. "What happened? Are you okay?"

Lily pulled the sleeve of her dress back down. "It was nothing. I fell."

Once Carlye's shoes were fastened, Lily said, "We have to go. Follow me."

Carlye wasn't used to wearing heels, so keeping up with Lily was nearly impossible. They went down the hall and through the door that was painted with the pine tree.

The carpet was thicker on the other side of the pine tree door. Her heels caught in the carpet as she tried to keep up with Lily and she almost fell, catching herself on the wall. They traveled down a flight of steps and then down a back hallway where there were more doors. It felt like a maze. At the end of the hallway, Lily stopped and motioned Carlye to come in.

Carlye was breathless as she stepped into the office. The lack of food, stress and whatever they had given her to keep her unconscious was draining the life out of her. She saw the woman named Dora sitting behind a large wooden desk. The office was much bigger than she thought it would be with windows overlooking a lush lawn just outside, a fringe of pine trees in the distance covered by a crown of mountains. In front of Dora's desk, there were two chairs. There were also two chairs back against the wall. She saw Lily slink back and sit in one of the chairs against the wall.

"You are on time. Good." Dora motioned Carlye to sit in one of the chairs directly in front of her desk. "You look better now that you are cleaned up. I wasn't sure what Nathan had sent us." Carlye watched as Dora started typing something on her computer. "Do you know why you are here?"

"No," Carlye whimpered. "I just want to go home."

"Well, you are going to be with us a while. Your parents are happy that you are here. You are part of a special Camp Hope program."

Carlye felt her spirits brighten, although something in her chest told her that something wasn't right. "What kind of a program?"

Dora suddenly got very stern. "Do not speak unless I speak to you first!"

Tears welled up in Carlye's eyes. She felt them drip down her cheeks and onto her blue dress.

"Stop crying. That will result in punishment. You will wear the clothing we give you. You will eat with the other girls if you behave. If you don't, you will be locked in your room. Is that clear?"

Carlye tried to stop crying. She really wanted to. A knot of fear welled up inside of her that engulfed her. The tears kept coming. She kept hoping that Lily would say something nice or that they'd tell her she could go home. "I don't want to be here..."

Dora stood up from her desk and walked around it. Carlye felt a tight grip on her arm. "Stop crying right now."

"I can't."

The slap came so fast that Carlye didn't have a chance to brace herself. Her left cheek burned. "Stop crying right now."

Carlye collapsed to the floor. "I'm sorry. I'm so sorry..." she whimpered.

She felt Dora's hand rubbing her back. "That's a good girl. Just do what we tell you and everything will be fine. Now, if you can stop crying, we will call your mom."

Carlye wiped the tears from her face and got up off of the floor. She followed Dora to the other side of the desk where Dora dialed the phone and handed it to Carlye.

Carlye put the phone up to her ear and waited for it to ring. One ring, two...

"Hello? Carlye???" Carlye heard her mom's voice on the other end.

"Mom?"

The call cut out. Carlye looked at Dora who had put her finger on the switch, ended the call before Carlye could say anything else. "Now your mother knows you are okay. Lily, take her upstairs and get her ready for this afternoon. She's having her debut with Myra."

13

"Alana, slow down." Kat could hear Van talking into his phone. "Tell me again. What happened? Let me put you on speaker. Kat is with me."

Kat and Van were in the car, on their way to pick up Jack from Laura's house. Laura had picked him up from school for them while they met with the Morgans. Van pulled into a parking lot so they could both hear Alana.

By the time Van got the phone set to speaker, Alana was so hysterical it was hard to understand her. All they could make out was, "She called. She called."

"Alana, try to calm down so that we can understand you." Kat desperately wanted to know what had happened.

"I'm sorry. She called. All she said was 'mom' and then the phone cut out."

"Was there a number?"

Tim's voice came on the phone. "No, it said unlisted."

"Alana, are you sure it was Carlye?" Van asked.

"Yes, yes. I'm sure. It was her."

"Did they ask for anything? Ransom? Did she say where she

was?" Kat's heart quickened thinking that Carlye might have given them some clue where she was.

"No, all she said was 'mom' and that was it. It was like someone hung up the phone."

"Did you call the detective yet? If you haven't, you need to." Van had started the engine of the truck again.

"Yes, we just did. He's on his way over."

"We are too. We will be there in ten minutes." Without asking, Van swung the truck back into traffic heading back to the Morgan's house.

Kat called Laura from the truck. "I'm sorry, mom, can Jack stay a little longer? It looks like there is a break in the kidnapping case."

Without hesitating, Laura agreed and said Jack could spend the night. Kat could hear him in the background, "Can we watch a movie and make popcorn, Gramma?" Hearing him say that made her heart rise in her chest, a stark contrast to the sadness she felt when they talked to the Morgan's. With the promise to text later, Kat hung up. Looking up from her phone, Kat glanced at Van, his jaw set, muscles flexing. She knew he was fully immersed in Carlye's story. He had one hand on the wheel and the other was out the window. Kat's heart rose a little further. She was glad that he was in their life. She pushed her fingers under his thigh.

He looked over at her, "Cold?" he asked, grabbing her hand.

"Not so much. Just glad to be in this with you."

He smiled, lifted her hand and kissed it. "Me, too."

By the time they got to the Morgan's house, there were already two cars in the driveway. One was a police cruiser and one looked to be an unmarked unit from Aldham's police department. The uniformed officer opened the door.

"Hi, we're here to see Tim and Alana," Van said, stepping into the house. The officer motioned them forward.

Kat followed Van into the kitchen. Alana was perched on a stool, a box of tissues nearby. She had her hands wrapped around a mug of tea, the edges of a tissue showing between her fingers. Even though they had just been at the house a little while before, Alana looked totally different. Her hair, which had been neatly combed, was now in a messy ponytail. The sweater and jeans had been exchanged for leggings, a sweatshirt and slippers. Her makeup was mostly off, Kat guessed from crying.

Kat moved closer to Alana and almost ran into Michael, Carlye's brother. He was watching a video on his phone. He didn't say anything to Kat. He didn't even look up. His reluctance to make contact didn't stop Kat from noticing the haunted look in his young eyes.

Van moved over to the detective, who was talking to Tim. There was also a tech with them, who had set up a laptop on the other end of the counter from where Alana was sitting and looking at the display on their phone.

"Alana?" Kat whispered as she got close to the stool where Alana was sitting and staring. Alana surprised Kat by jumping off the stool and wrapping her arms around Kat's neck. Kat could feel Alana's hot tears as they hugged. Kat pulled back, her hands on Alana's shoulders.

"Let's sit down. Tell me what happened."

Alana did as Kat asked. She pulled a few new tissues out of the box and blew her nose. "I was just sitting here and the phone rang. It was the landline. We've kept it just in case of a power outage, you know..."

Kat nodded, trying to encourage her to continue telling the story.

"When I picked up there was a little pause. I felt like it was Carlye. Then, I heard her little voice say, 'Mom.' Before I could ask her anything, the line cut out. It was like someone hung up."

Kat nodded again. "Are you sure it was her?"

Alana stared at Kat. "You have a child, don't you?"

"Yes."

"You'd know your child's voice, wouldn't you?"

Kat instantly felt bad for questioning Alana. "I didn't mean…"

"It was Carlye. I know it. Someone has her."

KAT SAT with Alana for a few minutes, just letting her cry, until Van tapped her on the shoulder. "Can you come over here?" he asked, motioning with his head toward the detective, who seemed to be waiting for them.

Kat got off the stool and joined Van. "This is Detective Traldent. He's the one working on Carlye's case."

"Please, call me Lance." Kat shook his hand. He was very tall and very thin. He had on a black suit with a light blue shirt that looked like it barely stayed on his frame. His hair was cut neatly, very short, and he had a pad of paper in his hands. "Your husband was telling me…"

"We aren't married."

"Sorry. Let me start again. Van told me that the Morgan's reached out to you for some additional help. I've got no problem with that as long as we have some ground rules."

Kat was surprised. In her years of being a journalist, law enforcement usually had a problem with reporters getting involved in an ongoing investigation. They didn't want to have their evidence compromised or their leads exposed to the general public before they made an arrest.

"Go on."

"If you find out anything, you'll call me before you go to print. You won't do anything illegal that might compromise my investigation. And, you'll let me know if you get any new leads. Sound reasonable?"

"It does." Kat wondered why Lance was being so accommodating. "Let me just ask you this -- why let us get this close to the investigation? I'm just curious."

"Your reputation precedes you. I read the Apex article."

Kat saw a sly smile start to crawl across Van's face, "I'll bet he ran a background check too."

Lance chuckled. "Yes, I did that as well. Thank you both for your service to our country." He flipped to a different page in his notebook. "How about if we go outside and I'll give you what we've got so far while the tech works with the Morgan's."

Kat and Van fell in behind Lance as he walked out the front door, nodding at the officer who was standing guard. When they were out of earshot, he said, "I have to tell you that we don't have a lot of information to go on at this point." He flipped to another page in his book. "When we got the initial report, we suspected a runaway or that maybe Carlye had just gone off with a friend to camp overnight without telling the counselors. After we sent out the Amber alert, which got no results, by the way, we've been pretty much dead in the water. We've checked into the camp, the counselors and the staff. Doesn't seem like anyone has a history."

Van interrupted. "Did you notice that the camp director has only been alive for two years?"

Lance squinted, "What do you mean?"

"We did a little of our own background work. Isla McCall, or whatever her name is, only has a profile anywhere that is two years old. Check her social media accounts and her financials. You will see what I mean."

Lance scrawled a few notes on his paper. "Yeah, I didn't see that. We have techs looking at that right now. Have you found anything else?"

Kat looked at him, wondering if he really didn't have any

other information. "We think that the family is credible. Tim and Alana seem legitimately upset and grieved."

"I'd agree with that."

"The son seems too young to have a part in what is going on."

Lance nodded. "Anything else that you've come up with?"

Van shook his head, "No. We had only left their house a little while ago when Alana called about Carlye. Do you think it was the real deal?"

"I'd like to think so. We are looking at their call history now. The call came in as a restricted number. My tech is working to see if we can figure out where the call came from. It might take some time, though. It may require a warrant. We'll have to get a judge to sign off on that before the carrier will give us any information."

Kat heard Van sigh. "If it really was Carlye, what does that tell us?"

Lance grimaced and tilted his head to the side. "Not much, other than she was alive when she called."

14

Detective Lance Traldent said goodbye to Van and Kat with the promise that he'd let them know if anything broke with the case. He got into his department-issued car and headed back to the office, his suit coat neatly folded on the backseat.

As he was driving back to the station, he realized that not having many serious cases was a benefit to working in Aldham. Less heartache. Less headache. People always thought that police officers were able to just do their jobs and then go out for a beer after. It didn't work that way. Not only did the officer suffer through the case, many times the officer's family did too.

That was the reason that he and his wife had split up.

A particularly difficult case had haunted Lance for a year after it went cold. The murder of two people by a river. A man and a woman. There were no leads. There was no surveillance. The man's body had fallen back into the water after he'd been shot point-blank in the head. First on the scene, Lance had gone into the water to pull him out, hoping he was still alive. He wasn't. Lance found himself sitting in the back of an ambulance getting checked out and the man's blood cleaned off of him.

He didn't know why the case had hit him so hard. It was just the unsolvable nature of it. With little evidence and no leads, there was no way they could move forward with an investigation. It ate at him night after night. He didn't sleep. He couldn't eat. He saw a doctor and a therapist after he'd lost thirty pounds.

It seemed so senseless.

A casualty of the case was his marriage. He and his wife, Ronna, weren't divorced yet, but he knew that if he didn't get himself together, that would be their next step.

Lance parked his car in the officer's parking lot and used his ID to get through the backdoor of the department. It wasn't a big police department. About forty full-time officers, three detectives, a K-9 team and a couple of part-timers along with some administrative staff. They were usually busy with small collars -- drinking, speeding, two kids getting it on in the back parking lot of a building where they thought their parents wouldn't find them. Missing kids wasn't the norm.

He nodded at a couple of the other guys as he went back to his desk. He stopped in the break room and made himself a cup of coffee, juggling the mug and his notebook on the way to his desk. Once he sat down, he pulled up his notes and logged into his computer, adding the newest information to the case file. Hopefully, all of the information would amount to something at some point.

It was a helpless feeling being a detective. He wanted so desperately to be able to do something for the Morgans. He knew in his gut that something terrible had happened to Carlye. He just needed enough information to make a story out of it. Something he could hang his hat on so they could find her. He wasn't sure he would have that chance. The longer that a child was missing, the worse the outcome usually was.

One of the admins, Jenny, interrupted his train of thought,

"Hey Lance, there's a mom and daughter here to see you. I put them in room three."

"What about?"

"I'm not sure. Said they could only talk to you."

"Thanks."

Lance closed his computer and stood up, pulling up his pants. He'd have to try to remember to eat. He stopped by Jenny's desk on the way to see the mom and the daughter. "Can you do me a favor?" Jenny nodded. "Can you call Duke's and order me a turkey sub and have them run it over?"

Jenny smiled. "Put it on your tab?"

"Yup."

"I'll get you fries and a cookie too."

"Thanks." Apparently, his weight loss hadn't gone unnoticed in the department. He made a mental note to work on that.

Lance had barely gotten into the interview room when the girl blurted out, "You have to help Carlye!"

Trying to be as calm as possible and quickly realizing that this could be the break he was looking for, Lance set down his coffee and notebook and said, "Do you know Carlye?"

"Yes, but I don't know what happened to her."

Before the girl could say anymore, her mom interrupted. "Detective, I'm so sorry. I'm LaDonna Jenkins. This is my daughter, Holly. She thinks she was at camp with the girl that you have been looking for."

"It's nice to meet both of you," Lance opened his notebook. "Give me one second, please."

Lance got up and opened the door, giving Jenny a nod that told her to turn on the interview room surveillance. If this was about Carlye, he'd want to watch it again later. "Sorry about that, please go on."

"It took some work for my husband and me, but we finally

convinced Holly to tell you what happened. Holly said she would come in and talk, but it had to be only to you. She saw you on television. She's afraid and doesn't want anyone else to know."

"That sounds perfectly reasonable." Lance knew that in situations like this it was better to let people tell their story and ask questions later. If Holly did have anything to say, that is. "Holly, I'd love to listen to what you have to say. Is that okay?"

"I guess so." Holly was a beautiful girl with a wild mane of black, curly hair that framed her face.

"Were you at camp with Carlye, the girl we are looking for?"

"Yes, I told you that! Weren't you listening?" Holly erupted.

"Holly Jean..." LaDonna said.

"Sorry, mama."

"I know you are upset, but please remember your manners."

Lance watched the two of them, appreciative of the fact that LaDonna was quick to help her daughter stay calm.

"Holly," Lance said carefully, "Can you tell me what happened?"

Holly straightened up in her chair and closed her eyes for just a moment as if she was trying to gather herself. "It was about a week ago or so. Carlye and I had become friends at Camp Hope. She was new there. She needed someone older."

Lance started writing in his notebook. "You said you are older. How old are you, Holly?"

"I'm fourteen. Carlye is eleven."

Lance nodded, encouraging her to continue.

"That afternoon, Nathan, one of the camp counselors, told us to be ready at seven o'clock. We were going to get to go and do something special. Carlye and I got ready and met him at the front of the lodge door. We got in the van with him."

"Did you know where you were going at that time?"

"No. We just got in the van. He was one of the counselors, you know? We were supposed to be able to trust him." Holly's voice cracked.

Lance saw LaDonna lean over and whisper into her daughter's ear. Lance could barely make it out, "You are doing just fine, baby."

Holly straightened again. "So, we went to the party and met this guy named Mitch. I think that was his name."

As he wrote the name down, Lance couldn't tell if she was going to continue the story. "You said his name was Mitch?"

"That's right."

"What happened then?" Lance looked up from his notes. LaDonna was staring at Holly. She looked like she was willing her daughter to speak.

"Mitch said there was food in the kitchen. I was hungry so I went to go get something to eat. There was a woman there wearing an apron. I guess maybe she was making the food? I went to the counter to grab a sandwich and she came up behind me. She grabbed my arm and pushed me toward a side door that was in the kitchen. She whispered, "Run! Get away from here as fast as you can! They are trying to take you." Tears started to run down Holly's face.

Lance got up and retrieved a box of tissues and a small bottle of water from the counter behind the table. "Here." He gave her a moment and then leaned forward on the table. "Holly, you are so strong for coming to us and telling us the story. Can you tell me what happened next?"

Holly wiped her eyes and sighed, "I was so scared. We were out at some house in the woods. I ran and ran. I was so worried about Carlye, but I was too frightened to go back to the house. The lady told me to go. I didn't even know what she meant. It was dark, and I fell a couple of times, but I made it out to the highway. There was a gas station there. The man who was working let me call my parents and hid me in the back until they came to find me."

Lance felt a glimmer of hope for the first time in weeks. Holly knew what had happened to Carlye. It had almost happened to her. Questions were lining up one after the next in Lance's mind. Before he could ask them, LaDonna pushed a piece of paper toward him. It had an address on it. "Here's where we found Holly. We are truly sorry that we waited to come forward. After what happened, we were just so scared. I hope you understand."

"I just appreciate that you did come forward. It took a lot of courage."

Lance saw Holly look down at her lap, "I'm so worried about Carlye. Do you know anything else? Has anyone seen her?"

"We do have a lead that we are following up on. But you have given us so much more to work with." Lance reached out and squeezed her hand. "Now, would you be able to stay for a little bit longer? I'd like to have you work with a sketch artist on a picture of Mitch and get some more information about Nathan. Would that be okay?"

"Yes, I think so."

"Good. Now, are you hungry?"

Holly nodded. "Great. Let's get some lunch in here for you and your mom to eat while we finish up. Just give me a minute, okay?"

Lance got up from the table and stepped outside the room. "Jenny?" he called. She was sitting at her desk. "We've got a break in the Morgan case. I need Stu in here to work with Holly on a sketch right now." Jenny nodded. "And, we need food for these people. Can you help me out with that while I get some things organized?" Another nod.

Lance went over to the door and stuck his head in, "It will be just a moment, ladies. Jenny will be in to chat with you about lunch and Stu is coming to help you with a sketch. We will be right out here if you need us." He closed the door and went and sat down at his desk, his mind racing with the new information. Was this the break they needed? He wondered if they were too late.

15

After the sting of the slap and hearing her mom's voice, Carlye could barely hold it together. She followed Lily out of Dora's office and they went back upstairs, through the door with the pine tree on it. Neither of them said a word. Carlye occasionally sniffled and tried to wipe her nose with her hand. When she put her hand down, it was covered in pink lipstick.

At the other end of the hall from her room, there was a small dining area. It had two cheap tables and plastic chairs pushed in against them. There was a small refrigerator at one end of a counter and a sink. "This is where we eat," Lily said quietly, although there was no one else in the room. "There are crackers and juice for breakfast and lunch. We get some meat and vegetables for dinner."

Carlye wasn't sure she could eat. She felt sick to her stomach. Lily must have picked up on her unwillingness to eat. "I know you probably don't feel hungry, but you should have a little something. If you get too weak, they will send you away." Lily's body stiffened and her face became pale. Carlye knew that getting sent away wasn't a good thing.

"I can try some juice, maybe," Carlye said, sitting down at the table. Lily handed her a small cup with some orange juice in it and sat near her. The cool liquid felt good going into Carlye's stomach. She couldn't remember when she had eaten last. All she remembered from the last few weeks was waking up somewhere, being allowed to use the bathroom, and given a little food and water before she'd feel the pinch in her arm that knocked her out.

"What is going to happen to me this afternoon?" Carlye asked as soon as she finished her juice.

Lily looked away, "I don't know. Just listen to Myra. She will help you."

Terror reached up and pulled at Carlye's insides. She had to fight to keep the juice down. More tears welled up in her eyes. She thought that Lily might try to help her, to at least tell her that she would be okay, but all she did was stand up. "We have to go." Lily walked over to the counter and pulled an anti-bacterial wipe from the container on the counter. "Dora will get mad if we leave a mess."

Carlye watched as Lily scrubbed the table, her face just inches from the table, looking for every little spot. She carefully checked each chair and the floor for any sign they had been there. She put their cups and the wipe neatly in the trash. "We need to go," Lily repeated, whispering. Carlye stood up to leave, ready to follow. "You have to push your chair in. I told you, Dora will get mad," Lily hissed.

"Sorry," Carlye whispered back. Carlye followed Lily down the hallway and back to her room. "Go in and don't come out unless someone comes to get you, okay? If you don't stay in, they will lock you in." Carlye nodded and watched Lily go to the end of the hall and enter a room on the right-hand side of the hallway. Carlye clicked the door closed and sat down on the bed. There was nothing else to do but wait.

16

The next few hours at the station were busy. Stu, the department's sketch artist, met with Holly and LaDonna and worked on an image of the man named Mitch -- if that was his real name. Lance moved in and out of the room asking questions and getting more information. The lunch that Jenny got for them, pizza and salad, seemed to perk up Holly and LaDonna enough to keep them talking. That's what Lance needed right now. Witnesses who would keep on talking.

As he was walking toward his desk to run a background check on Nathan the camp counselor, LaDonna caught him.

"Everything okay?" Lance asked.

"Oh yes, yes. I just wanted to apologize again for not coming forward sooner. You have no idea how scared Holly was when we found her."

Lance perched on the edge of the nearest desk. "Can you tell me more about that night?"

LaDonna nodded, "We got a call at about nine o'clock. Her dad and I were just watching some television. There was a man on the other end of the line. He said that he had our daughter there and that she needed to talk to us. It was an emergency."

Lance saw LaDonna's chin quiver. "It's okay. You are doing fine."

LaDonna nodded, "Holly got on the phone and was hysterical. We could tell it was her, but we couldn't make out what she was saying. It was so bad that her dad told her to put the man back on the phone. He gave us his name and the address of the gas station. He said he'd stay with her while we drove out to get her. It was the longest hour of my life..."

"I'm sure it was. What did you find when you got there?"

"The guy at the station walked us back to the manager's office. I gave you his name already. He was very nice. He took us to the back where the offices were. Holly was hiding under the gas station manager's desk, curled up like a scared kitten. We could barely get her out."

"Did you go straight home after that?"

"Yes. We packed her up, wrapped her in a blanket we had in the back of the car -- she was shivering even though it wasn't that cold. I sat in the back with her while her dad drove."

"When she got home, was she any better?"

"Not really. She ran up to her room and locked the door. Has barely been out of it since. I think not knowing what happened to Carlye has been eating at her, but she keeps saying that she's afraid that the men will find her. She's basically been locked in her room for the last week or so."

"How did you finally get her to agree to come in?"

"We started seeing the information about Carlye on the news. We put two and two together. Her dad wasn't sure Holly could handle the information, but I know my girl. She's tougher than she looks. I knew it was eating her up inside. I called our pastor and told him to get to the house right away. He'd already been over to talk to her a few times, but this time he and I showed her the stories about Carlye. She cried and said she needed to do something. That's how we ended up here."

Lance took a minute to process the information that LaDonna had shared. Whatever had happened to Holly in that house had been enough to spook her into being silent. "Thank you, Mrs. Jenkins. I appreciate what you have done."

She put her hand up in a dismissive wave and walked back to the room where Holly was. Lance barely had a chance to check through his notes when the tech officer that had been at the Morgan's with him a few hours earlier stopped at his desk, "Bad news."

"What happened?"

"The call from this morning, we can't track it. They used a VOIP system and bounced the call all over the place. Best we can get is the western United States. Sorry."

As the tech walked away, Lance frowned. Tracking a VOIP call was nearly impossible. They were routed over the Internet and couldn't be traced most of the time. Carlye might have called her mom, but there was no way to track it and no way to tell where she was. Fourteen days was a lot of time to travel. She could be anywhere.

17

"Thanks for the update. We are on our way."

Kat watched as Van stopped pacing on the other side of the window and ended the call on his cell phone. After leaving the Morgan's house, they had stopped for a quick dinner. Detective Traldent's call came just as they were finishing up. Van had gone outside to take the call, but Kat had been watching the entire time, trying to make out what Van was saying.

"What's going on?" Kat probed as soon as he got back to the table.

"There have been a couple of developments. If you've had enough to eat, we should take a ride."

Kat smiled, "I know that you already told him that we were on our way..."

"Reading my lips again?" Van laughed and gave her a quick kiss. "Yes, I did tell him that we are on our way, so whenever you are ready."

"That would be now." Kat got up, grabbed her bag and pushed her blonde hair behind one of her ears to get it out of her face. She pulled the sunglasses that had been resting on her head off and put them in her bag. It was starting to get dark now. She wouldn't need them.

Van started up the truck. They pulled out of the restaurant parking lot and Kat could tell they were headed to the highway. "Where are we supposed to meet Lance?"

"It's a gas station. He said he would tell us more when we get there."

Kat searched for the address on her phone and realized it would be about a forty-five-minute drive if they didn't hit traffic. Van always had music playing in his truck. She heard him humming along to a song that she didn't recognize.

Staring out the window, Kat escaped into her own thoughts. She briefly wondered what Jack and Laura were doing, hoping that Jack was okay. Woof was with them, too. That always made Kat feel better.

The countryside passed by them in almost a blur as they made their way out of Aldham. Best as Kat could tell from her search results, the gas station they were going to was closer to Bryson, where Camp Hope was located. Trees and shrubs passed them on each side of the road. Kat wondered about Carlye. Was she still alive? Fourteen days was a long time for a child to be her own. Especially one who was only eleven. Had she been taken? Had she run away? Although Alana seemed to be sure that her daughter had been kidnapped, they didn't have any evidence of that yet. Kat hoped that Detective Traldent had information they could all act on, or at least as much as he'd let them.

Kat knew this was a police investigation. She knew that in the eyes of the law, she and Van were just journalists. She also knew that for some reason -- maybe because of their military backgrounds -- Traldent was willing to keep them in the loop.

Kat rounded her back to stretch it out, trying to shake the achiness she was feeling from the stress of worrying about Carlye. Kat wondered where she was and what she was doing.

A prickly feeling rose in Kat's stomach. She took a couple of deep breaths to try to force her own anxiety back into its place.

Ever since the Apex story broke, her own PTSD from the fiery IED attack she'd survived in Afghanistan had improved. She didn't know why. What used to be debilitating memories had now faded. Her therapist guessed that the fact that she saved Jack's life had returned her life to something of its normal axis, whatever that meant. Kat had thought and thought about her therapist's comment. It had been rattling in her head. The only thing she could figure is that she no longer felt like a victim.

Not that she was happy that she had killed someone. She'd have to carry that weight for the rest of her life. The only thing that made it better was that Jack's life had been in imminent danger. There had been a knife to his throat. It was justice. Kat just wished that she hadn't had to be the one to deliver it.

She rolled her wrist a couple of times. "Is it bugging you again?" Van asked. He knew that Kat had a habit of rolling her wrist, the one that had been shattered in Afghanistan, when she was having a bout of PTSD.

"Naw, I'm okay. I was just thinking about Carlye."

Silence enveloped the truck. It was a reality that neither of them wanted to think about. Carlye wasn't at home with her family. She wasn't getting ready to start middle school. She was somewhere they couldn't see and couldn't find. Kat hoped they could get to her in time. If there was any time left.

The truck's tires made a grinding noise as they pulled off of the two-lane highway and into the gas station. After leaving Aldham, the traffic thinned and the four-lane road narrowed to two lanes. Van pulled the truck into the station and parked the truck off to the side. "We are here."

Kat could already see Detective Traldent's car parked right in front of the door to the station's mini mart. A police cruiser from Timborough was sitting in front of the garage bay doors. They got out of the truck and headed to the door.

A bell, suspended from the closer on the door, chimed as they walked in the door. It smelled like a gas station mini mart, the combination of grease and sugar wafting through the air. Kat hoped she didn't need to use the bathroom. Gas station bathrooms weren't always very clean. She wasn't sure that the Timborough station was any different.

Detective Traldent gave them a head nod when they came in. He was standing by the checkout counter talking to another officer. He waved them over. "Kat, Van, meet Officer Norland from Timborough."

"Nice to meet you." Van and Kat took turns shaking his hand.

"Officer Norland was able to get here sooner than I could. He's been holding down the fort. Let's go outside so I can give you an update."

Kat followed Van and Lance back outside. The outdoor lights for the station had come on. A red car pulled in to get some gas, the driver peering at the police cars. It pulled out slowly and kept on driving down the road. Kat couldn't tell if they were just staring at the commotion from the police, but she wondered if they were connected to Carlye's disappearance.

"I guess I'm not good for business," Lance chuckled, pulling his notebook out of his pocket.

Kat saw Van smile and then look right at Lance. "What's going on?" Van asked. "Why are we out here?"

"I'm getting to it. Hold on for a sec so I can pull up my notes."

Lance thumbed through his notebook. There was something about his old-school note taking that fit him perfectly. It was like he came from another time and another era. She almost expected him to wear men's pajamas, slippers and a robe when he was at home.

"Here's where we are. You know about the call that came in just after you left the Morgan's the first time. Here's the data we have. It lasted for nine seconds. Mrs. Morgan picked up, said hello and then heard Carlye's voice say 'mom.' The call ended right after that."

"Were you able to trace the call?" Kat immediately jumped to finding Carlye. Was she here at the gas station?

"We tried. The call was placed over VOIP. There is no way to trace it. The best that we got was the western United States. That's it."

Kat saw Van's brow furrow, "Are we sure that it was Carlye that called? Do we know if she was with anyone else?"

Lance shook his head. "All questions I'd love to have an answer to."

A thought passed through Kat's mind. She hesitated before saying it, "Are you sure it was Carlye? I asked her and she said it was. I wondered what you thought?"

Lance chewed his lip. "That occurred to me as well. I'm not sure it was, but Alana is one hundred percent positive. We didn't have a recording device attached to their phone, so I don't have a definitive answer."

Van shifted from side to side, "So why are we here? What does this gas station have to do with Carlye?"

"That's where things get interesting..."

18

An hour passed, maybe two. Carlye was too frightened to do anything except sit on her bed. Even if she had the energy to do something, there was nothing to do. A few times she had walked to the door and turned the knob to make sure it was unlocked. She didn't dare open it. The reality of her situation was sinking in. She didn't know where she was. She didn't know who these people were or what happened to Nathan or when someone would take her home.

She had just started to think about home, trying to push the tears back down her face when the door opened. A girl walked in the door, wearing a similar blue dress to Carlye's and the same pink lipstick. The girl whispered, "Carlye?"

"Yes?"

"It's time. Come with me. I'm Myra."

Carlye got up off of the bed and followed the girl who had come to get her. She felt numb, but her heart pounded in her chest.

Myra didn't walk quite as fast as Lily, so Carlye was able to keep up a little bit better. They passed through the pine tree door but stayed on the same level as the room she had been staying in. As Carlye followed her she noticed that Myra's dark brown hair was braided. She looked exotic to Carlye, like she was Latin or Indian. Questions tried to form in Carlye's mind, but she was too exhausted and scared for them to come out of her mouth.

A few more turns and Carlye followed Myra into a dark room that was lit by candlelight. There were two cushioned tables and a large armoire with white robes in it against the wall. "We will go out first so Mr. Maifer can see us and then if he approves, we will come back in here to change." Carlye didn't say anything. "It's really important that you don't say anything. Do you understand? He doesn't want to hear us speak."

Carlye felt confused and even more terrified, but she followed.

On the other side of the room was a door that led right out onto a patio. Carlye realized from the view that they had to be on the second story of the building. The view was beautiful, like the ones she had seen on nature shows. She saw mountains in the distance and tall trees brushed right up against the patio railing. But her heart sank as she realized that she was nowhere near home.

Carlye stepped forward, following Myra. The patio was enormous. Bigger than any she'd ever seen in her life. There was a covered area that had couches and chairs. There was a kitchen area where a woman in a white apron was standing, arranging some food. Off to the side, there were two cushioned tables, just like the ones that Carlye had seen in the room they passed through on their way to the patio. As Carlye looked around her surroundings, she saw two men sitting and laughing. As they got closer, Myra glanced towards her, "Don't say a word."

Carlye nodded. The men were older than her dad, she thought. They had drinks in their hands and seemed to be relaxing. There was a tray of food in front of them. Seeing the perfectly laid out tray of appetizers made Carlye's stomach growl. Somehow, she didn't think they would share.

Carlye followed Myra until they got close and then they stopped right in front of one of the men. He had thinning gray hair and was wearing a white shirt and black slacks. His legs were crossed. Carlye noticed that his face was scarred. The sleeves of his shirt were rolled up and he held a short glass with something in it. Carlye guessed bourbon. Her father had bourbon on holidays. It looked like the same color.

When Carlye and Myra got close, the man and his friend stopped talking. Myra pushed Carlye forward so that they were standing next to each other. The man looked at her for what felt like a long moment and nodded. Immediately, Myra turned and walked back the direction they came. Carlye felt her grab her hand and pull her to follow along.

Back in the room they had started in, Myra said, "We have to hurry up. Take off your dress and put this robe on."

Carlye felt self-conscious. She didn't have any underwear on or even a t-shirt underneath the dress. "Should I leave my shoes on?"

"No, you can take those off." Myra paused, tightening the belt around the white terry cloth robe that she put on. "Don't worry. You are going to be fine. Today shouldn't be too bad."

"Who is that man out there?" Carlye asked.

"Mr. Maifer. This is his house." Myra didn't offer any other details.

Carlye struggled into the robe. It was too big for her. Myra fixed the collar and helped her secure the tie around her waist. Carlye felt like she was going to throw up. She swallowed hard a few times, trying to make the feeling go away. She didn't understand this. She didn't understand what she was supposed to do. She wanted to go home.

"Follow me," Myra said.

Carlye didn't know what else to do. She didn't want to end up in Dora's office again. As they walked back out onto the patio, she tried to tell herself that maybe if she was good and did what Myra said she'd get to call home again. Tears started to well up in her eyes. She just wanted to be home with her family. She sniffled once, as quietly as she could, as she followed Myra across the patio.

"Just do what I do," Myra said, leading Carlye over to the cushioned tables. She didn't know what they were for. They stood to the side and waited.

In a moment, the men came over, the woman in the white apron bringing them fresh drinks, which she put on a small table nearby. The men started to take off their clothes. A fresh wave of nausea followed Carlye. She watched as Myra took the man's shirt and pants and hung them on a stand nearby. Carlye did the same for Mr. Maifer. As she got close to him, she could smell alcohol and cologne. The smell made her nearly retch.

The men laid down on the tables, only wearing their underwear, and Carlye watched as Myra pulled up a blanket over the man's lower half. Carlye did the same. Myra pulled a small bottle of what looked to be oil out of a cabinet and put some on her hands. She nodded for Carlye to do the same.

The oil smelled like flowers or something, Carlye couldn't tell exactly what. She watched as Myra began to knead the man's shoulders and back. Carlye froze. She didn't want to touch Mr. Maifer. It seemed wrong. He was old. Her stomach turned and she swallowed hard to avoid being sick.

When she didn't immediately start the massage, she saw Myra look her way, her eyes big, as if she was willing Carlye to do what she was doing.

Carlye nodded and closed her eyes. Myra was right, it wasn't too bad. She didn't know exactly what to do, but she just rubbed his back the way that she had seen her mom rub her dad's shoulders when he had a bad day at work. She didn't know what else to do. She kept going, watching Myra the whole time.

All of a sudden, Carlye heard Mr. Maifer clear his throat. Myra stopped what she was doing and walked over to a coat rack that was near the cabinet that held the massage oil. She whispered, "Hang up your robe here."

Carlye felt her eyes go wide. "I don't have any clothes on."

"I know. It will be okay."

Carlye did as she was told. The warm air touched her skin. Even though it was a nice day, she felt like running. She needed to get away from this place. Though she was screaming inside, she felt paralyzed. She followed Myra back to the table and put more oil on her hands, the warm air touching her entire body.

After a few minutes of rubbing Mr. Maifer's back, she saw Myra move to stand in front of the table, massaging the other man's shoulders. Carlye did the same. The tile was cool on her feet. As she got into the same position as Myra, she could feel Mr. Maifer looking at her body. He didn't say anything. He didn't touch her, but she could feel him staring. It was the most uncomfortable feeling she had ever experienced. At one point, she felt a tear roll down her cheek. She quickly used the back of her hand to wipe it away.

The better part of an hour had gone by, no one saying anything. Carlye just did as Myra did, massaging the men. The girls moved over the back of their bodies rubbing oil all over them. Carlye had withdrawn into a deep place inside herself. She was no longer looking at Mr. Maifer. She wasn't thinking about the sick feeling in her stomach. She was just doing what Myra did.

From behind her, Carlye heard the door open. Two more girls came out onto the patio. One of them was Lily. They were both wearing the same robes that Myra and Carlye had put on before the massages started. Carlye heard Mr. Maifer clear his throat. Myra instantly stopped working, put on her robe and motioned Carlye to do the same and follow her. The other girls started to move towards the table. Carlye didn't know what they were doing. Maybe more massage?

Once they got back into the changing area, Myra said, "You did just fine. The other girls will finish for you since it is your first day."

"Finish what?" Carlye asked.

"Helping them to feel good…"

19

"Apparently there was another girl with Carlye the day that she was taken. The other girl, Holly Jenkins, got away and hid here at this gas station until her parents were able to come and get her."

Kat felt her heart rise. She knew this was a major break in the case. Not only had Carlye apparently called home, but they now knew that it wasn't a runaway situation. She had been taken. Why they didn't know yet. What they did know was that it was possible that Carlye was alive. It was a start.

"Who is this girl? Why did she wait so long to come forward?" Kat could tell that Van was impatient for details.

Kat saw Lance refer to his notes, "As I said, her name is Holly Jenkins. She was at the police station all afternoon. What she told us was that she was at Camp Hope with Carlye when one of the camp counselors said they had a special field trip for the girls."

"How old is Holly?" Kat asked, her stomach sinking.

"Fourteen."

Lance continued the story. "Apparently, they drove for

about an hour or so from Camp Hope with one of the counselors. His name is Nathan. We are running him down now. When they got to the party, there was a man there that Holly thinks was named Mitch."

"Where was Carlye when this happened?" Kat wondered how the girls got separated and Holly escaped.

"Holly said she was hungry, and this Mitch sent her to the kitchen to get food. When she went into the kitchen there was a woman who shoved her out the side door, telling her to run, that someone wanted to take her."

As the news settled on Kat, she felt like she had been punched in the stomach. These girls were so young. She imagined how terrified Holly must have been. "How did Holly get to the gas station?"

"She said that she ran and ran and finally found this place. She showed us places where she'd been scratched up and had fallen. Her story checks out. The mom came in with the address of this place and the name of the guy that kept Holly hidden until the mom and dad could get here."

"Wait, I don't understand," Van started, "Why did she wait so long to come forward?"

Lance sighed. "Her mom apologized for that. She said that Holly has basically barricaded herself in her room since they got her home. She's been afraid that since they knew her at the camp they could come and find her. She hasn't left the house in a week."

"What got her out of the house?" Kat asked, picturing Holly curled up in her bed, hiding from the people that wanted to take her.

"Finally, LaDonna -- that's the mom -- called their pastor and they showed her the news stories about Carlye. They told her that she was home and safe, but that Carlye wasn't. That was enough to make Holly come in and talk to us."

"Man, I wish she had done that sooner." Van scuffed a couple of pieces of gravel with his boot. "The trail is practically cold now. I don't know if we will ever find Carlye."

20

The girls didn't say much to each other after they changed back into their blue dresses. Carlye watched Myra hang up her robe. She did the same. Out of a drawer in the cabinet where the robes were hung, Myra pulled a tube of lipstick. She reapplied hers and handed it to Carlye, who did the same.

Without a word, they walked back through the pine tree door and back to their rooms. Carlye watched Myra go to the end of the hall. She paused, giving her a silent wave before going into her room.

Carlye closed the door. She was all alone. There was nothing to do. The room, other than the beds and bathroom, was completely empty. Carlye pulled her shoes off and saw red blisters had formed on her heels. She crawled up into her bed and pulled the covers up. She didn't know what to do next. She was too tired to try to figure it out. Hopelessness draped itself over her. Carlye had no idea how to get home.

The warmth of the blankets had almost convinced her body to sleep when a quiet knock at the door yanked her out of her rest. Carlye looked up to see Lily, "Come on," she whispered. "Dora wants to see you."

Smoothing her dress over her thighs, Carlye put on her shoes, limping because of the pain of the shoes. "I can't wear these," she told Lily.

"You have to."

"I have really bad blisters."

Lily just shook her head and waved that Carlye needed to follow. Once out of the room, the girls were silent, going through the pine tree door and down the hallways at the back of the house.

They stopped outside of Dora's door and Lily barely made a noise on the door. "Come," Carlye heard Dora call.

Carlye stood in front of Dora's desk. She turned slightly and could see Lily sitting in the chair behind her. "Don't look at her. You are to look at me."

All Carlye could think to do was to look down.

"Mr. Maifer said that your debut went well. You will get a special dinner tonight. Your work will begin tomorrow. That is all."

She heard the door creak open and turned to see Lily standing in the doorway, motioning her to come forward. Carlye limped her way to the door.

Dora hissed at Lily. "Get her some band aids. It is your responsibility to make sure that she is ready for Mr. Maifer. You know that."

Carlye looked at Lily. The color had drained from Lily's face. Carlye immediately felt a combination of relief and fear. She was glad to get some help with her blisters, but what did Dora mean "ready for Mr. Maifer?" Carlye limped behind Lily all the way back upstairs. She wanted to take her heels off, but she was worried about the consequences.

It seems there were always consequences…

Carlye began to realize as her heart sank that this wasn't a special assignment from Camp Hope, this was a prison.

21

"What exactly happened once Holly got here?" Kat asked, pulling out her own notebook and starting to write.

"Let me show you," Lance said, motioning them to follow him inside the station. They walked past the aisles of candy and chips and through a door in the back that was marked Employees Only. At the end of the hall on the right, they entered a room that had a sign saying it was the office. Lance walked behind the desk and pointed under it, using his pen to show where Holly had hidden.

Kat saw Lance look through his notes again. She had to give him credit. He was thorough at least, especially when sharing information with them. She followed Lance behind the desk.

"She barricaded herself back in this corner." He pointed to a spot on the dirty, worn-out carpet." It was hard to imagine anyone would want to sit on it, let alone hide there. "The gas station attendant reported that he wanted to call the police, but Holly begged him not to. He told her that if he could reach her parents that he'd wait for them."

Kat nodded. "If I was a scared young girl, I'd probably want to see my parents, too. How old is she again?"

"Fourteen. She's sweet and pretty. Unfortunately, I can see why someone would want to take her. The question is, for what?"

Kat and Van said goodbye and thank you to Lance and got back in the truck. On the way home, Van had his window cracked open. Kat could smell the change of seasons coming. Though they didn't get huge sweeping changes of season like areas of the north, Aldham did get their share of a change of seasons. The heat of the summer had given way to cooler fall weather.

Kat and Van seemed lost in their own thoughts for miles of road stretching ahead of them. They didn't say a word. There was no music on in the car. The only sound was the truck engine propelling them forward and the wind whistling through the window Van had opened.

After nearly half the distance towards home had elapsed, Kat felt Van reach for her hand. "Are you cold? Do you want me to close the window?"

"No, I'm good." She squeezed his hand. "The breeze is nice."

Quiet covered them again until Kat broke the silence, "What do you think those people wanted with Holly? I wonder if the same people still have Carlye."

"I think we have to think about what we know for sure."

Kat nodded. Van's reliance on facts was comforting. It helped her to rein in her thinking, which was running wild with emotions and questions.

Van stared ahead at the road. "What we know is that Carlye, or someone who sounded like her, called home today."

"You don't think it was Carlye?" Kat snapped, angry that

Van would even call the contact into question. She pulled her hand away.

"That's not what I said. What I believe is that Alana wanted it to be Carlye. Is it likely it was? Yes. Do we know for sure? No. We wouldn't actually know unless Carlye told us that."

"I'm sorry, I didn't mean to snap." Kat sighed.

Van reached for her hand again. "It's fine. I know this is upsetting. Are you sure you want to continue with the case? We can tell the Morgan's..."

Kat didn't give him a chance to finish. "Yes. I want to see this through." Kat leaned back in the seat. "What we know for sure is that Carlye might have called." She heard Van laugh. "Why are you laughing?"

"It was just the way that you put it 'we know she might have.' Cute."

"Pay attention to the road, buddy." Kat slapped his hand away. One thing that she loved about their relationship is that they were able to have fun together. "Getting back to the case, what about Holly? What do you think about her story?"

Still staring at the road, Kat saw Van raise his eyebrows. "I think that she saw something that terrified her. I think she feels guilty about leaving Carlye." He glanced at Kat. "We should talk to her tomorrow if she will let us."

A few more miles went by before they spoke again. Kat's mind was racing with sadness and fear and questions. She knew she was getting attached to this story. She also knew that the emotion she was thinking could cloud her judgment. But there was one question she had that kept rattling in her brain. She almost didn't ask the question, but she couldn't restrain herself... "Van, do you think Carlye is still alive?"

"I have no idea."

BY THE TIME they got back to the house, it was late. Kat slipped out of Van's truck and back into the house. She turned lights on as she went. Van followed and quickly stepped ahead of her, checking each room to make sure that nothing had been disturbed. After the Apex story landed, they had become very careful. Van always checked the house.

"Are you heading to bed?" Van asked.

"Not sure I can sleep. I'm going to work on my computer for a bit."

"I can stay for a while if you'd like. I've got some work to do anyway."

"That's fine."

Kat opened her laptop and started a pot of coffee. There were a few emails about other stories that she was working on in her inbox. She ignored them. She realized she was hungry and started to make some eggs and toast. She found Van in the family room, his laptop open and his legs propped up, the television turned on to local news. "Do you want some eggs?"

"That would be nice, if you are making them..."

A smile passed across her face, "Happy to."

Kat wandered back to the kitchen and cracked some eggs into a pan and put some

bread into toast. The smell of food cooking made Kat's stomach rumble. As soon as the eggs were done, she put some on a plate and took it to Van with a cup of coffee. She had never done that with Steve. She'd never wanted to.

Van had been very respectful in the days after Steve's arrest. The shock of being married to someone who had been paid to be in the relationship was something that sent Kat's emotions flying. It was worse knowing that he had willfully turned Jack over to the Apex thugs who had nearly killed him.

Six months had gone by and Kat had healed some, but not totally. Steve was out of the picture. Kat had sole custody. The thought saddened Kat. She had been intimate with a man who had been paid to be with her and to father a child. Steve told

Kat's lawyer that Kat was never supposed to get pregnant. He even tried to claim that Jack wasn't his. A quickly completed paternity test proved otherwise.

After Steve's arrest, Van started coming by the house regularly to check on Kat and Jack. He knew they were alone. He had been there when Kat had shot Edgar to save Jack. After his time in the military, Van understood how Kat was feeling. Though she did what she needed to do to save Jack, she was still worn and scared after that night.

About two months of Van coming by regularly led to their relationship deepening. They spent evenings outside watching Jack play, Van would bring cartons of Chinese food for them to eat or they would go to the park together. Kat liked his company. He was easy to be around. No matter the circumstances, he was always happy, or at least wasn't unhappy. That was totally different than Steve, who had been moody nearly all the time.

As Van reached for the plate, he said, "Thanks. Do you want to come in here and eat?"

"Naw, I'm going to get on that computer of mine and do a little research."

"Okay," he mumbled through bites of food.

Kat went back to the kitchen and piled eggs and toast on her plate. She took it over to the kitchen table where her computer was waiting. She took a bite of eggs and started to type into the search bar, "child abductions." The search led to images of children who had gone missing. Down farther on the page, there were articles listed. One by one, Kat started to click on those, trying to wrap her brain around Carlye's disappearance and why someone would take her.

The articles listed a lot of different reasons that children disappear. One article mentioned runaways because of abuse. Kat clicked through and read a few paragraphs. The author said that children who are abused tended to run away because they couldn't solve the abuse on their own. That didn't appear to be the case for Carlye.

Kat scrolled down, taking a bite of toast, and started to read an article on drug addiction. That didn't fit either. Another article mentioned parent abductions. As she looked at the article, the authors mentioned that in cases of divorce, one parent might steal the child away where they couldn't be found so they didn't have to comply with custody arrangements.

At the bottom of the page was a small article, "The Hidden Reason Kids Disappear." Kat clicked on it. As the page loaded, she saw an image of a girl who was covered in bruises. Her face was obscured, but you could clearly see that her arms and legs had been hit repeatedly, some of the spots bright purple and blue and others that had faded into a yellow color. Kat scrolled down and saw more images, stopping to read the paragraphs in between. The next image was of a young girl, maybe eight, who was sitting in a wheelchair. As Kat read the content, her stomach turned. The article read, "Her 'owners' as they called themselves, had paralyzed her chemically so that she wouldn't run away."

Those girls had been trafficked.

Kat left that article and went to another article on sex trafficking. This time, the article talked about the prevalence in the United States. "You'd think that sex trafficking was something only for the seedy streets of Cambodia or Thailand," the author wrote. "You'd be wrong." As Kat read, she saw that girls of all ages were being either brought into the country or kidnapped inside the United States to be trafficked. The article went on to discuss that the difference between sex trafficking and prostitution is that trafficked kids are offered up for sex by force or deceit.

Kat leaned back in her chair for a moment, letting the information sink in. Was it possible that the men who almost took Holly wanted to traffic her? The idea swirled around in Kat's head. She stared back at the screen, pushing her half-eaten meal away from her, and dug in to do more research.

As Kat scrolled through a few more articles, she saw that even infants were trafficked. And, girls were not the only ones that were vulnerable. Young boys were increasingly being trafficked in all parts of the world. While some "owners" only worked with girls, other ones liked having boys around for their clients.

Kat stood up from her chair and poured herself another cup of coffee. It was past three o'clock in the morning. She had been at it for hours, but she knew she couldn't sleep. She walked into the family room, wondering if Van had left and she had been so focused that she hadn't noticed. He was slumped to the side of the chair, sound asleep, the television still on, the screen of his laptop still open but black. Kat lifted his laptop off of him gently as not to wake him and put a blanket over his legs. She took his plate back to the kitchen and got back to work.

22

Carlye had been back in her room for a few hours. There was a soft knock on her door. "I brought you some band aids," Lily said. "It is time for dinner. We have to go now."

Carlye got up off of the bed without a word -- she had been curled up on the top of the bedspread trying to rest -- and followed Lily.

In the room at the end of the hallway, there were pans of food that had been set up on the counter. The girls, each wearing matching blue dresses and their signature pink lipstick, sat silently at each table. It was odd that no one talked, Carlye thought. Lily pointed to a table at the back and whispered to Carlye to sit down. She did as she was told. In a minute, Carlye was back with a small plate of food for her. There was rice, a tiny piece of chicken and a few green beans. Carlye picked at her food, not wanting to eat. She looked around at the other girls.

There were eight of them in total. One entire table was empty. The girls looked to be her age or a little older. Some of them were blonde like her, others were dark. No one spoke and no one looked up from their food. One girl, long and lanky with porcelain skin and a long blonde braid, got up from the table and took her dish to the sink, washing it and putting it away. She pushed in her chair and silently padded out the door.

Lily leaned over and whispered, "You'd better eat. There isn't another meal until tomorrow unless Mr. Maifer feeds you tonight."

Carlye's stomach flopped when she heard his name. She had seen Mr. Maifer. She had touched his shoulders. She didn't want to be near him. Why did they mention tonight? What would happen? Fear crawled up through Carlye like a vine.

When she was done with her food, as much of it as she could eat, Carlye washed her dish like she had seen the other girl do and padded down the hallway, not saying anything more to Lily. She closed the door to her room and stood up on the bed, trying to see if she could get the window open. It would open just a crack, just enough to smell the fresh air. There was some sort of lock on the window and iron bars on the outside of it. Carlye looked down and realized that even if she could get the window open, there was nowhere for her to go. The fall out of the window would be enough to kill her. She was trapped unless she could find a way out or unless someone came to rescue her. Before tears could fall down her cheeks, another knock came on the door. It was Lily. "It is time to go," she said.

With the door closed behind her, Carlye could talk, "Where are we going?"

"You are having a private meeting with Mr. Maifer."

"What does that mean? Lily, I'm scared!" Carlye sat down on the bed and started to cry.

"No, don't cry. He doesn't like it when the girls do that."

Carlye saw Lily kneel down in front of her. "You will be okay. He will give you something to make it easier. Just do what he says, and you will be back here before you know it."

With that Lily stood up, her face hardened. "Put on your lipstick. We have to go now."

Lily rushed Carlye out of the room, down the hall and through the pine tree door. The fear in Carlye's throat was nearly choking her. She moved like she was a robot. The little girl inside of her, the one that liked to play dress up, kick a soccer ball and eat spaghetti with her family, retreated deep inside of her.

Carlye followed Lily through a few more halls and down a side stairway until they got to an area of the house that looked more like a home. The stairway had left them near what looked to be the front of the house. Carlye had never seen anything like it. The ceilings were three stories high and there was artwork hung above a sweeping staircase. A chandelier was lit up. Just beyond the entrance was a kitchen with the same high ceilings. As Carlye glanced in the kitchen, she saw a woman with long dark hair cascading down her back, wearing purple satin pajamas leaning against the kitchen island, staring at her. She didn't have time to ask Lily who it was. She couldn't without fear of getting into trouble.

Lily stopped in front of two tall, wooden doors. They looked like doors to a castle to Carlye, carved and arched. She rapped on the doors quietly. Two knocks only. A male voice inside said, "Come." Lily pushed the door open.

Inside was a large room filled with plush furniture. A couch and two overstuffed chairs were set in front of a fire. There was an enormous wooden desk set off to the side. Carlye could see that Mr. Maifer was sitting behind the desk, wearing the same white shirt and slacks from before. She followed Lily to the front of the desk.

"That will be all." Mr. Maifer nodded to Lilly, who looked at Carlye with a stare that told her not to move.

Carlye was alone in the room with Mr. Maifer. She took a minute to look around but could hardly breathe. There were tall windows that looked outside. Although it was dark, a few lights outside made it look like they were on the first floor. If she could only get out, she thought, she might be able to get away. There was another door in the back of the room, but it was closed. Before she could look anymore, he broke her concentration. "I know you are confused about why you are here," he said, motioning for her to follow him to the couches where he pointed for her to sit down. "You'll see why you were chosen soon." Carlye felt his hand brush the hair back from her face. She tried not to move. There were two short glasses on the table, filled with a brown liquid. He picked up one and handed her the other. "Drink that. It will help you to relax."

Carlye licked her lips and picked up the glass. She tilted the glass to her lips and took a sip and then tried to set it down. "I told you to drink that," he growled. Carlye quickly picked up the glass and took small drinks until the cup was empty. The liquid burned in her throat and had a bitter taste that almost made her gag. "Good girl," she heard Mr. Maifer say.

The liquid had made her feel warm inside. She had never had alcohol before except for a sip of her mom's red wine last Christmas. She leaned back on the couch and suddenly felt groggy and sleepy. As she passed out, she felt the warmth of Mr. Maifer's body coming toward her...

23

By the time that Van woke up, Kat had already been for her run and was out of the shower, dressed and ready to start the day. "I wondered where you went." He motioned toward the family room, "Sorry about falling asleep. I didn't mean to stay over."

"No problem," she smiled. Van hadn't spent the night at Kat's house. Not with Jack. Not with all of the confusion that Jack was dealing with around Steve. Though their relationship had been building, Kat wasn't in a hurry to rush into anything at all.

"Did you have a good run?" Van asked, sitting down at the kitchen table.

"I did. I needed to think. I think I know what happened to Carlye."

Kat poured coffee out of a fresh pot that she had just made, one for her and one for Van. "What do you know about sex trafficking?"

"Honestly, not much." Van furrowed his brow, "Wait. Is that what you think happened to Carlye?"

Kat tilted her head to the side, raising her eyebrows, "It

seems like a possibility." She pulled up some of the articles that she had read last night, showing Van the information about kids being taken from their families, while they were on vacation, at college and even on school trips. She gave him a couple of minutes to process the information.

"I had no idea. I thought this was just something going on in the far east."

"I did too."

"How did you come up with this?" Van kept clicking on articles and scanning them while he asked.

Kat chuckled.

Van looked up from the computer, "Why are you laughing?"

"You just went into total editor mode."

Van laughed too, "Caught. Anyway, answer my question."

"So, I was searching for the reasons that children get abducted, or how it happens. I ran across this." She leaned over the computer, went back to the search results and showed him the article about the girl that was paralyzed and the little boys.

Kat heard him suck in his breath, "This is really bad. Really, really bad." Van looked up at her as she stood over him, "If this is what has happened to Carlye, we have to do something."

The idea that they needed to do something brought up a wave of panic in Kat. She didn't say anything. She just walked out the back door to sit on the patio furniture. It was a cool morning and she could hear birds chirping in the tree by the back door. Her heart was pounding in her chest. She sat down on one of the patio chairs and pulled her legs up, hugging them to her.

"What's the matter?" Van said, following her out the door.

"I just can't, Van. I mean, this story, Jack -- it's just too much." Kat felt hot tears run down her face. She didn't know how much of it was the lack of sleep or the case or what had just happened with the Apex story that was causing her to react.

Van pulled up a chair next to her and put his arm around her. He didn't say anything. Neither of them did for a few minutes.

When one of them did speak, it was Van, "Tell me what has you so upset, Kat."

She hadn't moved. Her head was buried in her knees. She raised her head and said, "It's wasn't too bad when I started reading about it, but then when I saw that they take boys, too. All I could think of was Jack."

Van didn't say anything for a few minutes. He just let her sit with her feelings. He was good that way. "Maybe that's the reason we should try to help."

"I just want to be here to protect him. I don't want to be running all over the place and he's exposed. He has to be safe..." More tears ran down her cheeks. It was as if a tug of war had broken out in her body. Part of her wanted to do everything she could to help the Morgan's find Carlye. Part of her wanted to stay at home and watch Jack like a hawk. She knew that she couldn't have it both ways.

"Jack has lots of people around him to protect him. You, me. He's going to be protected."

"But what about right now. I mean, he's at Laura's..."

"With that crazy dog that would eat anyone who would try to hurt him? That is one wild pup." Kat felt Van's hand stroke her blonde hair back off of her face. "Here's what you have to think about: Do you think that it is more important to stay with Jack 24/7 or try to find a balance and help some people along the way?" Kat started to say something, but Van stopped her. "And, you have to consider what you want Jack to see you doing. Worrying? Helping others? It's a choice, Kat."

For someone who'd never been a parent, Van had a lot of wisdom. He was hard to argue with. "I want Jack to be safe and I want to help a little."

She saw Van nod, "That's where you have to find the

balance. Jack's your priority, but I bet you can squeeze in time to help the Morgan's."

The conflict inside of her resurfaced. A sadness covered her. "That's what I tried to do with Apex. Look what happened to Jack. He was almost killed."

"I know, but we know better now. We understand that if we go after truly bad guys that we've got to be prepared to protect our family."

Kat liked the way that Van said, "our family." "How would we do that?"

"Let's not worry about that right now. When the time comes, I have a few ideas that will work, I think." He stood up from the chair. "So, can we go in where it is a little warmer and finish talking about this?"

As soon as he said it, Kat realized that she was cold, too. "Yes," she said, using her sleeve to wipe the rest of the tears from her face. They stood up and walked back into the house, just as Kat heard a car door close.

The back door opened, and Woof charged into the kitchen, flopping over on top of Kat's feet and waiting for a belly rub, "Mama!" Jack yelled, running over to her and hugging her legs, "I'm so glad to see you!"

"I'm glad to see you, too, buddy. Did you have a good time at Gramma's?" Before he could answer, Laura walked into the kitchen, carrying Jack's overnight bag over her arm and a crockpot.

"Let me help," Van said, taking the crockpot from her. "What's this?"

"Just a little something for you guys for dinner tonight. Chicken soup. I thought it might

help."

Kat plugged it in on the counter. "Thank you so much. Did everything go okay?"

"Yup. Jack and Woof were great and great company. That dog doesn't leave his side."

Laura turned to Van, "You are here early, young man."

"Sorry, ma'am. I kinda fell asleep on the chair in the family room. Not sure Kat slept a wink last night."

"I didn't..." Before Kat could say anything more, Jack popped into the room.

"Can I have Paul over?"

Kat put her hand on his head, "Yes, for a few hours."

VAN AND LAURA left at the same time. Diane, Paul's mom from t-ball, came over to the house just as they pulled out. "See you in a couple of hours," Diane said to Paul. "Be good and listen to Mrs. Beckman."

"Yeah, okay mom..."

While the boys were playing, Kat wandered around the house. She was bone tired. She went upstairs and collected laundry and started a load. Just as she started to work on sandwiches for the boys for lunch, she heard yelling.

"No, you didn't!" Jack yelled.

"Yes, I did. I told you I wanted the yellow truck!"

The boys were both yelling. "We will solve this problem right now. Hand over the yellow truck." Reluctantly, Jack handed her the truck. "Now, why don't the two of you go outside and play. No trucks, just you two."

"Okay," Paul said, heading for their back door. Jack hung behind. "I'm not sure I like him anymore, Mama."

Kat squatted down to Jack's eye level, "You are doing fine. He's your friend. Sometimes friends disagree. That's okay. Now, go play."

Jack trotted off. As Kat stood up, she wondered if Tim and Alana had the same conversations with Carlye. They had said she had problems making friends. What if Jack was the same way?

The thought chased her as she went into the kitchen to continue working on lunch and laundry. She could see the boys on the swings in the backyard. They seemed to be okay. But the question was real. What if Jack had problems making friends? Would she take the same steps that the Morgan's did to help Carlye? What if the same thing happened to Jack? What if he was taken? A shudder ran up and down her spine. How many unknowing parents had exposed their children to the same risk?

The Morgan's were good parents, or at least they seemed to be, Kat thought, putting a couple of dishes in the dishwasher. They could never have known the day they signed Carlye up for Camp Hope exactly what they were signing her up for.

Now, the question was, would they ever get her back?

24

The sunlight streamed into the window above Carlye's bed. She rolled over and realized she was on top of the bedspread, not under the blankets. She woke up feeling groggy. Her head pounded. She felt a little nauseated like she had the flu. And the light from the window was so bright...

She sat on the edge of the bed and saw that she was still wearing the same blue dress she had put on yesterday. Her body ached all over, but she didn't know why. She couldn't seem to clear the fog from her brain. She was still scared, but the fear seemed far away.

A knock came on the door. Lily walked in without saying a word. In her arms, she had a yellow dress, yellow shoes and a yellow ribbon. She set them down on the empty bed next to Carlye.

Carlye watched Lily as she moved silently through her room. "Lily, how did I get back up here?"

"I don't know," Lily whispered. Carlye could tell that she didn't want to talk. "Please go take a shower and put these things on. I'll see you at breakfast."

Lily didn't give her a chance to ask any other questions. The door closed and Carlye was alone in the room again. There was no other option than to do what Lily asked unless she could find a way out.

Carlye turned on the water to the shower, pulled off the blue dress and realized that there were bruises on her legs. Bruises that hadn't been there the night before. She saw crusted blood between her legs and immediately got scared. What had happened to her? Why was she bruised and bleeding? Why did she feel so tired?

She retreated within herself again. All she could think of was getting to breakfast. That was the next step. She stepped under the warm water, used some soap to clean up the blood and quickly dried off, putting on the yellow dress. She looked in the pile of clothes for the day and in all the drawers. There weren't any. She tied her hair in the ribbon as best she could and put on the shoes, quietly making her way to breakfast.

When she got to the room, everyone stopped to look at her. The room was silent. Lily jumped up from their table and ran to a drawer, pulling out a tube of pink lipstick. She quickly handed it to Carlye who put a smudge of it on her lips. All of the girls resumed eating.

Carlye sat down at their table, almost too exhausted to move. She didn't even try to go get anything from the counter. There wasn't that much to eat anyway. Only crackers, the kind in the plastic packets that Carlye used to get with her soup at their favorite restaurant, and little cups of orange juice.

Carlye saw Lily staring at her, "You have to eat something," she whispered.

"I can't."

"You have to." Lily shoved two packets of crackers at Carlye and a small cup of juice. Carlye pulled open the packet and tried to eat the corner of one of the crackers. It was stale. She took a sip of the juice. It was warm. She thought back to the night before. She was sure that in that big kitchen they had real food. At her house, there was real food. At her house with her mom and dad and brother...

Carlye closed her eyes and looked down at her lap. She was trying not to cry, but the tears just wouldn't stop coming. She felt a strong hand on her arm. It was Lily, pulling her out of her chair. Lily dragged her down the hallway and took her to her room, closing the door behind her. Carlye fell to the floor in a heap. "You can't cry like that. We will get in trouble."

Carlye didn't say anything. She didn't even want to look at Lily. She just turned her head into the corner of the bedspread and let the tears roll.

There was no one to comfort her. Lily had left her again. She was all alone.

25

Once Jack and Paul were settled with lunch, Kat called Van. "I just had the most incredible realization. What if this happened to me? What if Jack has social issues and I choose a camp and this happens to him?"

"You would be careful about what camp you chose."

"But the Morgan's were careful. They did all sorts of research. They got references. They even visited the place."

"They did their best. That's what you will do, too." Van's voice had quieted.

Van's assurances didn't really make Kat feel any better. "Van, we have to find Carlye. We can't let this happen to another child."

"We don't actually know what happened to her yet, Kat. We can't make any assumptions."

"I know I'm right about this. I know it. She's out there somewhere and someone horrible is doing things to her -- things that no child should have to endure!"

"Slow your roll, there. Remember, I'm on your side."

"Well, if you are, then what are we doing about it?" Kat heard Van chuckle. "What's so funny?"

"Last I heard, you were making peanut butter and jelly sandwiches and now you want to save the world. You are funny. Love that about you."

Kat paused. She realized that she had gotten a little overheated about the subject but watching Jack and Paul fight made her realize just how vulnerable kids are to predators -- good kids from good families. Her heart sunk a bit, "I'm sorry, it's just that watching Jack and Paul fight... I mean, I try to be a good mom, but now that Steve's not here, he can't make decisions. I don't want him to, but what if I really mess up?" She heard Van hush her over the phone.

"You won't. And I'm not going anywhere. You've got me, too."

WITH THAT, they hung up. Van promised he'd be over in an hour to stay with Jack and Paul while she went to do some research. The next hour went quickly, Kat on her phone, checking her email and alternately checking on the boys to make sure they weren't arguing again.

By the time Van arrived, Paul was just about ready to leave. He waved to Kat and gave Jack a high-five on the way out the door. Kat leaned out, watching him get into Diane's car and pull out of the driveway.

"So, what's on the agenda this afternoon?" Van asked, picking up Jack and setting him on his shoulders.

Kat smiled. "Well, I'm going to leave you two troublemakers to go do a little research. I should be back in a couple of hours. Think you can hold down the fort for me?" Kat reached up and tickled the bottoms of Jack's feet.

"Yup, I think we can do that." Van spun around with Jack still on his shoulders, Woof nipping at Van's heels. "What do you say, Chief? Can we take care of Woof while Mom is gone?"

"Yes, we can!" Jack yelled as Van pulled him off of his shoulders and set him down on the floor. Woof smelled him all over, checking for damage.

Kat reached down and patted Woof's head. His long tongue was hanging out. "Yup, Woof, he's fine. We won't hurt him, I promise."

K<small>AT GATHERED</small> up her bag and headed out to the garage to get in her car. She drove out of their neighborhood and into downtown Aldham. In her research the night before, she'd realized that there was an organization that worked with sex-trafficked girls not more than twenty minutes from her house. In between helping the kids, she had called and asked to speak to the director. Explaining the story she was pursuing got her an invitation to stop by.

As Kat drove, she thought about what Lance had told them when they toured the gas station. From what he said, it didn't sound like Holly was a girl prone to drama or hysteria. It sounded like she was legitimately frightened.

Kat passed through downtown Aldham and headed out to the other side of the city. Aldham wasn't a large city, not in comparison to a New York or Los Angeles. The factories had pretty much gone out of business, but what had replaced it was healthcare. Kat passed the exit for Mercy Memorial, the hospital where Laura had been treated for her cancer. As she did, Kat found herself wondering how girls who had been trafficked regained their identity. Were they able to have normal lives? Hold down jobs? Have families?

A smudge of doubt crept into Kat's thinking. Maybe Carlye had just run away. Maybe she would turn up at a friend's house or a relative's cabin somewhere, just trying to live on her own. There was always the possibility that the Morgan's weren't who they said they were.

Although the thoughts passed through her mind -- after all

it was her job to ask the questions -- they didn't stick, not in a way that Kat would consider that they were viable. The only option she could think of where all the pieces fit together was trafficking. She just hoped there was enough time to help Carlye.

26

Night had almost fallen before Carlye woke up. Sheer terror and exhaustion had caused her body to shut down for the day. Lily hadn't come to get her. She didn't even know what time it was except for the fact that the sun was starting to go down. She didn't know if she had slept through dinner or if they had come to get her and just let her sleep. Her mom used to do that sometimes...

Carlye sat up knowing that she had to do something. She just couldn't stay in the room any longer. She got up from the bed and cracked the door. There was no one in the hallway. All the doors were closed. At one end of the hallway was Lily's room. The other end of the hallway, just past the dining room, had a staircase that looked to be on the outside wall of the house. If she could just get down those stairs and out the door, she could run for help.

A plan started to form in her mind. She closed the door and sat back on the bed. In a few minutes, it would be completely dark. It would be hard to see her once she got out of the house, or at least she hoped that would be the case. She looked around the room for anything that would help her. She tried to think back to her Girl Scout days, but the people in the house hadn't left her anything at all. Just the clothes on her back. She didn't have a coat or pants or the right shoes. It didn't matter, she realized. She knew if she stayed in the house, she'd die.

IT TOOK about an hour for the sun to fully set, the long shadows turning into inky blackness. It was so dark that Carlye wasn't sure they were near a city where she could get help, even if she could get away. She picked up the pair of yellow shoes, deciding to take them with her in case she needed them. Cracking the door open, she could see that the hallway was abandoned. All of the doors were still closed.

Carlye closed her door behind her with just a light click and slunk down the hallway, sticking to the wall. She passed the dining room, which smelled of stale food and antibacterial cleaner and past a few more doors before she got to the landing. She took her first steps down the stairs, looking below as best she could to see if anyone was there. She didn't see anyone. Her breath caught in her throat. She could see a door at the bottom that looked like it led outside, just before the stairs continued down into what Carlye guessed would be the basement.

Three steps, two, one... Carlye turned the handle on the door and pushed it open. The cool night air hit her face and she stopped for a moment, then started to run toward the driveway, hoping to get into the woods.

An arm grabbed her, pinching the skin, "Where do you think you are going?"

Carlye stared up at the man. It was Mitch. The man from the party a few weeks ago. She wrestled and screamed, trying to get away, but her eleven-year-old frame was no match for his raw strength. She dropped her shoes and clawed and scratched at him as he dragged her back into the house.

"You shouldn't have done that," Mitch growled at her. "I thought you were going to be one of the good ones."

Carlye felt him pull her down the stairs. He didn't take her back to her room. It was dark and smelled funny. There was just enough light to see. When they got to the bottom of the steps, Carlye fell. Crumpled in a pile, she tried to scramble back up, but Mitch caught her by the hair and dragged her. She felt dirt under her feet and fought to get away from him. Each twist brought new pain. She could feel her hair coming out of her scalp. "Stop! You're hurting me!" Carlye yelled, not caring who heard her. No amount of screaming helped. Mitch dragged her into the darkness.

He stopped for a moment and slid a large wooden door open, never releasing his grip. It looked like a door that Carlye had seen at a stable. As soon as it was open, he threw her against the back wall. She cowered in the corner, sitting in the dirt. Instinctively, she drew her legs up in front of her. Mitch came straight at her, his breath smelling like alcohol, "I didn't think we were going to have a problem with you. I guess I was wrong," he growled.

Carlye felt him grab the front of her dress. He pulled her up and pinned her against the wall. His hand drew back and slapped her across the face, hitting her hard enough that her ear started to ring. She could taste blood in her mouth as she crumpled to the dirt again.

"You are going to have to stay down here with the animals until you understand," Mitch said coming at her again. "You are an animal. You belong to us."

"I want to go home," Carlye whimpered.

"You are home. This is where whores like you live." He pulled her up and pinned her against the back corner again, this time pulling up her dress. "I guess you need to be taught a lesson."

He spun her around until she was facing the wall. She

didn't know what was happening. He bent her over. "You don't even know what to do. That's funny," Mitch muttered as he unzipped his pants. "I guess you need a little lesson from your Daddy, huh?"

Carlye felt pain inside of her like she had never experienced before. All she could do was groan. She nearly fell to her knees. "Oh no you don't," she felt Mitch pull her up. She turned inward, thinking about running down the field, chasing a soccer ball. She thought of her family and reading books with her mom.

A minute later, the pain was over. She laid on the floor, barely moving. She heard Mitch zip up and slide the door closed. "Thanks for the ride, missy," he said, leaving her in the dirt and the dark.

27

Kat pulled into the Blue Water Center at about two o'clock. It was a nondescript brick building on a side street just on the other side of Aldham. She parked and walked to the front door, where she was buzzed in. There was an armed security guard at the front door. "You need security at this kind of place?" Kat asked.

"You ever been here before?" he asked, searching her bag.

"Nope."

The guard grunted and let her pass where she was buzzed in through another door. The reception area was pleasant enough with a few couches and chairs and a desk with a red-haired woman sitting behind it. "Are you Kat Beckman?" she asked before Kat could say anything.

"Yes."

"I'll let the director know that you are here."

Kat watched the redhead walk back down a long hallway and then come back, opening a side door, "You can come with me," she said, holding the door open as Kat walked through.

"I'm Lacey. It's nice to meet you." Kat saw her lean a little closer, "By the way, I'm a big fan. I love your stories."

Kat smiled. It wasn't often that she had a fan. Before she had a chance to respond, they ducked into an office. "Jo, this is Kat Beckman. Kat, meet Jo Bennett, our Director."

Kat stuck out her hand to a slight woman with razor cut gray hair who was sitting behind a desk. "Hi, it's nice to meet you. Thanks for taking the time."

"Sure enough."

They both sat down. As Kat settled herself into her seat, she noticed the artwork in Jo's office. "The pictures you have in here are amazing."

"Thanks. Our guests did those for me."

Some of the art was truly spectacular. Some of it radiated joy -- bright colors and motifs of family and the outdoors. Some of it wasn't that cheerful. Kat's attention was caught by a small drawing that was framed and hung right near Jo's desk. It was dark, so dark in fact, that there looked to be only a pinhole of light in the work. "That one, the framed one over that. That's really interesting."

Jo smiled. "Yes, we had a guest who graduated from the program about a year ago. She did that during one of our art therapy sessions. When the therapist asked her about it, she said that that tiny bit of light was the only hope she had while she was being trafficked."

"I can't imagine."

"You're in good company. It's hard to come to terms with what these girls go through on a daily basis, let alone over weeks, months and even years." Jo picked up her cup. The entire office smelled like cinnamon tea. "So, you are doing research for a story?"

"Sort of... First, can you tell me why the name of this place is the Blue Water Center?"

"Sure. The women that are here feel like they have been hunted by sharks. We named it Blue Water to let them know that no predators are here."

Kat smiled. "That's a great story."

"So, how can I help?"

Kat told Jo about how Tim Morgan had come to find her at the park and how there were few new leads in finding Carlye. "Van, my editor, and I, are trying to assist the police with the investigation a little bit."

"That's unusual."

"Yeah, it's kind of a strange situation." Kat laughed a little. "We have a reputation with the police of being able to help them sort leads, I guess." Kat took a moment and stared out the window and then told Jo how she had come across the information about sex trafficking. "What I didn't realize was how prevalent this is in the United States."

"It is. There are major portals for trafficking in Detroit, over the border with Mexico and through ports in Florida."

Kat made a couple of notes. "How likely is it that Carlye was trafficked and not just kidnapped, do you think?"

"It's hard to know. Do you have a picture of her?"

Kat pulled out a picture and showed it to Jo.

"How old is she?"

"Eleven."

Jo whistled. "There's been no ransom demand? Her family isn't high profile?"

"That's correct."

Jo leaned back in her chair. "I think you can do the math. She's a pretty girl and she's in the right age range to be trafficked."

"So, who would take her? Are we looking at gang activity?"

Jo smiled. "For this girl? Probably not. Gangs do some of that, but they tend to bring their victims into the gang -- make them members -- and then abuse them as part of their membership." Jo raised her eyebrows. "This girl? If she was trafficked, and we don't know that, she was probably sold to someone with a lot of money and a lot of fetishes. Is her family supportive? I mean, do you sense that she might have run away?"

"Not based on her family that I can see. They seem supportive and devastated. Carlye did call home, but they didn't get to talk to her."

Jo wrinkled her forehead, "What do you mean?"

Kat sighed, "Well, the mom said that Carlye called yesterday, said 'mom' and then hung up."

"Are you sure it was Carlye calling?"

"That's the part that we are stuck on. The call was made over VOIP, so the police can't trace it. Alana -- the mom -- said it sounded like someone hung up the phone. But Alana is sure it was Carlye."

"VOIP is pretty sophisticated for a runaway. If Carlye did run away, you'd think that she'd ask for money or a bus ticket home or something. Whoever has her might have let her call and hung up as a way to get her to cooperate."

"So, this doesn't sound like a runaway to you?" Kat stopped writing and stared right at Jo.

"To be honest? No." Jo turned for a second and looked out the window in her office. Just beyond her window was a group of women walking through a small garden. It was fenced in. Kat saw the security guard outside with them.

"Does your security always stay with your guests?"

"When they are outside? Yes. These women are seen as property by their owners. They want their property back. That security guard is what keeps them away. That, and we have worked hard to be difficult to find." Jo turned back to Kat. "I don't think that Carlye has been kidnapped or has run away. Look at what you know and what you don't know. There's been no ransom, no demand for money or anything else. Carlye hasn't called her family looking for money. She's a beautiful girl. I think she's being trafficked."

Kat felt her stomach clench into a small knot. Thinking that Carlye was out there somewhere being exposed to men who would hurt her was more than she could really wrap her brain around. "If that is the case, what do we do? How do we go about trying to find her?"

"I think the first thing you have to accept is that you may not be able to. She could still be in the U.S. or she could have been shipped overseas. The other thing you have to accept is that even if you can find her, she's not coming home the same fun-loving little girl that she left as. Depending on what they do to her, she's going to be broken. This will be a lifelong journey for the family. I'm not saying that you shouldn't try. And I'm not saying that the family should give up on her. I've just seen too many families that think that when their girl comes back a little therapy will put her back to how she was. That's usually not the case." Jo opened a desk drawer and pulled out a business card. "Take this." She handed it to Kat. "He might be able to help."

Kat read the card. FBI Special Agent Sean Hollister. "Who is this guy?"

"He's an agent that I trust, Kat. I don't trust all of them, that's for sure. If anyone can get you and your editor on the right track, it's going to be him."

"Thanks," Kat said. "I've taken up enough of your time."

They both stood up. "If you need anything else, let me know. Processing this -- even if you are trying to help -- can be tough. But I'm glad that you are trying to help. Lots of people don't." Jo followed Kat out of her office and back to the reception area. "Lacey, will you make sure that Kat gets signed out okay?"

"Sure."

Kat signed out of the facility and Lacey buzzed the door open so she could leave.

. . .

On the way back to the house, Kat thought about all of the things that she and Jo had talked about. Jo's point that the lack of evidence that Carlye had been kidnapped or had runaway made it more likely that she was being trafficked was a good one. As a journalist, Kat knew that the lack of facts was often just as compelling as the presence of facts. What Kat didn't know was how to start to follow Carlye's movements after the last time Holly saw her. Every time she started to think about it, her thoughts hit a brick wall. There didn't seem to be any way forward. They knew Carlye was gone. They had some sketchy information from Holly, but the police hadn't found the house where they had been yet or at least she didn't know if they had. There had been one untraceable phone call. That was it. It was almost like Carlye had vanished into thin air.

Kat slammed her palm against the steering wheel. There had to be something that she could do. There had to be a lead that they hadn't followed up on that would take them to the next step. None of these criminals were perfect. Many times they were just lucky. Kat's anger and frustration grew inside her.

After talking to Jo, Kat knew that she couldn't just abandon Carlye. The drawing that was in Jo's office surfaced in her mind. That pin dot of light that was in the image, that was what Kat was for Carlye. Kat's determination was the only hope that she had. The question was what to do next.

Kat pulled in the driveway, still feeling frustrated when her phone rang. It was Detective Traldent. She tried to be upbeat. "Hey. How are things going?"

Lance sighed. "I have to be honest. This is a tough one. I wish we had more leads to go on."

"Me too."

"I do have one new piece of information."

Kat felt her chest tighten. She was excited about the idea that there was a thread they could pull. "What's up?"

"I did a little more digging on this Isla McCall, the camp director. Turns out, you and Van were right. Her background is only two years deep. I've got our tech guys working on figuring out who is she really. I don't know if it will lead to anything, but I thought you should know. We are probably going to interview her at some point."

"Why not pick her up now?"

"If she's tied to the kidnappers, then we don't want to spook her. We want to be able to watch her."

"Lance, I don't think that Carlye was kidnapped."

"Really? Why?"

Kat told Lance about her visit with Jo, the Blue Water Center director. "In essence, what she said was that the lack of facts that support kidnapping or a runaway situation, the more it looks like sex trafficking to her."

Lance grunted. "If that's the case, that creates a whole new set of problems."

"I realize that but think it through...there's been no ransom demand. The Morgan's aren't exactly people who have a lot of means or a high-profile lifestyle. From all accounts, their home life is stable and pretty basic. There's not been a lot of drama or anything that might make Carlye want to run away. See where I'm going?"

"Yeah. I was hoping this wasn't the direction this would turn, but I think you are right." Lance paused for a moment. "Let me get an update from my tech guys on this Isla McCall and I'll get back to you."

"Okay. Oh, before you go, any location on the house they went to yet?"

"No, Holly was cooperative to start with, but she has

clammed up again. We can't get her to give us any more than she already has."

Kat made a mental note that maybe she and Van should go visit with Holly. "Okay, keep me posted."

"Yep. Do the same, okay?"

"Yep."

28

After Mitch's vicious attack, Carlye pushed herself back in the corner of the room she was in. In the dark, it looked like he had locked her in a stall, the kind you'd find in a horse barn. Her entire body hurt. Her face stung and her ear, where Mitch had slapped her, was still ringing. She was having trouble opening her eye. There was dirt and sweat caked all over her. She felt something warm streaming down between her legs. When she tried to wipe it away with the corner of her yellow dress, blood and a clear liquid came off onto the hem. She started to whimper and hid in the corner.

Hours must have gone by. By the time that Carlye woke up, there was a glow from tiny windows that were at the top of the room where she was trapped. Carlye put her fingers in the dirt and realized that it wasn't dirt at all, it was sawdust. Like you'd find in a stable. She didn't move from her huddled position in the corner, but she tried to look around.

Now that the light had come up, she could tell from the wood plank walls and the sliding door that the area had been designed for horses. It smelled vaguely like hay. Carlye remembered the last time she had gone riding was with her family on a vacation the summer before to a national park. They had rented horses and spent all afternoon following a guide.

She pushed the thought out of her mind. She felt sick and turned her head to throw up. She didn't have the energy to try to stand up. Her head hurt. She touched her scalp, wincing. She realized that it was not only her face and eye that hurt, but there was blood caked on her scalp. Mitch pulled enough hair out to make her bleed.

"Hey," Carlye heard a whisper and backed up even further into the corner of her stall. The voice was coming from the stall next to her. Carlye turned her head and saw a set of eyes looking at her from between the slats. "Are you okay?" Carlye didn't answer. She just turned back to the corner. "I saw what he did to you."

"I just want to go home," Carlye whispered. "I don't feel good."

"I know. They've done it to me too." The eyes moved back and forth in the slat, "Can you come over here? Just slide along the ground if you can't get up."

Carlye was scared. She felt her throat tighten. She didn't know who this girl was or what she wanted. Everyone in this place wanted something from her. Carlye slid about three-quarters of the way over. She didn't want to give the girl a chance to get close to her. "I can't come any farther," she whispered.

"I just wanted you to know that you aren't alone down here, that's all." The eyes moved away from the slats and Carlye slid back to her spot.

As soon as she got back to where she had slept the night before, the overhead lights went on. "Time to feed the animals," Mitch said.

Under the stall door, a tray appeared with a small bottle of water, moldy bread and a half-eaten apple. "Leftovers from dinner last night."

The girl that was next to Carlye threw the food back at Mitch, screaming, "You can't keep me down here. I was one of Mr. Maifer's favorites! He's going to want to see me. When he does, I'm going to tell him what you did to all of us!"

Carlye huddled back into the darkest corner of her stall. She heard the stall door next to her slide open. "Really, what are you going to do about it, animal?" Mitch growled. "Are you going to call Mr. Maifer on your cell phone? Oh, that's right, you are caged down here until I decide you can come back upstairs."

"Stay away from me! Don't touch me!" the girl cried.

"I will do what I want with you. That's my job."

Carlye could hear the sound of Mitch's hand hitting the girl next to her. The girl cried and begged, "Ow! No please, stop!" Carlye couldn't look, but it sounded like the girl was being kicked.

The beating went on for what sounded like a half hour. After the first few minutes, the girl next to Carlye didn't make any noise. All Carlye could hear was the sound of fists hitting her body. Carlye knew that the girl was on the ground. She could hear Mitch's boots making a thudding sound against her sides.

When he was done, Carlye heard the stall door close, "Damn animals. They don't know their place."

Carlye didn't look up from where she was hidden. She didn't want Mitch to come near her. She felt warm tears run down her face, even through her swollen eye. Maybe they were animals...

The lights went off and Carlye tried to fall asleep. It was the only peace she had. The only place she was safe. She saw that her breakfast was still under the door and she realized how thirsty she was. As she slid over to get the bottle of water, moving as quietly as possible she silently leaned over to look under the wooden slats at the stall next to her, wondering how the girl from the stall next to her was doing. "Are you okay?" she whispered.

She didn't hear anything, so she peered through the slats. The girl had landed in a pile on the floor of the stall. She was on her side, her black hair back behind her, her arm flung in front of her body. Carlye could see that her pink dress had been pulled up to her waist. A blood stain between her legs had run down onto her thighs. Her fingers were bent in a strange angle as if they were broken and turned the wrong direction. As Carlye's gaze moved up her body she looked at the girl's face. There was blood at the corner of her mouth and on her temple. Her eyes were open and staring. She was dead.

"Oh God," Carlye whispered, huddling back in the corner of her stall. She had never seen a dead body before.

Carlye began to cry and rock herself, trying to find someplace safe within herself to hide.

29

"Where's the new girl?" Jackson Maifer had called Mitch to his office to talk about plans for the day. Over paperwork piled on his desk, he said, "I have guests coming. I would like to use her."

"She tried to escape last night. She's downstairs."

Jackson looked up from his paperwork just in time to see Mitch's eyes dart to the floor. A billionaire, Jackson Maifer wasn't accustomed to having his wishes denied. "How much damage did you do?"

"I didn't get a chance to check on her this morning. I'm sure she's fine. I was dealing with another problem."

"Get her up here. Get her cleaned up and ready."

"Yes, sir."

Mitch turned to leave the office, but Jackson stopped him. "Mitch?"

"Yes, sir?"

"Remember that we allow discipline, but not damage. I own these girls. They are like my prized Thoroughbreds. They are an investment. Are we clear?"

"Of course, sir."

Mitch went directly from Jackson's office downstairs to the stable where he kept the girls that weren't compliant. When the house had been built, Jackson wanted his horses inside the house so he could visit them no matter the weather. When he tired of them, the stable had been cleaned out. Mitch had appropriated the space for his own use. It had started with putting a girl down there for a few hours to get her to cooperate. Jackson and his friends liked them submissive. As Mitch's role grew, Jackson allowed Mitch to offer his own brand of discipline to the ones that weren't cooperative. Jackson might not have liked it when they misbehaved, but Mitch did.

His boots clumped down the stairs. He flipped on the lights, the overheads coming on. He opened the door of the first stall and saw Carlye cowering in the corner. "Come on, precious. Mr. Maifer wants you cleaned up."

Carlye didn't move. Mitch walked across the stall in two strides and reached down to pull her up. "I said, we have to go."

In the light, he could see that her left eye was swollen shut and she had bruises on her arm where he had dragged her. Down the side of her head was clotted, crusted blood where some of her hair had come out. Her eye, the one that would open, was wide with terror. As he pulled her out of the stall, she stopped.

"Don't make me hurt you again," Mitch growled.

Carlye didn't say anything, she just pointed to the stall next to hers.

Mitch's eyes narrowed. Why would Carlye be interested in what happened this morning? That girl was always mouthy. Hopefully, he had broken her of her bad habit.

"Don't move," Mitch said to Carlye as he slid the stall door open and saw the girl, still on her side, her eyes open, staring.

"Damn." Mitch took a couple of steps into the stall and

poked at the girl with his foot. She was completely limp. He looked back at Carlye. "Do not move." The last thing he needed was the girl Jackson wanted to try to run away again.

He pulled his phone out of the back pocket of his jeans. "Can you bring the tractor in? I've got something to go out back."

Within about a minute, Mitch could hear the rumbling of a tractor start outside. A garage door opened, and the front loader came rumbling down the aisle. Originally, Mr. Maifer had bought it so that the workers could muck out the stalls. Now, they just used it for chores around the estate.

Mitch moved out in front of the tractor, waiting for the bucket to line up with the stall door. "Hold it there."

A young man in a baseball cap got off of the tractor. "What's going on?" he asked.

Mitch pointed.

The tractor driver didn't say anything. They were paid to keep quiet. Mitch led him into the stall and they each picked up an end of her body, one grabbing her arms, the other grabbing her ankles. Her head dropped to the side as they lifted her up. She looked like one of the horses they had to put down. Carrying her out of the stall, they threw her body into the tractor bucket. The young man got back on the tractor seat, started it up and pulled it back out of the stable area. He closed the garage door when he got just outside.

Mitch looked at Carlye. "Let's go."

As they walked upstairs, he made Carlye walk in front of him so he could keep an eye on her. From behind, he could tell she was dirty and bruised. He hoped that Dora could clean her up enough to make her presentable. He gave her a little push at each turn to let her know which way to go.

When they got to Dora's office, he didn't bother knocking. He just pushed Carlye in the door. She fell to the floor.

"What the hell did you do to her? She just got here!" Dora exploded.

"I told you she tried to escape."

"You can't do that. She has to be ready for Mr. Maifer. He's having an event tonight."

"Not my problem."

30

Although Dora had slapped her, Carlye felt some relief being in her office instead of the stables. The little relief she felt didn't stop the terror that was churning through her body. She had heard the girl next to her get beaten. She heard her cries and realized she might have been the only one there when she died.

When the door closed and Mitch left, Carlye didn't move. She had quickly learned that moving without being told would cause pain.

"Get up," Dora said.

Carlye did as she was asked, leaving a few flakes of sawdust on the floor of Dora's office.

"Let me look at you." As Dora came close, Carlye leaned away. "Don't move."

When Dora moved back behind her desk, Carlye felt relieved. She watched as Dora picked up the phone. "Lily," was all she said.

Within a minute, there was a quiet knock at the door. "Come," Dora said.

As Lily entered Dora's office, Carlye saw her look her way

and then avert her eyes almost immediately. "I need you to take care of this. She has to be ready for Mr. Maifer's event tonight."

Lily left without saying a word. Carlye didn't know what to do, so she didn't move. She saw Dora look up from her desk, "Did you not hear? Go!"

That was the only invitation Carlye needed. She padded quietly behind Lily, having lost her yellow shoes somewhere along the way. As they passed through the back portion of the house, Carlye saw the same woman that she had seen in the kitchen the night before. She was wearing leggings and a grey tank top. Her black hair was piled in a messy bun on the top of her head and she had earbuds in, staring down at her phone. She looked like she had been working out. Carlye paused for a moment, stopping in the hallway. As she did, the woman looked up at her. She didn't say anything. Carlye didn't move, the dirt and blood still on her face, the bruises on her legs and arms all different shades of grape and black.

Carlye felt someone pull on her hand. Lily dragged her forward. As they passed, Carlye could feel the woman's eyes on her. Carlye looked down and followed Lily.

Up one more flight of stairs and they passed through the pine tree door. Lily led Carlye back to her room. As she opened the door, Carlye noticed that a new deadbolt had been added to the frame. It only opened from the hallway side. "Go in and take a shower. I'll be right back," Lily said.

The minute that Carlye crossed the threshold, the door closed behind her and the lock clicked closed. She was, at least, back in her room.

31

After she hung up the phone with Lance, Kat went into the house, throwing her bag over her shoulder. As the garage door closed behind her, she called out, "Anybody home?" There was no response. She walked into the kitchen and put her bag on one of the chairs. Van's truck was in the driveway. The boys had to be here somewhere.

She heard laughter in the backyard. Kat looked out the window that was over the sink and saw Van, wearing a leftover Halloween mask, chasing Jack around the backyard. Jack was laughing and running just as fast as his five-year-old legs could take him. He had his plastic lightsaber in one hand and a truck in the other. Kat watched for a minute, thinking about how great it was to see Jack relaxed and playing like a child should.

The therapist that they had seen after Jack had been kidnapped told Kat that it would take a while, but that she was confident that Jack would rebound. He'd always remember what happened, but since he was so young, he'd only hold onto the parts that his small mind could understand. As long as there was no more trauma, he would recover.

Kat moved over to the patio door, chewing her lip. She

didn't want to interrupt them, but she did have things she wanted to tell Van. Another moment passed and they spotted her. "Mama," Jack yelled, aiming right for her. Kat slid the door open.

"Hey, you two. Looks like a lot of running going on."

Van walked up to the door, pretending to be winded and tired. "Yeah, Jack has been trying to kill me." Van fell over and pretended to be dead.

Jack jumped on top of Van. Van grabbed him in a bear hug and hoisted him onto his shoulders. "Tell you what... how about if we go in and make some sandwiches?"

"Yes! Sandwiches!" Jack yelled, sprinting into the house.

"It always amazes me how the smallest thing can entertain a kid," Kat said.

"Yeah. I wonder where we lose that?" Van put his arm around her and gave her a little squeeze. "How did things go at the center?"

"It was good. I learned a lot. The director, her name is Jo, she thinks that we are on the right track. She said that the fact that there's been no ransom demand and Carlye hasn't called for money or a ticket home makes her think that she might be a victim of trafficking."

They passed into the house and Van pulled up a chair while Kat started getting sandwich stuff out of the refrigerator. "That's sort of good news, I think?" Van furrowed his brow. "At least we have an idea what direction to look."

"And Lance called. He said they have verified that Isla McCall, the camp director, has only had a background for the last two years."

"Did they go talk to her?"

As Kat reached for plates out of the cabinet, she said, "Not again after the first interview. Lance is worried they will spook her. He's got his tech people working on it. There was something else that was interesting, though..."

"What's that?" Van stood up and stole a piece of ham out of one of the sandwiches.

"He said that Holly has clammed up. They can't get to her for any follow-ups."

"Really? That sounds like an opportunity. Think she'd see us?"

Kat thought for a second. "Maybe. It's worth a shot, huh? She's really the only one that has any idea who the players are and where Carlye might be." Kat sliced one of the sandwiches in half. "If Carlye is being trafficked, I can't imagine what she is going through. I keep thinking about her, wondering where she is and what she's doing. She has to be so scared." Kat found herself fighting back tears. Being a mom and trying to hunt down traffickers was taking its toll on her.

Van grabbed her in a bear hug. "It's okay. I'm here. We are going to do this one step at a time. All we can do is not give up."

Kat wiped her nose with the back of her hand. "Yep. You're right."

Jack came in and they put the sandwiches on the table. Kat's phone buzzed. A friend had invited Jack to come over for the afternoon. Van looked at Kat. Through bites of his sandwich, he said, "Holly?"

Kat nodded and got up from the table. A quick text to Lance got her LaDonna Jenkins' phone number and the go-ahead to interview her. "If you have any luck, let me know," the text from Lance read.

Within a few minutes, LaDonna had texted back and invited them over. Kat and Van dropped off Jack on the way to the Jenkins' house. They lived about a half-hour outside of Aldham. They were quiet in the truck on the way over, both of them lost in thought.

When they got to the house, LaDonna Jenkins met them at the door. "I'm glad you called. I haven't been able to get Holly out of her room since we went to the police station. I'm not sure what else to do for her. Maybe you can talk to her?"

Kat saw LaDonna look right at her. "You think she'd talk to me?"

"She might. Would be good to have a woman's touch." LaDonna looked at Van. "No offense, of course."

Van put his hands up in surrender. "None taken." He pointed to a couch in the living room. "Okay for me to take my position over there while you ladies do the hard work?"

LaDonna rolled her eyes. Kat liked that she had a sense of humor. "Typical. We do the work while the men rest." Her laugh trilled through the air. "Yes, of course. There's coffee in the kitchen if you want a cup while you wait."

Kat followed LaDonna upstairs. She could almost feel the fear seeping out from beneath Holly's door. LaDonna knocked, "Sweetie, I have someone here to see you."

"I don't want to see anyone," the voice from inside answered.

"Holly, it's time to open the door." LaDonna's voice took a more definite tone. "The woman that is here is a reporter. She may be able to help Carlye, but you've got to let her try."

Kat could hear the floorboards squeak inside the room. The door didn't open. "I don't want to talk to anyone," Holly said, from behind the door. "I just want to be left alone."

LaDonna started to talk, but Kat held up her hand encouraging LaDonna to let her speak. "It's okay if you don't want to talk to me, but if I sit out here, can I tell you my story? If you think that maybe I can help, then you can open the door and we can talk. If you don't think so, then I'll leave. I promise. Sound good?"

"Okay," said the voice behind the door.

Kat slid down, her stomach in a small knot. She sat leaning on the door. LaDonna stood a few feet away down the hallway. "Holly, I'm not going to tell you that I fully understand what happened to you. What I do understand is how it is to be so scared you aren't sure you can go on."

"You don't understand," Holly said from behind the door. Her voice was barely above a whisper.

"Give me a chance, okay?"

"Okay."

Kat sighed, trying to keep tears from forming, "I'm not just a local journalist. I was an embedded journalist in Afghanistan. I went over there to write stories about the people that were there. The Afghanis, our troops, the community." Kat looked up at LaDonna for a second. LaDonna had her eyes closed, a tissue in her hand. "I worked for a month or so there, getting to know the troops and seeing what they went through every day. One day, I went out with a group of SEALs who were doing some reconnaissance. I thought I saw something up about a mile on the road. I told the guys I was with about it. They took a look and decided we should go up farther on the road. It was a trap, Holly. The vehicle in front of us blew up and ours did too. My wrist was shattered and the SEALs had to pull me out of the truck. I was so scared I couldn't move. They had to pull me out of the wreck and drag me to safety. I've had years of nightmares and counseling. Holly, I understand what it feels like to be scared. The way that it crawls around in your belly and your head."

Kat waited for a moment, trying to listen to what was going on in Holly's room. When she answered, the voice was nearer this time as if she was sitting just on the other side of the door.

"My mom said you had to shoot someone," was all Holly said.

Kat looked at LaDonna, who nodded. "That's true. An organization named Apex was blackmailing my family and my editor. They took my son hostage."

"How old is your son?"

Kat finally felt like they were getting somewhere. Holly was asking questions. "He's five now. He was four when it happened."

"What did you tell him?"

"About what had happened to him?"

"Yes..." Holly's response drifted off like she was far away.

"I told him how much I loved him, that I'd do whatever it takes to protect him. He was scared too."

"Is he okay now?"

"He's better. Thanks for asking. We all are. We told him he did what he needed to do to stay alive. I'd say the same to you." Kat took a deep breath. No matter how hard it was, she had to stay calm so she could help Holly. She heard a click and the door opened just enough that she could see Holly's legs. She was sitting on the other side of the door, leaning up against the wall.

"Do you really think you can protect me?"

Kat stood up, brushing off the back of her legs. "I think I need to hear your story. Once you talk to us, then we can figure out the next steps. Just like I did for Jack."

Holly stood up. "How could you protect me?"

Kat pulled up her shirt and showed Holly the holster on her hip. She looked at LaDonna, "Sorry I didn't ask. I've been carrying it with me everywhere."

"Not a problem. I grew up in Texas. Guns everywhere."

Kat looked back at Holly. "My editor, Van, is downstairs. He was a Marine. He was the one that was with me when we took out Apex. Will you come down and tell us your story? You might be the only one who can help save Carlye."

32

There was nothing else that Carlye could do except what Lily said. She felt frozen. She walked into the bathroom and turned on the water for the shower. She pulled her clothes off and caught a glimpse of herself in the mirror. Her eye was definitely swollen. She touched it and pain pushed back through her head. There was matted blood all over her.

She couldn't look at herself anymore. She stepped under the stream of water and tried to clean up. Once out of the shower, she wrapped herself in a towel and sat on the edge of the bed. There were no clothes in her room. She didn't want to put on the yellow dress again.

Outside the window, the tree branches were moving. A breeze must have come up out of the valley. Carlye could see storm clouds on the horizon, plodding across the sky. She remembered sitting and watching the clouds on the horizon at her house, sitting in the bay window that faced out into the backyard. It was one of her favorite places to rest when she was home. She wondered if she would ever have that chance again.

Tears didn't come this time. There was just a sense of sadness and emptiness.

Before she could spend much more time thinking about it, Lily came back into her room carrying a tray with some food on it and a pile of clothes. She set it down on the bed next to where Carlye was sitting. "Here, put this on." Lily handed Carlye a pink dress.

When Carlye stepped out of the bathroom, she saw that Lily was sitting on the other bed, the one that wasn't occupied. "I brought you a sandwich. Dora wanted you to have something to eat. Just don't get it on your dress."

Carlye sat down on the bed and picked up the sandwich. It was peanut butter and strawberry jelly. She ate a few bites and left the rest. There was a small bottle of water with it. She drank it down and then refilled it in the bathroom sink.

"Are you done?" Lily stood up and came near.

"I guess."

Lily picked up a tube of ointment that was on the tray and dabbed it on Carlye's forehead and eye. "This should help."

"Downstairs..." Carlye started and then stopped, her voice cracking. Maybe she shouldn't talk about it, she wondered. Something in her needed to say what had happened. "Downstairs there was a girl."

Lily didn't say anything. She handed Carlye a pack of ice for her eye. "Hold this here."

"The girl downstairs..." Carlye started again.

Lily looked at Carlye. Carlye realized it was the first time they had made eye contact. "Mitch?" Carlye nodded. "Stay away from him."

"Did you know her name?"

"Jenna." Lily didn't say anything more.

Carlye wanted to ask Lily questions about where she was from and how long she'd been at Mr. Maifer's house. How they could get away. If any of the girls got to go home. She didn't.

Asking those questions would have meant that there was hope. Carlye wasn't sure there was any. Not after what she'd seen Mitch do to the girl in the basement.

The girls sat quietly for another twenty minutes or so, Lily helping Carlye with her ice pack and making sure her lipstick was on. "Lily, I just want to sleep."

"You can't sleep yet. Mr. Maifer is having a party."

Lily stayed in the room with Carlye, laying back on the empty bed in her room. Carlye didn't know why she was there. Maybe Dora wanted Lily to keep an eye on her. Either way, Carlye was grateful for the company. Although she couldn't tell the time, after a while a soft knock came on the door. Lily jumped off the bed and motioned for Carlye to follow.

When they walked out of the room, they followed three other girls through the pine tree door and out onto the patio where Carlye had her debut. As they walked, Carlye felt her hands start to shake. She clenched them into fists, afraid of what they might do to her if she didn't cooperate.

From the looks of it, it was early evening. The sun was starting to set and the patio was lit with subtle lighting and a fire. The clouds that had cluttered the sky had blown over without a drop of rain. There was a buffet of food and an aproned bartender serving drinks off to the side. Just ahead of the line of girls, there was a group of men standing around talking, each with a drink in their hand. Carlye gazed around, counting the five men, wondering which one would take a turn with her.

Carlye was the last one in line. The girls in front of her were different heights, with different hair and skin. Carlye guessed that some of them were a little bit older, but none of them looked more than sixteen. She thought she was the youngest. What they had in common was they were all wearing the same pink dress, the same pink lipstick.

As they got close to the group of men, Carlye saw one of

them turn. He looked like he was the same age as her dad. He was wearing shorts and a polo shirt with a sweater around his shoulders. He had on a big watch, the kind that she used to see in her mom's fashion magazines. He had a drink in his hand. As he turned to look at the girls, he smiled right at her. It wasn't a smile that Carlye liked. Her stomach turned. She looked down at her feet, the toes of her pink shoes peeking out from underneath the hem of her dress.

The girls stopped about ten feet away from the men, all lined up. Mr. Maifer was in the center of the group. "I've got a little present for you, gentlemen. Ready to have some fun?" he said, nodding towards the girls. Immediately, the first girl in line, the one that looked to be sixteen, started walking back to the changing room. Once they got there, the older girls pulled their dresses off and hung them on hangers. They weren't wearing anything but their shoes. Carlye immediately looked away. She didn't want to take off her dress. She couldn't. Lily touched her arm, "Get ready. We can't go out without everyone."

Carlye's throat tightened. She pulled off her dress and followed the other girls back out to the party. The night air was cold on her skin. She followed the line of girls over to the chef, who gave them trays of food. Carlye followed Lily and took the food over to the men only wearing her high heels.

Mr. Maifer and another man had sat down by this time. Carlye kept following Lily and passed by the men, holding the tray out, but not looking at anyone. As she passed by, she heard Mr. Maifer say, "See anything you like?"

The man replied, "What's not to like!"

Laughter filled the air, "I told you this would be the best party you've ever gone to." The clink of glasses toasting bounced off the patio.

Carlye circled back, following one of the other girls. On her second pass, she heard Mr. Maifer say, "Do you have one in mind?"

"That one."

Carlye realized that he was pointing to her. She stood, startled, and dropped the tray on the ground. Fear flooded through her. She didn't want to be punished. Mr. Maifer laughed, "She's new. Very new."

"That's what I like," the other man replied.

After the food was served, there was another round of drinks. Some of the men were talking to the girls, but Carlye and Lily stood off to the side while Mr. Maifer and the man that had been eyeing Carlye talked.

Carlye felt frozen. It wasn't a physical sensation, although she was cold. It was an emotion, like someone had turned her off. She was seeing what was happening in front of her without really seeing it.

One of the older girls was straddling the man that was sitting next to Mr. Maifer. She was laughing and Carlye could see his hands on her bare buttocks. Mr. Maifer leaned over to her and said something, nodding towards Carlye. The girl smiled and stepped off of the man, went to the bar and walked over to Carlye and Lily, holding two glasses. "Mr. Maifer would like you to join the party."

The girl didn't say anymore. She returned to the group of men. Carlye followed Lily, her glass in hand, her heels clicking on the stone pavers of the patio. When they approached the men, Mr. Maifer pointed right at Carlye, "Is this the one you want?"

The man with the sweater nodded, "Yes. Unless you want her?"

Mr. Maifer waved him off, "And deprive you of some fun? No. I can have her whenever I want." He motioned for Carlye to come closer. She leaned down, "Do what he tells you." As she stood up, his hand brushed her body.

Carlye walked over to the man like a robot and stood near him, facing away. She didn't know what else to do. Carlye looked over at Lily. She was sitting on Mr. Maifer's lap. He was rubbing her back. The man that had chosen Carlye stood up. "Let's take a walk." Carlye followed him to the other side of the patio. She hadn't been to that side yet. "Sit here." She sat down on the couch, the cool fabric hitting her bare skin. Out of a pocket in his shorts, he pulled a vial. "Give me your drink," he said. Carlye handed it to him, not saying a word, paralyzed to do anything but what he said. She saw him pour powder into the glass. "Drink this. It will help you to relax. You want to relax, don't you?"

Terror gripped Carlye so hard that she could hardly think straight. She tried to drink but ended up spilling some of it down the front of her chest. The man reached over and wiped it off of her. "Your skin is so soft. I can see why Jackson chose you. Finish your drink. I'm ready to have some fun."

Carlye started to feel the same warm groggy feeling she had the day before when Mr. Maifer offered her a drink. She could feel her heart beating in her chest, the man's hands on her…

33

The door opened. Holly finally emerged, looking drawn and tired. She had on an old sweatshirt and leggings. LaDonna put her arm around her daughter as they walked down the stars. Kat walked behind them.

As they got to the bottom of the steps and walked into the living room, Van stood up. Kat watched him. He stood in place, not moving. Kat came out from behind LaDonna and Holly. "Van, this is Holly."

Van stretched out his hand. "It's nice to meet you. Thanks for seeing us."

Holly plopped down on the couch after she shook Van's hand. LaDonna disappeared for a moment and then came back with a coffee for Kat and a tea for Holly. "This will help to settle you, honey." She set the tea down in front of her. "Chamomile," she said to Kat.

Van leaned forward on the couch. "I can't imagine what you have been through. Your mom told us how worried you are about Carlye. Do you think you can tell us what happened? Even the smallest detail may help us with our story and the police with their search."

"You are going to tell the police everything, right?"

"That's right. Is it okay if I record this so they can hear?" Van said.

Kat interjected, "Holly, we are working with the police. It's not a normal situation, but the detective that you talked to, Lance, he's a good guy. He's really working hard. We all have to work hard to so that we can find Carlye and bring her home."

That reassurance seemed to give Holly the confidence she needed. She started the story over again, telling them it was okay to record her. She told them about what she and Carlye had been wearing, the van they had ridden in and gave them a more detailed description of Nathan and Mitch.

Kat touched Holly's shoulder, "Can you tell us more about the house? Any landmarks that you saw? We have to try to find the house that you were in."

Holly closed her eyes for a moment. "It's not a tall house. Looked like it was only one floor. White on the outside, with a one-car garage. There weren't any other houses. It was like the only house on the street. The kitchen was to the right when you went in the front door. Oh, and there was a screen door on the front. I remember because it slammed when I went inside the house."

"How about anything outside that would help us to identify it from the road?" Kat was jotting things down in a notebook from her bag.

"The road was rough. Like it was a dirt road. The driveway too. It was the same." Kat saw Holly's eyes light up for a moment. "There was a red mailbox on a black pole right at the top of the driveway."

Kat paused. "Holly, do you remember the numbers on the box?"

There was a pause. "Not. Maybe a two or a three?" Holly sighed and crumpled into a smaller ball, "I can't remember."

Kat closed her notebook. "You did really good. This is great information. Now, will you do me a favor?"

"Okay..."

"You remember how I've been scared?"

"Yes."

"I got over it by being around people I could trust. You can do that too. Just be with your mom and dad and your pastor. But you need to come out of your room. Okay?"

Holly nodded. Kat wasn't sure she would actually do it, but she hoped that her words would sink in and help Holly to move forward.

Kat and Van thanked LaDonna and walked out to the truck. Kat picked up her phone to call Lance before they even pulled out of the driveway. "Traldent."

"Lance, it's Kat."

"Hey there."

"We just got done talking to Holly. We've got some more details on the house where she was taken and a recording. Can we stop by the station? Are you there?"

"Sure. I'll be here. We've been working on narrowing that down. See you soon."

THE DRIVE to the station didn't take long. Just long enough for Kat and Van to share their thoughts about the visit with Holly. As they pulled in, Lance was outside talking on his phone. "Thanks," he said, as they walked up, ending his call.

"News?" Van asked.

"Not too much, although we've got some help now. Come with me."

Inside the department, Lance used his ID to get them through the secured doors. Kat and Van followed him to the back, where they went into a conference room. There were people setting up equipment in the room, aerial images taped to the walls. Kat felt like maybe someone was finally taking Carlye's disappearance seriously. "Kat, Van, meet Special Agent Sean Hollister of the FBI."

Kat smiled, "I've heard a lot about you."

Sean Hollister smiled, a wide, toothy grin that didn't fit the profile of a Special Agent of the FBI. He was blonde with green eyes and had his FBI badge on a chain around his neck. "Really, how's that?"

"I met with Jo over at the Blue Water Center. She said you're the guy for these kinds of cases."

"Yes, I did hear from Mama Jo today about this case." Sean looked at Van but didn't say any more about Jo. "You look to be a military guy." He stuck out his hand.

"That would be right. Marines. I'm Van Peck. Kat and I work together."

Sean sat down on the edge of a table that was in the room. "Lance told me that you just interviewed Holly Jenkins."

Kat pulled out a chair and sat down, watching as other FBI agents booted up laptops and pulled files out of their bags. It looked like they were serious. "Yes. She agreed to see us. We got her out of her room. I think we've got a few more details on the house that she was taken."

Sean got up and walked over to the images he had attached to the wall. "We think that finding the house will be the next key in finding Carlye. Based on where we found Holly, which is here," he pointed to a spot on the map where the gas station was, "and the approximate timeline that she gave us, we think that the house should be in this area." Sean stopped, looking at the map, "What we don't know is which direction from the gas station. We have no way of knowing if Holly got turned around at any point and if the direction that she approached was actually the direction that she came from."

Kat could see from the maps on the walls that the area where the gas station was had different housing characteristics depending on which direction you looked. To the north, there were a few housing developments off of a side road that was closer in toward town. To the east, there was nothing but the two-lane highway. On the west side, there were a couple of commercial properties along the highway and then a side street that had a few houses and a farm. To the south, there wasn't much. From the map, it looked to be a narrow road with a smattering of houses.

Kat got up and squinted at the maps. Van joined her, the two of them staring at the area. "How big of a circumference is this?" Van asked Sean.

"We did ten miles -- five miles out on each side of the gas station. See anything?"

Kat traced her finger on the north side. "I don't think it would be here. This looks too developed." She stood back from the map. "Sean, do we know what kind of road this is to the south?"

Sean sat down at his computer and pulled up a more detailed image. "Looks like a dirt road or maybe gravel."

"Any others of those near the gas station?"

Kat waited for a minute as Sean scanned a more detailed view of his maps on his computer. "Doesn't look like it." Kat shot a look to Van who nodded.

"I think that's the area. Holly told us that the road to the house was bumpy. So was the driveway. Everything else is paved."

Sean closed his laptop. "Great. Let's take a drive."

Kat and Van followed Sean and Lance out to the back parking lot of the department. "Ride with me," Sean said as he and Lance jumped into a Black Suburban. Two other Suburban's with agents who had just been milling around quickly got into their vehicles and followed.

"Geez, you guys don't mess around, do you?" Kat said.

A toothy smile emerged on Terrell's face through the rearview mirror. "No, ma'am. This is the FBI."

"On the way out to the area where the gas station was located, Sean took a couple of calls, as did Lance. Kat sat quietly with Van in the back seat. She reached for his hand.

A spark of hope was lit in her chest. She hoped that Holly's description had been enough to get them to the right area. If they could find the house, the best outcome would be that Carlye was there and they could rescue her.

Kat saw out of the window the gas station they had been at. She tried to imagine Holly running in the darkness to the lights in the distance. Kat wondered if Holly even felt the barbs and scratches that had covered her arms and face from running through the woods. Had she been so terrified that she didn't feel anything? Was she in shock? Kat realized that in some sense, shock was the biggest mercy of them all.

The turn off to get to the area that they wanted to find was just east of the gas station. It was a small road that was without a street sign. The Suburban bumped and jolted as they made their way down the street. Sean pulled the SUV off to the side, the partner vehicles staying right behind. He took a look at his phone. "Based on the information we have, there are three properties down this road." He scrolled up to show Kat and Van. "The first one is a farm with a couple of outbuildings and a house or two." He scrolled again. "Down here there are two other properties with what look to be small houses on them."

"I'm not sure it is the farm," Kat said, instantly wondering if she should have kept quiet.

"Why do you say that?" Lance asked.

"Sorry, I don't mean to interfere, but Holly said she didn't see any other buildings."

"That's good intel," Sean said. "Since we are here, we'll take a look, but we can lean toward the other properties. Might as well clear them while we are at it."

Sean rolled down the window and waved to the other SUV telling them to proceed to the first property. It was a dilapidated farmhouse with a half fallen down red barn and a couple of outbuildings sandwiched between. The agents pulled in the driveway and got out of the vehicles. "You can get out, but stay by the cars," Sean said.

Kat and Van slid out of the back seat and waited. They could see the agents moving from structure to structure, working in teams of two. Calls of "clear" and "nothing here" echoed back to the cars. Within a couple of minutes, they were all back at the cars. "There's no sign they were here. Let's keep looking." Sean said.

A minute later, they were back in the vehicles and moving down the road. They stopped at the second potential address, but an older couple answered the door. A quick check of the premises yielded no results.

Kat could feel the frustration building inside of her. They had to be on the right track. The road was unpaved. They were within a reasonable distance to the gas station. There were heavy woods all around -- exactly as Holly had described it.

The team continued down the road to a third property. It was owned by a single man who was in a wheelchair. He let the agents in and still, there was no evidence that Holly had been there.

While they waited, Kat caught Van looking at her. "You okay?" he asked.

"I just want to find this place. Do we have the right road?"

"I don't know. These things can take time."

The agents returned to the vehicles and they got back in again. It felt like they had been at it for hours. "I think there is one more place we can try before we have to head back and regroup," Sean said.

The mood in the SUV was somber. They all knew that time was ticking. No one knew what had happened to Carlye or if she was still alive. They needed a break and they needed one soon.

The SUV caravan pulled down the road further, turned around a bend and started to accelerate to get to the last property when something caught Kat's eye. She saw a flash of red. "Wait!" she yelled. All of the SUVs stopped. "What's the matter?" Lance said.

Kat's hand was already on the door handle. She jumped out and pointed. "Look, over there!" Kat pointed as the agents joined her. Under several sprawling trees was a small white house with a screen door and a single car garage. In front of the house -- the red flash that Kat had seen -- was a red mailbox. "That's the house Holly described!"

Van put his hand on Kat's arm and pulled her behind the SUV as the agents and Detective Traldent quietly took up positions around the house. Kat didn't speak. All she could do was watch and wait, hoping that the agents would bring Carlye out.

34

The light came into Carlye's room, streaming across her face. She felt groggy again and pushed aside the memories of the night before. She took a minute to determine if she hurt anywhere. Her face felt better. The swelling in her eye seemed to be down. Between her legs was another issue. The pain was so intense that she wasn't sure she could stand up.

Carlye limped her way into the bathroom and tried to take a shower. The warm water soothed the aches she felt in her body, although she had a pounding headache so severe she felt sick.

In the shower, she saw new bruises on her thighs and arms. She pushed the thoughts of the night before out of her head. The naked bodies, the men. The one man that had chosen her and taken her off by herself. The powder he put in her drink. She didn't want to know what happened to her after that. She didn't want to know how she ended up in her bed or who put her there.

Carlye felt herself withdrawing deep inside again. It was

her only safe space. Out of the shower, she dried off, put on the new dress -- lilac this time -- and crawled back into bed.

35

All Kat could do was wait while the agents searched. Kat checked her phone to see the time, "How long have they been in there?"

Van shook his head. "Maybe twenty minutes? I don't know."

Another ten minutes passed as Kat watched the agents move around the building and in and out of the doors. Finally, Special Agent Hollister approached the SUVs wearing a set of rubber gloves on his hands. "Here's what we have: The house looks like no one lives there permanently. It does look like someone has been there recently. There are food containers that haven't been taken out. From the smell, it's been a while. That might fit our timeline for Holly and Carlye."

"Can we go in?" Kat practically took off running before he could answer.

"Yes, but wear these and don't touch anything. Stay with an agent. I've got to go and call for a Crime Scene Unit. Let's see what we can learn." Sean whistled for an agent to come over. "Take these two in the house. Don't let them disturb the crime scene, but they get free rein. If they mess anything up, you are going to be reposted to South Dakota." Another toothy grin and Kat and Van were off with the agent to look inside the house.

The house smelled like rotting trash. There were flies everywhere, especially in the kitchen. Kat and Van split up, each going with an agent. "Let's look on our own and then compare notes," Kat said.

With blue crime scene gloves on, Kat followed the agent around the house. Just inside the front door was a stained couch and a coffee table. On the table were empty beer cans and a bottle of whiskey. There was a door off of the living room area, if you could call it that, that led to the kitchen. White Formica countertops ran along the left side of the kitchen. On the wall directly ahead of her, Kat saw a back door and a refrigerator that was humming away. Kat looked at the door and then pulled the refrigerator door open. There was some lunch meat on the top shelf as well as one unopened beer out of a six-pack. Clearly, someone had been in the house recently.

"Can I check the date on the lunch meat?" Kat asked the agent.

"As long as you have your gloves on, you can. Just don't move anything," the grim-faced agent said.

Kat closed the refrigerator. She couldn't see the date on the package without moving it. She looked at the door that led out to the yard. She didn't want to touch the door handle to open it, worried that she might smudge any fingerprints that were on it. The woods were just beyond the door, only about twenty feet away, Kat judged. She could see a few broken branches but it was hard to tell if those were from Holly or from someone or something else. Kat decided to head outside to look at the yard. On the way out, she passed back through the living room area. Something shiny caught her eye that was under the corner of the couch on the floor. She leaned over. "Agent?"

The grim agent came over and knelt down. "I see it.

Someone get Hollister," he yelled. Within a few seconds, Hollister appeared.

"What'd you have?"

The agent didn't say anything but pointed. "Let's get that photographed and bagged right now. I want to take a look."

Kat stood back while the agents worked. A man wearing a digital camera around his neck and a blue FBI jacket came over and snapped several pictures while Hollister pulled an evidence bag out of his jacket pocket. "It looks like a necklace," he said. "One with a small bird on it. Anyone know if either of our victims had a necklace like this?" The agents around him shook their heads no.

"Before you put that away, can I take a picture of it?" Kat asked. Neither Holly nor Carlye's parents had mentioned it, but Kat had a feeling that it was part of the case. Before Kat could think about it too much, another agent called out. Kat followed.

The agent was in the single car garage that was attached to the house. "Look at this, Hollister," she said pointing to the ground, "There is a relatively recent oil leak on the ground." She clicked her flashlight on pointing the beam of light to the hinges of the door. Kat tilted her head to the side to see what she was looking at. There were three strands of long blond hair that had been caught in a splinter of wood.

"Jesus," Hollister said. "Get everyone out of here. I want a forensic team here now. This is now a hot zone."

Kat followed the agents outside as they waited for the forensic team to arrive. Hollister pulled off his gloves and joined them. "It looks like this is the house where Holly and Carlye were taken. I want the forensic team to go through it before we disturb anything else or miss something important." He looked at Kat and Van. "I'm going to do something totally unorthodox. Can you two go talk to the Morgan's and show them the picture you have of the necklace? See if it is Carlye's? I can send you with one of our agents."

Kat nodded, excited that they had found something and that it at least felt like they were making progress. She looked at Van. He nodded. "Of course. We can go right now."

Kat and Van jumped into the SUV with the female agent. The drive to the Morgan's house didn't take too long, although to Kat, who was anxious to see whether the necklace was Carlye's, it seemed to take forever.

When they pulled up in front of the Morgan's house it was quiet. As Kat got out of the SUV with the FBI agent and Van, she noticed a stillness around the house. It felt eerie. Van led the way, knocking on the front door. Alana Morgan opened the door, saw the FBI agent and started to weep, "Oh my God, oh my God. What is going on?"

The agent stepped forward. "It's okay ma'am. I'm just their escort. We'd like to talk to you for a moment if that is okay."

"Yes, of course. I'm sorry. I'm just..."

Kat put her hand on Alana's shoulder as they walked into the house. "It's okay. We understand. Is Tim home?"

"Yes. He's in the den working on his computer. I'll get him."

Within a moment, they were all gathered in the living room. Van started telling the story. "The girl that was with Carlye when she was taken gave us some new information that we followed up on. The FBI is now involved. We did a search this afternoon..."

Tim interrupted, "Did you find her?"

"Not yet, but Kat has something to show you."

Kat pulled up the image of the necklace on her phone. "The Special Agent asked us to come here to show this to you." Kat passed her phone over to Tim. "Do you recognize this? Is this Carlye's?"

Tim didn't say anything, but the expression told Kat everything she needed to know. He passed the phone over to Alana, who looked at the picture and then began to weep quietly. "Yes, that's hers. We gave it to her on her last birthday." Kat saw Alana bow her head, tears running down her cheeks.

The agent with them looked at both Tim and Alana, "You are sure. This is definitely Carlye's?"

They both nodded. "The picture in the hallway – she's wearing it," Alana said, sniffling. The agent got up. "I need to make a phone call."

Kat moved over so that she could sit next to Alana. She put her arm around her as she shook with sadness. "I know this is so hard," Kat said. "You are both doing great. The FBI is on this and we are all doing everything we can to bring Carlye back."

While Kat sat with Alana, Van spoke, "Have there been any other developments? Has Carlye called again?"

When Kat looked up at Tim, she saw his face was gray with worry, "No. Other than that one phone call, we haven't heard from her."

Before he could say any more, the FBI agent came back in the room. "Kat, Van -- we gotta go. Hollister needs you back at the department."

Kat got up and walked with the agent and Van back to the door. "I promise, we will follow every lead as far as we can take it."

Kat felt Alana grab her hand, "I know you can't promise anything, but please, do what you can…"

THE AGENT DROVE them back to the department. They were quiet, Kat and Van processing their thoughts.

Van finally broke the silence, "So, what do we think the necklace means?"

The agent glanced at him while she was driving. "In these cases, it doesn't mean anything more than it means. That's what my training agent told me. All we know is that Carlye was there. We don't know anything more than that."

"What about the hairs that you found in the door jamb?" By Van's questions, Kat knew that he wanted to try to put the pieces together.

"Once we get them tested, that will just be more evidence that Carlye was there."

"Was there anything else you found?"

Kat caught the agent giving Van a sideways look that said she wasn't going to talk anymore. "I think it's better if you talk to Hollister. He will be able to give you a full picture of the house and the next steps."

When they got back to the police station, Hollister and his team, as well as Lance Traldent, were already in the conference room with new images of what they found at the house.

"Glad you could make it." Hollister gave them another grin. "How did things go with the parents?"

Van spoke first. "They are rattled for sure, but they confirmed that the necklace was Carlye's. They got it for her on her last birthday."

Hollister nodded. "The forensic team is at the house right now. I've put in a property request to figure out who owns that house. We are waiting for that information."

"Hold on a second." Kat's brow furrowed. "You should be able to get the owner on the property within minutes. Even I can do that. What's the holdup?"

Lance sat down at the conference room table. "The problem is that the company that supposedly owns it doesn't exist."

36

Jackson Maifer sat at his desk sipping coffee. The party the night before had led to some lucrative deals that could seriously add to his already billionaire status. The men that he made deals with expected some perks in order to sign on the dotted line. Most of them liked what he had to offer. He checked his emails to see if his assistant had sent him anything that required his attention. She had not.

Heavily involved in real estate, Jackson had houses all over the world. He also owned commercial property in nearly every major city in the United States, plus some in the most well-know, stable cities in the world. London, Toronto, Bogota, Beijing, Geneva, Tokyo -- his fingerprint was on places everywhere.

In addition to his real estate holdings, he played heavily in the stock market, taking hundred-thousand-dollar losses like they were nothing. It was just play money as far as he was concerned. He also had manufacturing companies, healthcare companies and technology firms that were part of his holdings. Not to mention all of the shell companies that kept things moving as much money away from the feds as he could legally move. Jackson didn't want to pay more in taxes than he already did.

As he closed his laptop, pulling out some financial statements that needed his review before his next board meeting, his wife, Maria came in. "Hey honey, what are you up to today?"

"Just taking a look at these financials. I may have to go to LA tomorrow..."

Maria sat down on his lap. "Really? Can I come and do some shopping?"

"I think that would work... How much is it going to cost me?"

"I don't know, baby, how much am I worth?"

"You are everything to me."

Jackson saw Maria get up and close his office door, "Let me make a little prepayment," she said, pulling him over to the couch.

AN HOUR LATER, after Jackson sent Maria off to get her hair done, he returned to his desk. His phone chirped, an alert coming through. Jackson quickly sent a text to Mitch. A knock on his office door came a minute later.

"What's up boss?"

"Someone is tracking Mill Run Holdings. I want to know who." Jackson's mind began to swim. He had layers of protection over his off-book activities but knowing that someone was tracking him was unnerving.

"Of course. Let me make a couple of calls." Mitch turned around and left the room.

Jackson got up from his desk and started to pace the room. He needed to know who was looking into Mill Run Holdings and why. If they did a deep dive into the company, they would discover that it was held by another company and that one was held by another company, too. It was a shell game. Most people that had his lifestyle did the same. They usually did it for tax reasons. Jackson had his own reasons.

It wasn't something he could worry about now. He had people he paid to do the worrying. Jackson got up and paced between his desk and the fireplace. He had everything he wanted – beautiful homes, a successful business, a gorgeous wife and his girls. He couldn't want anymore. He clenched his fists. Anyone who tried to separate him from the life he built would pay. He would be sure of it.

37

The team had been working at the home ownership issue for hours. They had tracked the white house with the red mailbox to an initial listing of Mill Run Holdings. A deeper dive into the company didn't give them anything. No owner. Just an attorney. It looked like the majority shareholder was another company.

Kat stopped her own research as Lance slammed his hand on the conference room table, "What is this? I've never seen so many holding companies in my life. How is this possible?"

Hollister stepped behind him. "Did you find another?"

"Yes! We are down to the fifth level. Who is this guy?"

Kat and Van had been sitting together working on the attorney angle. There were different attorneys listed for every single company. They all seemed to have different legal firms, which was getting them nowhere.

Van pointed, "Wait! Stop there!"

Kat stopped scrolling down the screen in front of her. "What is it?"

"I've seen that name before."

Kat looked closely at the screen. Scott Norquist was the

attorney of record on the property with a firm called Wealth-Share Property Holdings."

Kat waited while Van did a search on his own laptop. He whistled, which brought Lance and Sean over to him, "Did you find something?"

Van nodded, "Maybe. These guys listed on the companies all seem to work for different law firms. I'm not sure that's the case. Look here..."

Hollister snapped his fingers, getting the attention of one of the agents. "Right now. I need a subpoena for corporate records for these law firms. We need to know who works for them. Think you can get that for me?"

The agent that Hollister barked at nodded.

"Continue, Van. Whatcha got?"

Kat noticed that Van paused. It was something that he did when he was still formulating a thought. "I'm wondering if the law firms are shell companies, too. There has to be a hub somewhere. A place where these holding firms and law firms all hit a nexus." Van clicked on his phone and pulled up an article from a Japanese business magazine. "See this guy? His name is Scott Norquist."

"Who is he and who is he with?" Lance asked.

"He is the founding partner of a prominent law firm called Norquist and Adams. I've read about them before. They are involved in the highest levels of business and Washington politics. These guys are more than attorneys, they are fixers."

"Who is the guy he's with?" Kat was intrigued by the information that Van had unearthed.

"That's billionaire Jackson Maifer." Van leaned back from the screen and continued, "I don't know a lot about the guy. He might not even be involved, but that's the level that Norquist plays on."

Kat could feel the team take a moment to digest what Van had said. "What you are saying is that you think Norquist is connected to all of these businesses that own all of these properties, which really just filter down to where we found Carlye's necklace?"

"That's a long way to say it, but yes."

The female agent that had driven Kat and Van over to the Morgan's house interrupted, "Hollister, you need to see this."

After a minute of looking back and forth between the attorney of record list and the information on the agent's screen, Hollister yelled, "Bingo!"

Kat tried not to laugh, but Hollister's pure joy at doing his job was infectious. "What did you find?"

"Our attorneys of record -- all seven of them -- have ties to the same firm. A pizza goes to the person who guesses it first!"

Van spoke up, "I'll bet it is Norquist and Adams, right?"

Hollister pointed directly at him, "Yes! That man wins a pizza!" Kat saw Sean look around the room. "We've been at it for hours. Let's take a break, get some food and be back here in an hour. We've got to figure out who the client is."

38

Jackson stayed in his office much longer than he normally did, waiting to hear from Mitch. An hour went by, Jackson continuing to pace until Mitch came back into the office.

"Mr. Maifer?"

"What did you find out?" Jackson growled.

"Mr. Norquist is going to be calling you in a minute if that is convenient."

Jackson could tell by Mitch's sniveling that there was something wrong, but that he wasn't going to share the news himself. Dora had stopped by and told him about the loss in the basement. It was bad enough that Mitch had wrecked one of his favorite girls. He couldn't deal with it now. After he figured out who was tracking his real estate holdings linked to the girls, he'd deal with Mitch. It might be time to replace him.

While he waited, he stopped to think about the girls. He didn't love them. He knew that. He prized them, the way that he used to prize his racehorses. The horses were what had given him the idea in the first place. Although his third wife, Maria, was a stunner with her long black hair and her even longer legs, she just wasn't enough despite their twenty-year age difference.

He had been at the track entertaining work associates, watching the muscles ripple on one of his horses as they walked by and then followed the horse and handler back into the stable. On one of the aisles were two blonde girls wearing tight jeans, working together to brush down one of the horses. It hit him like a landslide. He needed girls to entertain him and his friends. It would be better than horses.

Jackson's move away from horses as entertainment had started off with high priced escorts. The cost was exorbitant, but they were professionals. They just didn't have what Jackson, or his friends for that matter, wanted. They wanted new and fresh. Jackson had Mitch ask their escort agency for younger girls. They couldn't give him what he wanted. He ended the contract and then sued them for not fulfilling it. That is when he started building his own stable of girls. Literally.

The ring from his cell phone interrupted his thoughts. "Norquist?"

"Hey Jackson, how are you today?"

"I'm not happy. Who's sniffing around?"

"Is this line encrypted?"

"You know it is."

"The short answer? FBI."

Jackson took a minute to process that, neither man saying anything. "What are they looking for?"

"I'm not sure yet. I've got our investigators working on it. It looks like they are trying to see who owns some of your properties. They are digging deep on this one. You might want to have a chat with Mitch about which one of the girls is the troublemaker."

As Jackson hung up the phone with Scott, he motioned to

Mitch. "We have a problem. One of the newest girls isn't playing nice. You need to figure out who it is and deal with it."

"How do you know it's one of the newest girls?"

"We haven't had any problems recently. Has to be. Fix it." Jackson looked back down at his work and growled. "Fix it now."

39

Mitch left Jackson's office with a hole in his stomach. He could tell that Jackson was mad. Choosing the right girls from the right families -- ones that wouldn't make too much of a fuss -- was Mitch's job. One of the families was clearly fussing.

Mitch walked outside to smoke a cigarette. He needed to think. The last girls to come in were from that camp that Isla worked at. Mitch knew that he needed to figure this out and fast. Jackson had been none too happy. Jackson saw the girls as his Thoroughbreds. Mitch shook his head. He didn't see them that way. They were just a piece of tail. That was it.

Mitch walked down the driveway about halfway to the gate. It was a nice day in Colorado. The warm days had let Jackson entertain outside the last few weeks, but Mitch knew that the colder days would be coming. He didn't know, he never did, if Jackson wanted to keep the girls here or move them to another site. Sometimes he kept girls in more than one place. He'd even sent his jet to pick up a girl and move her if he wanted her for a particular guest, or more likely, for himself.

Mitch thought back to the last girls that had come in. He

and Nathan had brought the young blonde from Camp Hope. She was the one that tried to escape. What was her name? Hailey? No, it was Carlye. Jackson seemed to like her a lot. The other girl, the black one, she got away. Mitch didn't bother to tell Jackson about that. If the girl had enough spunk to run away, Mitch was sure that Jackson would have loved to have her, but Mitch just let her go. Jackson hadn't been at the pick-up site. He never was. He'd never know. She was more work than she was worth. They would have had to drug her the entire way to Colorado. She might have even ended up like the girl in the stables the day before.

As he crushed out his cigarette butt and buried it under some mulch, he felt a little bad about the girl that he had killed. It was her fault really. If she had just cooperated and done what she had been told, things would be different...

Mitch shook off the thought. They got one girl a year, it seemed, that just couldn't behave. Those girls never went back to their families. Mitch usually took care of them. They were troublemakers and Mitch knew that Jackson had worked hard to develop his stable of girls quiet. His unusual tastes weren't for everyone.

What did surprise Mitch over time was how many of Jackson's friends, if you could call them that, seemed to like the younger set. You'd think they'd like girls with a bit of curve to them, Mitch thought walking back toward the three-story retreat perched on the side of the mountain. And Jackson's wife, Maria, she was a looker. Why Jackson wasn't satisfied with her, Mitch didn't know.

Mitch shook his head. He knew that Maria was just like Jackson's other wives and girlfriends. Just looking for money. Well, maybe not his first wife, Shelly. Mitch had never met her, but he had heard that she died from a blood clot when their two kids were little. The kids were grown now. Jackson and Maria only met them when they went to Florida. The kids never came to Colorado, they never really interacted with Jackson. Mitch could only remember one time they did, and it was only because Jackson Jr., wanted to go skiing. It had been a nightmare. Mitch had to move all of the girls to another location.

The thoughts in his head led him back to which family was causing problems. He had success in the past finding young runaways or girls that had just come across the border. He'd bring them in and Dora would get them cleaned up and ready for service. Then Jackson decided he liked ones that were blonde and thin. The very young ones. There was one on the way that he was sure that Jackson would like. But she was very, very young. The youngest he had ever brought out to Jackson's estate.

Mitch wandered back into the house and went straight to Dora's office. "I need a minute."

"I need a million dollars, but you can't always have what you want," Dora replied as she looked at her computer. "Actually, I do have a million dollars. So, what do you really want?"

"The FBI is digging. Any ideas which family might be causing the problem?"

"Who was last in?" Dora asked absentmindedly.

"The blonde from Isla's camp. What's her name?"

"Carlye. I don't know her last name though. Let me pull it up." A minute went by as Dora looked for Carlye's records. "Carlye Morgan. Yes, she came from Camp Hope. Want me to reach out to Isla?" Mitch nodded as Dora picked up her phone. The conversation was short. "Isla said the local PD has been out to the camp, but it was just one officer from some podunk department. You really think Carlye's family is the one that's causing the problem?"

"We have to figure it out. Jackson is mad."

Dora tapped the end of a pencil on her desk, "He has a party tomorrow. Heavy hitters coming in." Dora leaned back in her chair. Mitch saw her staring at her. "By the way, take it easy on the merchandise, okay. She was pretty messed up when you brought her to me."

"Yeah, yeah." Mitch stood up and walked to the office door, heading out in the hallway. As soon as Dora was out of earshot, Mitch mumbled, "That girl needed to be taught a lesson."

40

The afternoon passed. Carlye stayed in her room. Lily came to check on her a few times, making sure she had showered and had some crackers and juice. Most of the day, Carlye stayed in her bed. Sleep was becoming her friend. It was the only place that she was free. Her waking hours were filled with a combination of rules and pain. There was no point in being alive.

A knock came on the door just after dinner. The sun was beginning to set. Lily unlocked the deadbolt and stuck her head in, waving Carlye to follow her. Lily motioned to Carlye to put on her lipstick and waited as she did so. Carlye followed Lily past the dining room. They walked down the stairs and out the side door that Carlye had tried to escape through. Waiting just outside the door, Mitch was perched on a utility vehicle. It was green and had four seats plus a small bed in the back. Carlye followed Lily as she got in the back seat. Behind her, she could see a wicker picnic basket, the kind her parents used to use when they went to the park.

Mitch didn't say anything when she got in. The cold air seeped through Carlye's white dress. Mitch had a jacket.

Neither she nor Lily had one. "Where are we going?" Carlye whispered to Lily.

"Mr. Maifer wants you at the honeymoon house tonight."

Carlye didn't know what the honeymoon house was, but her stomach turned as they lurched over a few bumps in the road. Her mind raced and then completely stopped as if it had shut off. She didn't want to think about what might happen to her tonight. She couldn't.

They turned off into the woods, the driveway winding farther away from the main house, flanked by a line of hemlocks. The evening had turned cool. Goosebumps traveled up and down Carlye's arms and legs as the air moved through the vehicle. Up ahead, a small wooden cabin appeared through some trees and branches, as immaculately maintained as the main house, lights glowing from the inside. Mitch pulled up to the front door. "Get out," he growled. "Don't screw this up."

Carlye followed Lily up to the front door as she pushed it open. Warm air hit her skin as soon as she stepped inside. As her eyes adjusted, she saw a living room, complete with candles lit and a bear rug in front of the fireplace, a warm fire already burning. The kitchen area, which was open to the living room, had a long counter covered in plates of fruit, cheese and crackers plus an array of liquor. It looked like something out of a decorating magazine her mom might have read. Carlye tried not to think about it. Lily pointed to her left, "There are two bedrooms. You use the one in the back. I'll stay in the other one."

"What's going on? I'm afraid," Carlye whimpered, the words barely making it out of her mouth.

"Just sit on the couch. Mr. Maifer is sending you a special guest. I'll be here when it is over."

They could hear the approach of a vehicle coming to the front door. Lily went right to the second bedroom and closed the door. Carlye walked over and sat on the couch just as the door opened.

A dark-haired man walked in the cabin. "You are already here. Good."

Carlye didn't know what to do, so she sat stock-still on the couch.

"Come here so I can look at you," the man said.

As Carlye got closer she could smell cologne coming off of him in waves. He had almost black eyes and was wearing a suit. His nose was long and tapered and he had thin lips.

"You can call me Talib."

Carlye didn't say anything, she just nodded.

"That's good. Don't talk. I don't want to hear your voice. I've had a stressful day and I need to relax." Carlye watched him as he walked over to the bar and made himself a drink. "I'd offer you one, Jackson said I should." He pulled a vial of powder out of his suit coat and put it on the bar. Carlye recognized it as the same vial the other man had used. She wondered if Mr. Maifer gave all of his friends those vials. Talib looked at the vial and then looked at Carlye. "I think you have enough experience to enjoy this, don't you? You don't need this tonight." He poured liquor over some ice cubes in a crystal glass and swirled it around. "I want you awake and it's my party."

Carlye watched as he took off his suit coat and hung it over the back of a chair. He took off his tie. She couldn't move. She felt like she was frozen.

"In my culture, the women do as they are told. You will do as you are told. I've had a difficult day. I've had difficult decisions to make and I expect you to obey. Do you understand?"

Carlye nodded. The man's tone had changed. He sounded angry. Carlye was confused. She hadn't met him before. He seemed nice just a minute before.

"Go stand in front of the fire. I want to start our party there."

Carlye did as she was told. Talib brought over a kitchen

chair and made her stand on it. "You are smaller than Jackson described. Stand on here."

Carlye climbed up on the chair, facing Talib. As he set his drink down on the coffee table by the couch, he looked at her, staring. He leaned toward Carlye putting his hand on her hip. "No, you don't need any powder tonight, do you?"

Carlye looked away. She felt the sting of a slap on her face. "Don't ever look away. That is a sign of disrespect."

Trying not to cry, Carlye looked at him. He leaned in and tried to kiss her. She turned away. He grabbed her chin and stuck his tongue in her mouth. She could smell his cologne and feel his rough hands on her skin pulling her closer. When he pulled back, she tried to remember to look at him. He reached toward her and grabbed the neckline of her white dress yanking down so hard that it tore right down the middle of the fabric. Her naked body was exposed.

Talib's hands were all over her and then he stopped to take his shirt off. Grabbing her, he muttered, "I'm feeling more relaxed already, baby."

His hands moved over her body. Carlye tried not to think about it and didn't move, standing completely still, shrinking back inside herself. As he was kissing her, he grabbed the back of her hair and lifted her off the chair, slamming her down on the rug. "I like it rough. How about you?"

Again, Carlye didn't say anything, trying not to cry. Her head pounded from being slammed against the floor. She started to push away. "Leave me alone," she cried. "You're hurting me!"

Talib slapper her face again and grabbed both of her arms and pinned them down above her head. "Jackson said you were new, but I didn't realize this new. I'm so lucky, aren't I?"

Stunned, Carlye didn't move. She couldn't even if she wanted to. She heard the jingle of Talib's belt being loosened and his zipper being pulled down. She turned her head away and then felt the grip of his fingers on her jaw, "What did I say about looking at me?" he shouted. As Carlye tried to look back at him, she felt searing pain between her legs and groaned. "Oh, you like it now. That's right, baby."

Carlye just laid still. She couldn't move because of the pain and the throbbing of her face and head. She felt Talib's hands around her neck. "This is the best part."

As his hands started to squeeze, she panicked and tried to fight him off. The entire time, Talib stayed on top of her, rocking back and forth. Carlye felt her vision narrow as she tried to breathe and then nothing...

41

Jackson's personal cell phone rang. It was Scott Norquist, the attorney who coordinated all of his business dealings, both legitimate and off-book.

"I have some news for you."

"What's that?"

"You were asking who is looking into you?"

"Yes."

"When we got the subpoenas for the house that Mill Run owns, we did a little digging of our own to see who was asking. It looks like it is an FBI agent named Hollister and a local LEO -- Traldent. But here's where it gets interesting. There are other people on the case."

Jackson stood up and started to pace his office. He'd been working since early in the morning, trying to deal with an issue in one of his Asian businesses. "What do you mean other people? Like a PI?"

"No. It is a reporter and her editor. Kat Beckman and Van Peck."

"I'm not worried. What could they do? They don't have access to our information." Jackson heard Scott pause.

"I wouldn't be so sure. These two just leaked a big story. Beckman actually killed someone to save her son. They were both deployed in Afghanistan. These are serious people, Jackson. We need to discourage them from continuing their efforts."

They hung up without saying another word. Jackson texted Mitch and called him to his office. Jackson had his email open. Scott had sent him an encrypted file on Kat Beckman, the reporter. Jackson spun the computer towards Mitch so that he could see her face and information. "She's hunting us. She and her editor, this guy," Jackson pointed to another image on the screen. "They need to be discouraged. Do what you need to do."

MITCH NODDED and walked out of Jackson's office. He liked these kinds of assignments. Jackson didn't really want to know what he was doing. He just wanted it done. He could do that, and more.

The van that Mitch rented smelled like cats, but he didn't care. In the back were a few boxes and some tools. He had put the West Road Electric signs on the side of the truck about a block from where he rented it. He nodded to himself, appreciating how official the van looked. Magnetic signs were the best, he thought, realizing that all the people he passed on the road had no idea what he was about to do.

He had Nathan, from the camp, had started sitting on Beckman's house as soon as Jackson said she was a problem. Mitch had said to Nathan, "I think she will be easier to scare than her editor."

Nathan had called about a half-hour ago from the car he was watching the house from and let Mitch know that Kat and her son had left the house. It didn't look like anyone else was home.

Mitch pulled into her driveway in the van and got out,

putting on a hard hat to look the part in case the neighbors were watching. He went up to the front door, giving Nathan a head nod as he did, and put his toolbox down, pulling a lock picking kit out of his pocket. It took just a second to pop the door open.

Inside the house smelled like coffee and toast. Mitch would have loved to go through Kat's things, maybe even mess things up a bit, but he knew he needed to get in and out. He went directly to the bathroom and stood on the toilet, installing two cameras where they were pointing into the shower. As soon as he got down, he wiped the boot prints off of the toilet seat with a towel that was hanging nearby. It smelled like lavender. He stopped for a moment. Kat Beckman probably smelled good, too, he realized. He enjoyed the thought for a moment and left.

The whole process of installing the cameras took less than two minutes. He pulled the van out onto the street and checked his cell phone to make sure the feed was coming in. It was. He sent a link to Jackson with a text that said, "I'll explain later." There was no response.

Passing Nathan's car as he pulled down the street, Mitch tossed an envelope with two grand in small bills through the window. It was just a thank you tip for helping him out on short notice. Nathan was a good kid. He'd have to see if Jackson would hire him after college.

42

One of the agents had brought Kat home long enough so that she could stop and pick up Woof at Laura's and go pick up Jack after his first day in Kindergarten. It was hard to believe that he was big enough to go to school. They walked in the door, Woof in tow, Jack dumping his backpack on the ground to go find his trucks.

Kat set her own bag down on the floor and kicked her shoes off. There was just enough time for Kat to get a run in before dinner. She took the steps two at a time and put on her running gear. She used to love to run outside, but since Steve's arrest, she had been running on a treadmill. Steve had never wanted a treadmill and not one certainly in the middle of the house. That's where she had put it, in the middle of the living room. She flicked the television on, catching up with the day's headlines and pounded out three miles.

Sweaty and hot, she knew she needed a shower. She walked back up the steps this time, a little slower, still catching her breath, and turned on the shower. Stepping in, she started to lather up, taking her time, getting the sweat off of her. She started to think about Carlye and the case but decided to deal with that after dinner.

Kat turned off the water and stepped out, putting on a fresh set of clothes and combing her hair back behind her ears. She wondered how Carlye was and her mind drifted to Alana and Tim. She couldn't imagine their pain.

43

The cameras that Mitch had put in Kat's house kept footage for seven days. He was sure to get some good looks at her during that time. Just twenty-four hours had passed since he installed the cameras and got back to Jackson's place in Colorado. While he grabbed a sandwich in the kitchen, he took a look at the feed.

He leaned on the counter, fast-forwarding through all of the video until he saw Kat stepping naked into the shower. "You definitely have a runner's body, don't you," he muttered. He wasn't sure that Jackson was ready to use this. That was a subject for a later meeting. It would depend on how close the FBI got this time.

Mitch straightened up. The FBI had been on their trail before, but moving the girls always handled the problem. That, or getting rid of them. Mitch wasn't sure this time would be that simple. It felt different, somehow. He shook off the feeling and took a bite of his sandwich walking back to his office. Time would tell...

Now that Mitch was back in Colorado, he had more than

enough tape of Kat Beckman in her shower than he needed. He spliced a section of it together and typed out an email. Scaring off people like this never took much, Mitch thought as he clicked send.

44

Carlye started to come to, laying naked on the rug in front of the fireplace. Lily was sitting over her, waving smelling salts under her nose. Carlye sat up, coughing. Lily sat back and passed her a blanket. "Are you okay?" Lily asked. "Let me see your neck." Carlye let her look. "You are going to have bruises."

Carlye moaned. "What happened?"

For the first time since Carlye was taken to the house, she felt like she could talk freely. It was just her and Lily in the house.

Lily shook her head, "He's a choker."

"What does that mean?"

"He likes to choke the girls out. He likes it when they pass out."

Tears started to fall down Carlye's face. She couldn't hold them back anymore. "I want to go home. Will they ever send me home?"

Lily pursed her lips. "I don't know. Sometimes girls come and go, but I never know what happens to them. I'm just glad you are okay. We need to get back."

Since Carlye's dress was torn, Lily helped her wrap up in a blanket that was on the couch. As Carlye got up, she could see the chair that Talib had made her stand on, the indent in the rug where her head had been and blood on the floor. She looked away. They walked out the front door. Another man was waiting for them in a pickup truck. He didn't say anything, but Carlye wondered if it was the same man that drove the tractor down in the stable. She was grateful he had the heat on. Tears started to roll down Carlye's face. She leaned her head against Lily's shoulder. Lily didn't move, but the comfort of someone who wouldn't hurt her gave her a moment to breathe.

The pickup truck pulled up next to the door into the house. The girls got out without a word. Carlye followed Lily back upstairs, trying to keep up. Walking was difficult. She hurt all over. Her head was throbbing and every step sent a shooting pain up through her groin.

Lily opened the door to Carlye's room and let her in. There was a plate with a sandwich and a bottle of water on the nightstand. "They left you some food in case you didn't eat. Go take a shower. I'll see you in the morning."

Carlye didn't want to shower. She could barely stand up. She sat on the bed, naked except for her white high heels and the blanket Lily had given her. She tried to eat some of the sandwich and drink some water, but her throat was so sore from wheezing to breathe that every swallow was painful. She curled up on the bed, as small as she could, and escaped to sleep.

45

The next morning, Kat and Van arranged to meet Lance at a local diner to go over the case. "Well, we know for sure that Carlye was in that house a couple of weeks ago."

"That's good, but what's the next step?" Kat was frustrated with the length of time that the investigation was taking. It seemed like it was too long. It had been ten days since Carlye went missing. As much as she tried to go on with her normal life being a mom and a journalist, knowing that Carlye was out there somewhere was terrifying to her. She couldn't imagine how the Morgans must feel.

"I know you are impatient to find Carlye." Lance rolled a straw between his fingers, "but we have to do this step by step. Especially now that Hollister and his crew are involved. They think there might be a bigger picture here. We just want to make sure that we cover our bases in terms of procedures. That said, we've drilled down on the owner of the house."

Van spoke up, "Who is it, Lance?"

Lance curled his lip. "We think it is Jackson Maifer."

Kat saw Van's brow furrow, "Wait, the guy in the picture that I showed you? Him?"

Lance nodded. "Yep. It looks like he is the majority shareholder in the string of companies that own properties. We have lists of corporations like you wouldn't believe. We have been keeping the FBI busy, that's for sure."

Kat's stomach tumbled at the thought that they were getting close. "What do we do now? Do you know where Carlye is?"

"That's the problem. Now that we are digging, not only does Maifer know that, but he owns dozens of properties both here and abroad."

The reality that Carlye was likely being trafficked covered over Kat. "So, you think she's being trafficked? Is that the working theory?"

"Yes." Lance held up his hands, "But one that can't be published yet, okay you two?"

Kat and Van both nodded.

Lance continued, "The last thing we need is to alert this guy more than he probably already is. Getting subpoenas is a noisy business. The perp always knows we're looking at them. I'm sure Maifer has his attorneys warmed up already."

Kat frowned. She wasn't seeing a next step. "Wait. I don't understand. Are we just sitting around chasing paperwork while this poor girl -- and God knows how many others -- are being abused?" It didn't seem right that they had to wade through all of the procedural nonsense when a girl's life was in danger. Couldn't they do something now?

"We are most definitely not sitting on our hands, but we have to figure out where Maifer is right now and if Carlye is with him. We have to have more evidence in order to get a warrant to bring him in. I know you are impatient, but there is a process..."

Kat's brain was racing. She knew they needed to do something, and fast. From what she had learned from Jo at the Blue

Water Center, these sharks would become more and more abusive over time. The longer Carlye was with them, the worse shape she'd be in when she got home.

After they met with Lance, Kat and Van stopped at the Aldham police department to check in with Hollister. When they got there, Kat left Van in the meeting with Lance and the FBI agents. She needed a minute to think. As she stepped out of the department's front doors, a cool breeze hit her face. She walked down the block to a coffee shop, ordered a to-go pack of coffee, bagels and cream cheese. As she was walking back, her mind shifted back to her time in Afghanistan. A moment of panic chased her. She couldn't have a flashback here, in the middle of the street. She couldn't. Kat started to walk a little faster, trying to get back to the station. But she didn't have a flashback. Not in the way that she had them in the past. There was no smoke in her nostrils, no blinding memories that took her out of her current reality. She just had this vision of TJ, one of the SEALs that she had been with, pulling his binoculars up to his face.

A few months before, her therapist, who had worked with her after she shot Edgar, the man that kidnapped Jack, told her that her flashbacks didn't have to be about her actual time in the Middle East. In fact, it might be her brain telling her something about what she was facing in her life now.

The feelings subsided and Kat kept walking. She still had the vision of TJ holding the binoculars up to his face. She couldn't shake it.

As she went through the front doors of the department, a female officer nodded and buzzed her through the door. Kat shifted the coffee a bit so she could pull the door open. Setting the coffee and bagels down on the table, she said, "We have to have a way to see what he's doing."

Lance stopped and looked at her, "What do you mean, Kat?"

"I'm not sure. I was walking back with this stuff and I remembered how much surveillance we did in the Middle East. Is there anything wrong with starting to watch some of Maifer's more likely properties?"

Hollister rolled his neck side to side, "Do you have any idea how many properties Maifer has? We are over a hundred right now."

"Can you project a map of those on the wall?" Having the FBI there meant that they had access to much better technology than just Aldham's police department. Within a minute, the tech support agent had pushed a map with dots on it up on the white wall of the conference room.

The map was of the continental United States. The agent said, "This is what we have so far tracking the holdings of the shell corporations that Maifer runs. This is just the U.S. It is likely that he owns properties around the world."

"If we bump into those, we'll need the State Department to give us a hand," Hollister said, sticking his hands in his pockets.

Kat walked over to the map and started to stare at it. "It would be likely that the girls would be where Maifer is, right?"

Lance stopped chewing his bagel for a moment. "Maybe. Maybe not. We don't know if he holds these girls for other people or if they are just for him and his cronies. He's got interests globally."

Van stood up from the table where he had been working on his laptop. "Hold on for a second. One of my postings was with psychological operations. We did profiles on guys like these all over the world. They usually traffic in more than one thing. Sometimes it's girls, sometimes it's guns, sometimes it's art."

"What are you getting at, Van?" Lance was fidgeting with the pencil he was holding.

"I know you guys have profilers, but just knowing the basics about this guy, I don't think he uses the girls for more than his pleasure. He might share with his friends, but it would be a close-knit circle."

"That's based on...?" Hollister had sat down again, his brow furrowed."

"So, listen, it's just a working theory, but I remember reading a piece on this guy. He's a collector. He loves the finest things. If it's not the best on the market, he doesn't want it." Van looked at the agent that was running the display. "Can you put up side-by-sides of Holly and Carlye?" The images changed over on the screen, huge pictures of the girls sprawled across the wall. "Look at these girls. They come from good families. They haven't been abused or abandoned. They were sent to camp because their parents wanted the best for them. These aren't your typical girls that would be trafficked."

Kat pulled up some of the information that Jo had forwarded to her about girls that were trafficked. "The information that I got from the director of the Blue Water Center says that most girls that are trafficked are from impoverished families. Or, they have been abandoned or have run away. These girls don't fit that profile."

Van stood up, slowly nodding his head as if a thought had taken hold. "Look at them. These are beautiful girls. Startlingly beautiful. These are prized possessions. Exactly like things Jackson Maifer would like to collect."

Silence settled over the room as everyone took a minute to think about what Van had said. Hollister was the first one to speak, "So what you are saying is that you don't think that Maifer has these girls all over the world. You think they travel with him?"

Kat watched as Van started pacing across the floor. "Think about it. This guy can have anything he wants. Literally anything. He has enough money to move mountains. Why would he want girls that were addicted to drugs or had a disease? I don't think he would."

"If our working theory is that he trafficks these girls, but they are for his own pleasure, then he'd keep them close." Lance sighed. "If that's true, that makes things a little bit easier."

Van looked at Hollister, "Now, that's not to say that he doesn't send the girls ahead of him or he might even send girls to the men that he provides that service for. I wonder if he uses these girls to help seal business deals?"

Hollister nodded. "Yeah, we've seen that before, but that kind of perp usually has all sorts of girls at their disposal. You are suggesting that his refined aesthetic causes him to only grab the good girls?"

"That's exactly right."

"If that's the case," Hollister said, standing up, "Then wherever Maifer is, there should be girls as well. Let's find this guy."

Kat and Van stayed with the FBI team and Lance as long as they could. The team quickly got down to business trying to figure out where Maifer was at the moment. It turned out to be a bigger project than they hoped.

"This guy has places everywhere," the tech support agent sighed.

"I know." Hollister walked over and stood behind the agent. "What we are looking for is places that Maifer would stay. If Van is right, then he's not going to go do a girl in the back of an abandoned drug house that he owns. This guy loves the finer things. He's gonna keep the girls close and clean. Make sense?"

Over the next couple of hours, the team removed commercial properties from their list. They narrowed their search specifically to Maifer's residences. "Once we get the possibilities down, we need to figure out his movements. Anyone have any idea where he is?"

"Doesn't the guy have a bunch of private jets?" Van asked.

"Worse. He owns a private corporate jet service," said the

tech support agent. "He literally could have taken any of those planes anywhere in the world."

"I guess that's one way to get away from bad airline service," Hollister showed his toothy grin again. "You just buy the airline!"

Kat saw the tech support agent roll her eyes.

When it got close to dinner time, they headed back to get Jack. He had been at his friend Paul's house since the school day ended. "What did you think of today? Do you think we made any progress?

Van raised his eyebrows, "It all depends on whether or not our working theory is right. If it isn't, then Carlye could literally be anywhere."

AFTER DINNER and getting Jack settled with his toys, Kat decided to take a look at her email. There wasn't anything too exciting in it -- a few emails from Jack's school about the start of the year and some notes from Van's assistant on the next publication dates. She was just about to close her laptop when she saw a new email pop up in her inbox. There was no subject line. She clicked on it and a video started to run. She squinted for a minute and then cried out, "Van! Van!"

Van, who had been in the garage looking for a wrench to fix the faucet in the bathroom came running. "What's the matter? Are you okay?"

All Kat could do was point. The video of her naked in her own shower ran over and over again, the same scenes repeating without stopping.

Van sat down in front of the screen. "The message says, 'Keep your nose out of our business.'"

Kat watched Van's color change. He didn't say anything and calmly put the wrench on the table. Kat followed him. He walked up the steps to the bathroom and quickly found the cameras that had been placed there. Before he disconnected the last one, he glared into it and gave it the finger.

"I'm going to call in a favor for a sweep." Van sent a text and a minute later there was a reply. "He will be here within the hour." Van finally took a minute to look at Kat. "We need to let Hollister and Traldent know about this. You could be in danger. That was a clear signal to back off."

The next hour was a blur. Before Kat could even process what had happened, TJ Weiss, the SEAL that had pulled her out of the Humvee in Afghanistan was at her house. He had bought a new house close to her and he and Van had become friends after the Apex incident. He was also a long-time friend, and at one time, more than that.

Kat, still rattled from the threat, was afraid to answer the door when it rang. Van nodded, letting her know that it was okay. "What are you doing here?" Kat wrapped her arms around TJ's neck. He used one hand to give her a bit of a hug. He was holding a bag of equipment with the other.

"I heard you might need an exterminator." TJ had a warped sense of humor, typical of many of the SEALs.

"That's one way to put it," Kat said, feeling herself relax.

As Van shook TJs hand and they moved into the house to discuss the problem, Kat felt her body begin to relax a bit. Seeing herself naked in the shower felt so violating, but she knew that Van and TJ would take care of the problem and protect her and Jack at the same time. She went back into the kitchen to start a pot of coffee.

46

Van was trying to stay calm. The whole situation with Carlye going missing had gotten out of control and he knew it. The fact that the people that had Carlye had the means to break into Kat's house and had the technology to not only film Kat but to threaten her, well, that was another level entirely.

Once TJ arrived, Van walked him through the house. "I'm not sure if they put anything else in this house, but I want it out. They got the initial film of her in the bathroom." Van handed TJ a plastic bag with the tiny video recorders that had been placed there and growled. "This cannot happen."

"Copy that," TJ said.

Since the incident with Apex, TJ and Van had gone out a couple of times for a few beers. They found out they had a lot in common, particularly their taste in music and cowboy boots.

Their meeting had been coincidental. Van had gone with Kat to where they thought the Apex people — the ones who were blackmailing her — were running their operation. Against Kat's wishes, they broke into the building and got caught. Van ended up bound and hogtied, out cold on the floor of the warehouse. The military had tracked her there because of her security clearance and TJ ended up on the team that came to get them.

What Van liked about TJ was his no-nonsense approach to anything and everything. He'd seen it in special operators over and over again. Their work required so much intensity that they learned to stay calm no matter what.

Van went into the kitchen to check on Kat. He wasn't feeling quite as calm as TJ was trained to be. Over the last few months, he and Kat had grown close. He hadn't pushed it with her. He knew that she needed time to heal. As if it wasn't bad enough that she had post-traumatic issues from her time in Afghanistan, she had to kill Edgar to protect Jack. Van knew that only the help of a really good therapist had gotten her through. He hoped that being around had helped too.

He wanted more from his relationship with Kat, but he knew that she needed time. She had lost her husband -- worse yet, she had been betrayed by him. Steve was currently in jail. Van had held her when she found out from the investigators that the only reason they had been married is because of her clearance. Apex had targeted her for years. Their entire marriage was a sham. As Kat cried, she told him that the only good things out of the last five years had been her relationship with Steve's mom, who had become like a mother to her, Jack and him. He was surprised when she said his name at the end of that list.

He found Kat in the kitchen, standing over the coffee pot. Van walked up behind her and put his hand on her shoulder. She spun around. He instantly felt bad. He had clearly startled her. "It's just me," Van said. "Just checking in on you."

"I'm okay."

Van knew she was lying. The video had scared her. Knowing that someone could find

you in your most intimate moment was something that had

rattled her. "TJ is taking care of it. We need to call Sean and Lance. They need to know."

"I know it's the right thing to do. I'm just..." The sentence stopped in mid-air.

Van leaned back against the counter, thinking about how beautiful Kat was. Her eyes were moist as if she was trying to hold back tears. "It's just what?" He tried to ask in the gentlest tone he could muster. Being direct could make it hard to deal with someone who was more sensitive.

"It's just that we have to show them footage of me in the shower. I feel embarrassed and ashamed."

"There is nothing to be ashamed about," Van said, a smile on his face.

Kat elbowed him. "You know what I mean!"

"I do." His tone became more serious. "But the reality is that they broke into your house and illegally took video of you that was meant to shame you, not to mention threaten you and Jack."

"Jack? What does he have to do with it?"

"You don't think if they can get in here, they can get to Jack?"

"You think they would?"

"You think they wouldn't?"

Van watched. Kat didn't say anything more. He could tell by the color draining from her face that though she had thought about it, the reality hadn't landed until that moment.

"Isn't having TJ here enough?"

"TJ can't stay here. You know that. And, Sean and Lance need to know what we are dealing with. It goes to the mindset and capacity of the people that have taken Carlye. As much as I want to shield you from this, I really think we need to let them know." Van gave her a moment to think. One thing he had learned about Kat was that he knew she wanted to do the right thing. She just didn't want to be told to do so. She came around to it in her own time.

"I know you are right. I don't like it though."

"I get that. Can I call them now?"

Kat nodded her assent. Van stepped out of the kitchen, pulling his cell phone from his back pocket. He walked past TJ, who was using a scanner to check for other bugs in the house.

The phone had barely connected when Lance said, "Traldent."

"Lance, it's Van."

"Hey man. I don't have any news for you. We are still tracking Maifer."

"I've got news for you, though. Is Hollister with you?"

"Yeah."

"Can you guys go to a private room and put me on speaker?"

"Sure enough."

A moment went by and Lance spoke again, "Okay, we are all set. What's going on?"

Quickly, Van told them what they had found in Kat's email. He heard Sean whistle as he finished the story. "That's quite the development," Sean said.

Lance interrupted, "So, let me get this right. Someone broke into Kat's house, put bugs in her bathroom, taped her while she showered and then used the videos to threaten her."

"Yep."

"We are on our way. Text me the address."

DETECTIVE TRALDENT, Special Agent Hollister and the FBI tech support person showed up at Kat's house a half-hour later. Van let them in. "She's in the backyard with Jack."

They followed Van out to the backyard where Kat was playing in the sandbox towards the back of the yard with Jack. The agents didn't say anything. They just waited.

Van saw Kat dust off her legs and walk toward them, Jack in tow. Jack ran ahead of her and then veered toward Van when he spotted the other men. Van knelt down and looked at Jack, "Pal, these guys are here to talk to your mom. Is that okay?"

Van watched as Jack looked the men over. He took two steps closer, "I'm Jack."

Lance and Sean both said hello to him and gave him fist bumps.

"Buddy, how about if you go check and see how TJ is doing. I bet he's up to no good," Kat said, catching up with Jack.

"Yes! I'm going to go get him!" Jack started to run off.

Sean stopped him. "Wait, if you are going to get him, you might need this." Out of his jacket pocket, he pulled a plastic child's FBI badge. "Now, hold up your hand like this and repeat after me. I, Jack, promise to be the best FBI officer."

Van smiled as Jack repeated it. Sean shook his hand and said, "Congratulations, Agent Jack. Now go take care of your mission!"

Jack ran off giggling, Woof in tow.

Van started the conversation. "As I told you on the phone, someone got into the house and installed cameras in the bathroom and took video of Kat, which they are now using to threaten her."

The three of them went into the kitchen. The tech support agent had set up her laptop on the kitchen counter and was waiting for them. "Okay that I'm set up here?" Van nodded. He knew the situation was embarrassing for Kat, so he took the lead. "Here's the email and the video."

"If you don't mind, I'm going to check on Jack and make sure he hasn't put TJ in cuffs yet." Kat walked away.

Van knew it was that she really didn't want all of the men to see her in the shower. Chasing after Jack was as good a reason as any to not have to be present. As soon as she walked away, Van clicked on the link and the video started playing.

"Geez, that's getting pretty personal," Lance said, shaking his head. "What did the message say again?"

The tech reread it off of the screen. It says, "Keep your nose out of our business."

"Van, I gotta ask. Is Kat working on anything else that would have prompted this type of response?" Lance leaned over the screen to read the text again.

He shrugged, "No. Everything else she's been working on has been local and low key. A story on busing for kids with special needs and some upgraded fitness trails in the parks. I've tried to keep it pretty calm for her since the incident."

Both men nodded. Hollister looked down the hallway, "Can you show me where the video cameras were?"

"Sure."

As they walked away, Hollister looked at the tech agent, "You are working on tracking this, right?"

"Of course."

The men followed Van up the stairs and found Kat, Jack and TJ near one of the bedrooms. Kat escorted Jack back down the steps to protests that he wasn't done arresting TJ yet. "I know buddy, but TJ has to talk to the guys for a minute, then he will be down."

Van took the men into the bathroom and showed them the locations of the cameras.

"Do you have the cameras?" Lance asked.

TJ pulled the bag out of his toolkit. "These are those. Van took them down and stuck them in here. I've done a sweep of the rest of the house. There's nothing else but some scratches to the front door lock. Looks like that's where they made entry. Standard door pick kit."

They all went back down to the kitchen. Hollister handed his tech the video cameras. "Mark these as evidence. And I want a copy of the video and the email logged as well." He took a moment and looked at Van. "Don't worry, this won't end up anywhere anyone can see it. I get the personal nature of this. We just have to log it."

There was a frown on Lance's face. "Are we sure this is from Maifer's crew? I mean, couldn't it be just a coincidence?"

"If they were going to threaten someone, it's a pretty personal way to do it, don't you think?" Van answered, feeling anger starting to form inside of him. "She's naked for God's sake. Don't you think that's pretty similar to what is going on with Carlye if they have her? To me, it's a no brainer."

"Let's trace this email and the cameras and see what we can find out." Hollister looked at the tech, "Get this fast-tracked."

"Already on it, sir."

47

Kat decided to take Jack in the backyard while the agents, TJ and Van were busy tearing the house apart and trying to figure out who had sent the email. Whether or not they viewed it as a connection to Carlye's case, she didn't care. She knew it was. Why else would they send her video of her in the shower?

She shivered. Being videotaped in your own shower was a deep, shameful violation. It was a kind of trauma that she hadn't experienced before. Clearly, the people behind this had resources and they weren't afraid to use them. Her stomach churned. While she knew that Sean and Lance had to see the video, she felt a sense of embarrassment. Jack's excitement about the park broke into her thinking.

"Mama, I'm going to the swings!" Jack yelled as he took off toward the swings, Woof chasing after him.

Kat trailed alongside him, her hands in the pockets of the light jacket she had put on before they went outside. There could be real repercussions from the video, she realized. If the video ever got farther than her computer and the FBI evidence room, it could ruin her career. Of a more immediate concern was how Sean and Lance would look at her. She sighed and tried to push off the thought. Everyone took showers, she said to herself, trying to push her worry back up on a shelf in her mind.

Telling herself that everyone took showers and not to be ashamed was something that her mother would have said to her. She hadn't thought about her in a long time. It had been a long time since her mom and dad died in a car wreck.

The wind caught in her hair and pushed it across her face. She tucked it behind one ear and walked over to Jack. It would be nice to be a kid again, she thought. There were people to take care of you, people to look out for you, people to shield you from danger.

As she watched Jack kick higher and higher on the swing, she realized that Carlye didn't have any of that. There was no one watching out for her. She wasn't that much older than Jack. And, if Kat had felt violated by some videotape, she couldn't imagine what Carlye was thinking or feeling.

48

The next few days became a blur for Carlye. She would get up and shower, put on the dress of the day and then try to eat some crackers and juice for breakfast. She and Lily were in charge of cleaning the dining area, so they stayed after at every meal, unless they had a party, checking to make sure each table was perfectly clean after the girls cleaned up after themselves. Any crumb or speck would cause them to miss a meal or worse, get sent to the basement.

Walking back to her room after breakfast, she saw Mitch pulling one of the other girls down the hallway. She was crying and screaming. As much as Carlye wanted to help, the look she got from Mitch told her to mind her own business. She quickly went back into her room and closed the door.

She wasn't alone.

In her room was a small child, a girl, huddled on the empty bed, crying. Carlye stood there for a moment, not sure what to do. The little girl, with long brown hair, didn't say a word. She just whimpered.

Finally, Carlye shook off her silence and whispered, "Hello.

Who are you?" The little girl started to speak, but Carlye put her finger up to her mouth. "You have to whisper."

The little girl used the sleeve of her jacket to wipe her eyes and said, "Addie."

"How old are you?"

"I'm five. I was on a trip with my daycare. I don't remember anything. Where am I?"

Carlye didn't know what to say. How could she tell Addie what was about to happen to her?

49

By the time she and Jack had gotten back to the house, there were even more agents with more cars parked in their driveway.

"What's going on?" Kat said, finding Sean, Lance and Van still in the kitchen. She absentmindedly turned off the coffee pot. It was empty.

"Hey, honey."

Kat turned to see Laura standing in the hallway, a suitcase in her hand. "Hi, gramma. What are you doing here?"

"Do you have Jack and Woof?" Laura asked.

"Yeah, we just got back to the park. Did you want to see him?"

Laura raised her eyebrows and looked at the agents, who hadn't said anything. Lance spoke up first. "Listen, Kat, we took a look at the tape and message you got. We think it is the real deal. We want to get Jack and Laura -- and you -- someplace safe until this is over."

"What? I don't understand..."

"Clearly, this guy has the money and connections to do what he needs to do. We will keep working the case, but we want you safe. There is no reason for you to be exposed to more trouble."

Van growled, "Nice choice of words..."

"Sorry, I didn't mean it that way," Lance said. "Why don't you go pack a bag and some of Sean's agents will take you, Laura and Jack to a safe house for a few days. Just until this blows over."

Kat turned to Van. "Is that what you think should happen?" She saw him blink, but he didn't answer. "You aren't going to answer?"

Van looked calmly at her. "It is up to you and Laura. But I think that Jack and Laura should go for sure."

"And what about me?" Kat knew she was pushing him. She could feel a ball of anger inside of her. She took a breath to speak ready to bark at him more and was interrupted.

"Honey, you need to stay here," Laura said. "You need to stay here and fight. You need to find Carlye and bring her home to her parents. Stop these animals." Clearly, Van and the agents had brought Laura up to speed on what was going on. "Jack and I will be fine. They are going to take us up to my cousin's house a couple of hours away. We will be fine. There will be three adults plus a slew of agents, isn't that right, Sean?"

By the look on Sean's face, Laura had taken complete control of the situation. If it wasn't so serious, it would be funny. "That is correct. Whatever you need, we will get."

"That is how it will be. Stay here with Van and end this. Now, let's go."

Nothing more was said. A trio of agents followed Laura out the door. She had Jack in tow, who ran over to kiss Kat and give Van's legs a hug. "See ya, mama! We are going camping!" Woof trailed behind them. Kat saw an agent try to wave him off. That agent got a stern look from Laura with a warning, "Woof goes where we go. That understood?" Kat saw the agent look to Sean for approval. He nodded. Woof jumped in the Suburban with Jack and Laura and they were off.

ONCE JACK and Laura were out of the house, Van stopped Kat, putting his hand on her arm, "You okay?"

"I guess so. I just can't believe how out of control this has gotten and how fast. Jack and Laura in protective custody? How does that happen?" She looked down at the ground. "Maybe I should have told Tim no and stuck to my local stories."

"You made the right decision, but these guys are for real, Kat. They are no different than the enemies we faced in the Middle East. They just happen to be here and have a lot of money to spend. That makes them all the more dangerous."

Kat nodded, silently grateful that Van was with her. She didn't know if she could face this alone. Did she want to face it at all? Without Laura's strict instructions to stay and fight, she wasn't sure she could.

She had walked outside and sat on the patio. Van had followed, silent. The yard felt so empty without Jack running around. Had she made the right decision? Was she strong enough to stay and fight? Maybe Laura had been wrong. Her memories of the Middle East, the fact that she had just killed a man a few months ago -- she wasn't sure she had any more energy to push forward.

"What are you thinking?" Van asked, reaching for her hand.

"I'm thinking that I just don't know if I can do this. I feel terrible for the Morgan's, but to put all of us through this for a story... Doesn't it seem like the FBI is working now? I mean that was the point, wasn't it? That's why Tim Morgan came to us in the first place."

Van nodded. "It was. Do you want to let this go? Do you feel like you have done enough?"

Kat didn't answer. She just sat with Van, the cool breeze

ruffling the waves of her blonde hair. She was tired. Tired down to the bones. She wasn't sure she had any fight left in her, and yet Laura was sure she did. Afghanistan, Apex and now this. Kat wasn't sure she had the strength.

Then her mind turned to Carlye. She couldn't stop thinking about the little girl that she had seen in the pictures at the Morgan's house. The terror and grief that the Morgans felt every day. And, Carlye's little brother. It was bad enough that Carlye was likely being abused as she sat outside, but to think that her family was suffering... That was almost too much for Kat to bear. She stood up, dusted off the back of her pants and looked at Van, "I think we'd better get back to work. We've gotta solve this so Jack and Laura can come home."

Van hugged her. "That's my girl. Let's get to it."

As they walked back into the kitchen, they noticed that the agents were packing up. "What's going on now?" Kat asked Sean as they headed back into the house.

"We are going back to the police station." He paused for a minute, "Are you guys coming or staying here?"

Van didn't say anything, but Kat piped up, "We will be right behind you."

THERE WAS a separate team of agents and detectives at the station. They had now expanded their operation to two conference rooms with people going in and out like bees buzzing in and out of a hive. Agent Hollister bellowed, "We are back, people. Where are we?"

The entire room stopped moving. One agent stood up and said, "Sir, we have been using the working theory that wherever Maifer is, the girls are."

"You can thank Mr. Peck for that bit of insight," Hollister said with a grin.

"Thank you, sir."

Van nodded.

"What have you figured out?" Kat saw Sean stare around the room.

"Well, we don't have anything particularly nailed down yet. As you know, Maifer owns his own jet company so whether or not he's on a plane we really don't know. The manifest could say he is, but he could be on another plane," the agent continued.

"Did you find evidence of this?"

"Yes sir," the agent nodded, handing over a sheaf of papers. Kat and Van leaned in to look. "As you can see here, we have a J. Maifer, Jackson Maifer and J. F. Maifer all listed on different flights. The thing is that these all happened at the same time or have overlap. I mean, he can't be on his way to Toronto, in Montana and heading to Florida all at once, unless he's got a clone." The agent giggled at his own joke.

Sean looked up at him from the papers. "Not necessary. We get the point."

"Yes, sir."

"So, where do you think he is? He can't be in all those places at one time. You are right about that."

Kat listened as Sean grilled the agent. Van passed behind her and walked over to the map that was being projected onto the wall with all of Maifer's continental United States real estate holdings. The options were about twenty once they removed the commercial properties. The analysts agreed with Kat and Van than Maifer liked luxury. He'd want his girls where he was.

The agent walked to the map and pointed a few locations. "We think the most likely spots for him would be his estate in Florida or this one in Texas."

"What evidence do you have?"

"The subpoena came back and these two properties show increased spending over the last month or so. Our assumption is that the extra money that is being spent is going toward living expenses and staff."

"Or they could be remodeling. Find out more." Hollister turned on his heel, heading out of the room. "And, get two teams to start to stake those properties out. Call the field offices and get them working. Tell them to be quiet about it. We don't need to spook him."

With Hollister out of the room, there was silence. A few people were on the phone. Kat guessed they were calling local field offices to get surveillance started. Less noise gave her a chance to stop and think. Staring at the map, she started to wonder, "Excuse me, has anyone located his wife?"

The agent she asked looked confused for a minute. "You mean Maifer's wife? Which one?"

Kat gave him a withering look. "His current wife. What's her name, Van?"

"Maria." Van glared at the agent, who quickly turned back to his laptop.

"She was last seen in L. A. They don't seem to be together all the time. We are thinking she's at their house there. I mean, if Maifer's got girls running around, she's not going to want to be there."

AFTER AN INITIAL DISCUSSION with the agents, Kat left Van at the station and headed home. "Are you sure you are okay being there alone?" Van had asked her before she left.

"I'm hardly alone with a detail of agents following me and staking out the house." Since Jack and Laura had been moved into protective custody, Hollister assigned a team of agents to stay at Kat's house and another truck full to follow her wherever she went.

"I guess you are right about that. Mind if I stay here and keep going through things with the teams?"

"Not at all. I'll be at home if you need me."

Van gave Kat a quick squeeze and sent her off with her agents who drove her home.

When she got to the house, two agents went in with her and checked the entire house. Once they were satisfied that she was alone in the house, they went back outside, telling her that they would be right outside if she needed them.

As soon as Kat closed the door, she felt her stomach grumble. She couldn't remember the last time that she had something to eat. She reached into the refrigerator and took out some turkey and made herself a sandwich. Sitting down in the kitchen, she opened her laptop and started doing a little bit more research on Jackson Maifer.

As she chewed, she saw that Maria, his current wife, was his third. He had expensive divorces with the other two. There were no children from the first wife, and she had died a few years before in a car accident. Maifer's second wife, Carrie, was the mom to a boy and girl -- both of them in high school. They lived in Virginia near her family. Kat moved on but made a note to reach out to the second wife. Maybe she'd know something.

Kat honed in on Maifer's third wife, Maria. There were pictures of them from a few charity events. She was a former model. With her long dark hair and features, Kat believed it. She was about twenty years younger than Maifer, according to the papers. From the pictures, Kat guessed that Maria was just arm candy, another acquisition for the billionaire's lifestyle.

Kat clicked on an article buried farther down in the search. Clicking on it, she saw it was dated from a few years before when Maria and Maifer had gotten engaged. The writer of the article, Jason Hughes, had spent more time focusing on Maria's background than any other article that she saw. Scrolling down the page, Kat learned that Maria was Spanish and had met Maifer while she was working Paris fashion week. They had started dating right after and were engaged in two months.

Questions started to form in Kat's mind. She checked the byline and clicked on it. The author of the piece, Jason Hughes had a direct email address through his paper, so she sent him a quick message explaining who she was and asking for more information about Maria. Kat didn't mention Carlye or her disappearance or their theories on what was really going on. There was no telling if he'd respond, but Kat wanted to know more about Maria. As soon as Kat got up to put her plate in the dishwasher, her phone buzzed. It was an email from Jason Hughes telling her to call him and giving her a number. Kat took that as a good sign and started dialing.

"Is this Kat?" the voice answered.

"Yes. Jason?"

"Yeah." From the background noise, it sounded like Jason was in a bar. "Gimme a sec to get outside."

Kat could hear the noise fade in the background. "Can you hear me okay now?"

"Yeah, now that I'm outside I can. So, you want to know more about Maria Maifer?"

"If you've got a minute to tell me..."

"Before we jump in, tell me a little bit about why you are interested in her?"

Kat thought quickly, "I'm working on a profile piece on Jackson Maifer. You know, people are always curious about the billionaire lifestyle. I wanted to focus it on the women in his life."

"That's a cool angle." There was a pause, as though Jason was thinking about something, "So Maria is interesting. She's not what you'd expect. Very smart. Very well educated. If I remember right, she has our equivalent of a Master's in Computer Science from the University of Barcelona. Her undergrad was in math. She's not your typical model for sure."

Kat furrowed her brow. "Your article didn't really cover that."

Jason chuckled, "Yeah, my editors weren't really all that interesting in her as more than a model or billionaire wife. We don't exactly have the deepest readers if you know what I mean."

"What else was interesting to you about Maria?"

"Other than she is super smart, she comes from a good family. Pretty religious. She's the oldest of six girls. I always wondered if part of the reason she married Maifer was so that she could support them."

"Why do you say that?"

"Well, her family has pretty good money, but nothing like what Maifer has. I mean, who does? The girls are just as smart as she is. As soon as she got married, Maifer started paying for the girls to go to really good schools. I think they may have some agreement that he will pay for their education."

"That's nice. Especially for five siblings."

"It's more than that. Remember, he's got two kids of his own. That's a lot of college bills to pay for if you ask me, but again, I'm not Maifer."

"Did you happen to talk to the second wife when you were doing your research?"

"Yeah. Her name is Carrie. She lives in Virginia with the two kids. A boy and a girl."

"Do they have a lot of interaction with Jackson?"

"Not much. They will go out to one of his houses once or twice a year. That's about it. Carrie said it is hard for them to see their dad with their school responsibilities and sports."

"Did you have a feeling about how much of a relationship Jackson has with his kids? I know they don't see each other that much, but do they talk regularly?" Kat was jotting notes on a pad nearby.

"I don't think so. Like many of these divorces, the kids were hurt. Carrie's really nice and really cute. I don't know why they broke it off, but while the kids love their dad, he seems to be too busy to spend time with them."

"One last question and then I'll let you get back to your beer."

"Sure."

"Did you sense that Maifer's on the up and up? Anything shady about him?"

"That part I can't answer. I was only looking at his marriages. I know there were some questions about his first wife's death, but no one proved anything. I'd have to check my notes, but I don't think she and Jackson were on the same continent when it happened."

Kat made a note of that and started to end the conversation. "Thanks again for the time, Jason. I appreciate it. Any chance you have contact info for Carrie Maifer?"

"Yeah. She goes by Carrie Stanton. The kids use her maiden name too. I can text it to you."

"Thanks again." With that, Kat hung up. Even more questions were swirling in her mind. Was there a possibility that Maifer's first wife had been killed? And what about the third wife, Maria? What was her story? How did a smart, beautiful woman get caught up in the life that Maifer had created? Did she even know what was happening right under her nose?

50

Carlye sat on Addie's bed for a long time, trying to get the little girl to calm down. She was so tiny and so afraid. Addie reminded her a little bit of her brother. She was just a few years younger. Carlye's stomach tightened. She had been trying hard not to think of home. Every time she did, she started to cry. She had to be strong for Addie.

Nothing happened for a few hours, as best as Carlye could judge. She wished there was a clock or a calendar. She had no idea how many days it had been since she had been at Camp Hope or when she had seen her family last. The alcohol and drugs seemed to cloud her system, not to mention that she hadn't had much to eat. Lily had told Carlye that Mr. Maifer liked the girls to be thin. Even if they had offered her a lot of food, Carlye wasn't sure she could eat it.

Carlye didn't know what to do with Addie. A dress had been put in their room for her. "Okay, Addie, we need to get dressed."

"Where are we going?"

"I'm not sure yet, but please whisper. I don't want to get in trouble."

"Okay." Just as Carlye stood up to get the dress, her door

opened. Carlye froze, instantly afraid that she was going to get into trouble for not having Addie ready to go. She was even more surprised when it wasn't Lily or Dora that opened the door.

A tall woman with dark hair stood in the doorway. She held out her hand to Addie, "Come with me."

Addie took her hand and followed. Carlye looked down the hallway and saw the pair go through the pine tree door and out of sight. Her mind was racing. Should she go after them? Then Carlye realized that the woman she saw was the same woman who had been in the kitchen the first night that Lily had taken her to Mr. Maifer. Her mind was foggy. Worried she would get in trouble, she closed her door and sat down on her bed.

A few minutes later, Carlye heard a car starting. Her bedroom was right above the garage. She saw the same woman who had just come to get Addie driving off the property. Carlye watched until the woman's car pulled through the gate and out of view.

51

The conversation with Jason Hughes was interesting, although not surprising Kat realized. Many billionaires had multiple wives and weren't shy about going after the most beautiful women they could find. What was interesting was that Maria was so well educated. That made her different than the rest of them.

Kat got back on her computer. She wanted to see if she could help narrow down where Maifer might have taken Carlye.

Before she had left Van, Lance and Sean at the police department, they had said they thought Maifer was in either Texas or Florida. Hollister's tech support agent had sent her logins to see their FBI research. It was limited -- not like what she had when she had her own military clearance -- but it wasn't bad for a guest pass.

Their entire theory had been that Maifer's additional expenditures were based on operating expenses, things like more food and staff as he moved from place to place. Kat already knew that they couldn't track Maifer's exact movements. He seemed to have perfected a shell game with his jets, several of them showing he was on them at exactly the same time. Apparently, anonymity was part of Maifer's game.

Kat sat back and rubbed her eyes. It had been a long day, but she knew that it was fruitless to try to go to sleep. All she'd end up doing would be tossing and turning. They needed a break in this case so they could find Carlye, and they needed it now.

Kat turned back to the wives. Jason Hughes had sent her the information about Carrie Stanton, Maifer's second wife. Although it was late, she decided to give her a call. Carrie picked up on the second ring, Kat apologizing for bothering her so late.

"It's okay. I'm kind of a night owl anyway. Who did you say you are?"

"My name is Kat Beckman. I'm a journalist. I'm doing a profile piece on wives of billionaires. Could I ask you a couple of questions?"

"Normally, I don't answer these types of questions..."

Kat was worried she'd hang up, "Wait -- Jason Hughes gave me your information. He said that you were very nice when he talked to you."

"Jason? Yes. I did talk to him a few months back. He is a nice guy. What is it that you want to know?"

Kat got Carrie talking. Sometimes you just had to get the conversation going. It would roll downhill from there. Carrie told Kat about the kids, their ages and what sports they played. She talked about living in Virginia. "How did you decide to live in Virginia after your divorce?"

"I've got family here and there are a couple of airports close by in case Jackson wants to see the kids."

"Does he do that very often?" Kat asked, probing.

"No."

Kat could hear the tension in Carrie's voice. "I know Jackson is very busy. That has to be hard on your kids."

"It is. Jackson has always wanted to spend more time with his friends at his parties than anything else. He'd work all day and go out for hours at night."

Anyone else who was listening would have thought that Carrie simply meant that Jackson liked to go out to bars or restaurants. Kat wondered if Carrie meant more than that. "Did you ever travel with him?"

"Always. Even if I wasn't staying in the same hotel, we were always in the same city. We'd bring the nannies with us too."

"You didn't stay at the same hotels?" Kat asked.

"Not usually. Jackson said that he didn't want the kids to disrupt his business meetings. He held them at the hotels that we were staying at until all hours of the night. Making the financial deals that he makes requires a lot of after-hours work. People flying in from all sorts of time zones, you know."

"Sure." Kat's gut told her that the reason they stayed at different hotels was much more than just his kids interrupting. "Let me make sure I have this right: Jackson always had you and the kids nearby."

"That's pretty much the case. It was very rare when we weren't all traveling together."

"Was that the same with his first wife?"

"I think so. Why do you ask?"

Kat scrambled to stay one step ahead of Carrie Stanton. "I was just wondering if that is hard on Maria. I understand that she's from Spain."

"I'm not sure what they've worked out, but Jackson is Jackson. He doesn't change. He just expects everyone else to change around him."

Kat thanked Carrie for her time and told her that she'd let her know once her editors approved her story.

Kat set her cell phone down on the table and began to look through the information that the FBI had sent over. They were looking hard at Jackson, but they weren't looking where they should -- at Maria.

Kat pulled on a pair of tennis shoes and ran out to the Suburban, startling the agents who were watching the house. "Everything okay?" one of them asked.

"Yeah, but you gotta get me back to the station. Will you tell Hollister I'm on my way back in?"

The Suburban roared to life as the transport detail did a quick U-turn, tires squealing on the pavement, and headed back to the Aldham police station. The agent in the passenger seat turned and looked back at Kat, "Special Agent Hollister said they will be waiting. ETA is twelve minutes."

Kat smiled as she leaned back into the leather seats. One thing about FBI agents is that they were precise. That was for sure.

Just a few minutes later, the agents dropped Kat off at the front door of the police station. "We will be right out here if you need us."

Kat nodded and went in. The station was pretty deserted. The new shift of officers was on, but Kat assumed they were out on the road. Most cities ran a skeleton shift at night, figuring that most people would be home in bed. It worked, most of the time. Lance met her at the desk and buzzed her in, "I didn't expect to see you until tomorrow. Thought you might get some shut-eye."

"I couldn't sleep." Kat followed Detective Traldent back to the conference rooms that the detectives and FBI had taken over. There weren't too many agents left. Hollister must have sent many of them back to their hotels to get some rest before they started again in the morning. Hollister, though, seemed wide awake. He was standing up, still wearing his blue shirt, dark tie, blue FBI windbreaker with his badge dangling around his neck. He had a steaming cup of what Kat guessed to be coffee in his hand.

"I thought you'd be home catching some sleep," Sean said, grinning.

"Naw. That wasn't going to happen."

"What brought you back here in such a rush?"

"I think you are all wrong about where Jackson is. You haven't found him, have you?"

Hollister stopped and squint his eyes. "No, we haven't. Do you have a better theory?"

Kat wasn't trying to insult Special Agent Hollister or his team. She just had a different take on what was happening. "I did a little research and think there might be a more efficient way to figure out where Maifer is."

"What's that?" Hollister said.

Kat described the discussion she had with Jason Hughes, the reporter, and Carrie Stanton, Maifer's second wife. "Here's the thing... we've always assumed that the wives didn't know what was going on. What we didn't know was that Maifer likes to have his wives nearby when he is traveling. Carrie said it was very rare when she and the kids didn't travel with him."

Van hadn't been in the room when Kat got back. He came in while they were talking, "Hey, what are you doing here?"

"I've got a theory that Sean needs to hear." It came out a little more strongly than she meant it to, but she was frustrated. She was frustrated that Carlye wasn't home with her family already. She was frustrated that any woman would have to go through this, no matter her age. She was frustrated that no matter how much expertise she had, the agents still had to move so slowly to preserve evidence. It was the right thing to do. Dotting all the I's and crossing all the T's was part of the job. But Kat just wanted Carlye back. "Sorry," she said, pushing her hair off of her forehead and looping it over her ear. "I guess I do need some sleep."

Van nodded, "It's okay. Just tell us what you are thinking."

"No one is tracking the wife. Maria. Carrie Stanton told me

that Maifer likes to have his wives near him at all times, no matter where he is. I'm guessing it's a control thing. That would be especially the case with Maria. She's a former model..."

The FBI tech support agent interrupted, "We know that part."

"What you might not know is that she has an undergrad in math and a Master's in Computer Science. She started modeling to pay off her student loans from the University of Barcelona."

Hollister whistled, "I knew she was a model from Spain, but I didn't know the part about her education. What are you implying?"

Kat sat down in a chair and sighed, "First, she's smart. She may know more than we think she does. Second, she has five younger sisters. She can't be blind to what is going on. She may be sympathetic to what has been happening, but not know how to help. Third, we now know, at least anecdotally, that Maifer likes to have his wife with him. We might not be able to find him, but have we looked for her?"

52

Carlye's door burst open. Mitch was wild-eyed. "Where is she?" Mitch had pushed the door open with such fury that it had left a dent in the wall. "I saw her on the video camera! Where is she?"

Carlye scrambled up on her bed, pushing herself back into the corner. "I don't know! Who are you talking about?"

"The little girl I put in here. Lily said she was safe and sound. Where is she?"

Mitch took two steps and was on top of Carlye, grabbing her by her hair and dragging her down the steps at the end of the hall. She screamed and cried, but he just dragged her all the harder, not even giving her a chance to stand up or to tell her what happened. Her arms and legs banged against the steps.

At the bottom of the steps, they didn't go through the doors to the stable, Mitch half carried, half dragged Carlye with him. Instead, he opened a door that she hadn't even seen there when he had taken her down the last time. A metal door clanged open and closed behind them. The room had one bulb in it, dangling from the ceiling, and it smelled like something was burning. Mitch threw Carlye to the ground, the back of her head hitting the wall. She slumped, terror rising in her throat. She felt a rough hand put a metal shackle to her wrist and close it. The room was cold and she started to shiver. Handcuffed to the wall, Carlye couldn't move.

Mitch's rant continued. "This is all your fault! You two have caused me nothing but trouble."

Carlye felt confused. Two? What was he talking about? When she looked up, she saw that she wasn't alone with Mitch. Nathan, her camp counselor was with them in the room, as was Lily. Lily was shackled to the wall next to her. Her face was bruised and her eye was practically swollen shut. She was naked, her green dress in a rumpled pile on the floor next to her. There were bruises on her thighs and a red mark that looked like she'd been kicked in the ribs.

"Lily," Carlye whispered, trying to get up.

Mitch took one step toward Carlye and slapped her across the face. "Shut up! I don't want to hear a word from you. I'm going to teach both of you a lesson!"

Carlye looked at Nathan. She was hoping for some sense of compassion from him. Instead, he just sneered at her.

Mitch started his rant again, enraged beyond what Carlye had ever seen in her life. He paced between the two of them. "You sluts are getting in the way of the work that we are doing. You..." he pointed at Lily, "are supposed to be responsible for her. You aren't doing your job. Her family is causing trouble and now she snuck one of the new girls out. We can't find her. That's a lost investment. Mr. Maifer isn't happy. That means I'm not happy." Knowing that her family was looking for her gave her a ray of hope that was instantly drowned in the darkness of the room she was trapped in. Carlye saw him stop walking. She didn't say a word. She didn't make a sound. She was worried he would turn his rage against her again. "This has to stop. I'm going to make it stop." Carlye saw him turn to Nathan. "Do you have it?"

Nathan nodded. "It's ready, boss."

"The video?"

Nathan nodded and pulled his cell phone out of his pocket. Carlye watched Mitch as he walked to the back of the room they were in. She could barely see his shape as he moved away from her. When he came back, he was holding a tool. It had a cord coming out of one end. Carlye couldn't see it well, but the other end looked to be metal and was red hot. Carlye felt herself shrink back into the wall as far as she could put herself. She was so terrified that she could barely breathe. What was strange to her is that a calm seemed to have come over Mitch. "Remember, don't get my face in this." Carlye saw Nathan nod. "Start it."

Nathan must have started the video because he came near Carlye and pushed the phone into her face. As he was doing that, Mitch growled. "We have your daughter. Stop looking for her. Your efforts are causing other girls to be punished." The camera pulled back from Carlye and she realized that Mitch had the branding iron in his hand and was walking toward Lily, Nathan following.

"No!" Carlye screamed.

It didn't do any good. Mitch grabbed Lily and pressed the white-hot tool into Lily's arm. She screamed as the heat seared her flesh. Tears streamed down Carlye's cheeks as Mitch stood up. "The little slut passed out," he chuckled. Carlye saw him look at Nathan, "Did you get it?"

Nathan nodded. "Yep, boss. No need for a redo."

"That's good. She'd probably freak again." Mitch didn't say anything to Carlye as he walked past her. He just kicked her in the leg and kept moving. When they left and closed the door behind them, there was nothing but darkness.

. . .

Mitch walked up the steps out of the basement and into Dora's office. "My God, take off your boots and leave them outside. What do you think this is, a barn?" Dora snapped as they came in. "You two smell awful."

Nathan took off his boot and put them in the hallway. Mitch didn't. "We got what you wanted. Nathan, send it to her."

"I already did."

Dora opened her email and found the video file that Nathan had sent her. She pulled it up and waited while it loaded. "What did you do?" she breathed. "I'm not sure that…"

Mitch didn't give her a chance to finish. "It needed to happen. Nothing good has happened since Isla sent us that Carlye girl. She's a problem. Send it."

"This is not going to get the feds off our back. You are going to make it worse," Dora argued.

Mitch took a step behind Dora and leaned over, hissing in her ear, "Send it!"

Dora looked down at her computer. Nathan realized at that moment that she was afraid of Mitch. They all were. All of them except for Jackson.

Dora loaded the video into their encryption file and typed a message. "Okay. It's done."

53

"Wait, slow down, agent." Sean had answered his phone while they were all still at the Aldham police department. "You are with the Morgan's?"

The entire room quieted. Kat moved closer to Sean hoping the next words out of his mouth would be that they had found Carlye. Her throat clenched, waiting for the news. As she waited and watched she saw the muscles move on the side of his jaw, his color becoming paler. Her heart sank. She knew it wasn't good news.

"Don't do anything. We are on our way." Sean said, hanging up the phone. "We've got to go. Right now." Before Kat could ask any questions, Sean was on the phone again, speaking so quickly that she couldn't hear from behind him what he was asking people to do.

Kat followed as he strode down the hallway and out the back of the police station. Van and a couple of agents followed him as well. Within a minute, they were in the Suburban headed to the Morgan's house. It didn't escape Kat that they were running with lights and sirens. She leaned forward as soon as Sean had gotten off the phone. "What's going on?"

"They've made contact. It's pretty bad." Kat was just about to ask a follow-up question, but Sean's phone rang again.

She felt Van's hand on her arm. "Just give him a minute. There are a lot of moving parts."

"I know. I just want to know what's going on."

"Easy, tiger. We will be there in just a minute."

THE FBI SUBURBANS pulled up in front of the Morgan's house. Armed FBI agents had taken up positions on each side of the house. It seemed like overkill to Kat as they followed Sean into the house, but then again, she didn't know what was going on.

"Update," Sean said to the team of agents that were huddled over a setup of three computers stationed on the Morgan's kitchen table.

Kat scanned the room while Sean talked to his people. Tim and Alana were standing against the wall, as though the agents had moved them away from the computers. Kat went to them. "What happened? Are you okay? Did they find Carlye? Where's Michael?"

Tim stared past Kat, his eyes fixed on the agents. He was glassy-eyed but pointed upstairs. Kat realized that he was in shock, but that he was telling her that Michael was in the house, probably in his room. "Van!" Van glanced her way and came right over. "I think they are both in shock. Let's get them sitting down, huh?"

"That sounds like a good idea." Van helped Alana over to the sitting area just off the kitchen and Tim and Kat followed. "Why don't you sit with them for a second, Kat? I'll just go see if I can find some water or tea or something."

While Van was going to the kitchen to find Tim and Alana some water, Kat sat down in front of the two of them. "What happened?" She searched their faces, but they were still both frozen.

Finally, Tim said, "There was a video. We got a video."

Kat tried to figure out whether or not that was good news by the look on his face. "Was it Carlye?" They both nodded. "Is she alive?"

Tim turned to her. "Yes..."

Van came back with a couple of glasses of water for them. An agent trailed behind with two mugs of tea. "Here. This should help." She looked at Van and Kat, "Why don't you go talk to Hollister. I'll stay here with them."

Kat felt reluctant to leave them until she noticed the red cross on the agent's jacket. She was a medic. "Okay. Take good care of them. Will you check on their son? He's upstairs, I think."

"Will do," she said with a smile.

KAT FOLLOWED Van over to the makeshift computer station that had been set up in the Morgan's kitchen. "What's going on? Is Carlye okay?"

Sean sighed, "She's alive. Her condition other than that is unknown." He nodded to an agent. "Show them."

The agent that was sitting in front of the computer screen that was closest to Kat and Van pulled up a video and hit play. As the video began, both Kat and Van leaned in to see it. The overall video was dark. Kat could see some movement, but she couldn't decipher what she was seeing right away.

"It's a little hard to see here for a second until the camera locks in," the agent said. "Just give it a second."

Kat stared at the screen. There wasn't any sound. No one was speaking. All of a sudden, the camera jolted and an image of a girl's face, pale and tired was on the screen. "Is that Carlye?" The agent nodded. Kat's gut turned. Carlye had clearly not been fed much. Her eyes were bulging out of her face in sheer terror. "Is that all they sent?"

The agent's face set in a mask. "No. Keep watching."

Kat sat down in a chair in front of the computer so she could get a better angle. A voice came across, low and husky, "We have your daughter. Stop looking for her. Your efforts are causing other girls to be punished." The man's face wasn't on the video, but his voice was the voice of a madman. The shot followed the man across the room where a young girl, beaten and bloodied, completely naked sat chained to a wall. Her eye was almost entirely swollen shut and there were bruises all over her body. In front of the screen, the man held up a white-hot branding tool. "This is what we do to sluts that cause trouble," he hissed. In the next instant, the brand seared into the arm of the girl in front of the camera. The shot cut out with the curdled screams of nerves being burned and flesh being charred.

Kat sat back in her chair barely able to speak. Nausea crawled up her throat. She swallowed hard. "Is that all of it? Who is that other girl?" The agent that had shown them the video simply looked up at Hollister, who had come in behind them as they watched the video.

"We don't know. We are running facial recognition right now. Now we know they have Carlye and at least one other girl."

Kat looked at Van and noticed his fists were clenched. "These people are animals," he said. "We've got to get them."

Hollister nodded, "Agreed." He looked behind him to see how close the Morgan's were. "I'm just afraid we are running out of time."

54

Maria Maifer thought about what had happened as she drove her red Mercedes away from the Colorado estate. She was miles down the road when she pulled over, opening the back of her SUV.

"It's okay. You can come out now," she said to the little girl who was huddled in a box in the back of her car. Addie, wild-eyed and dirty, looked like she was going to back away from Maria. "Really, it's okay. I'm going to help you get home." She helped the little girl get in the backseat and had her put on her seatbelt. Maria had stopped at a local fast food place and gotten water and a hamburger and french fries for her. There was no telling how long it had been since she ate.

"My name is Maria. What's yours?" Maria asked as she pulled back on the freeway.

"I'm Addie. I want to go home."

"I know sweetie. I'm going to help you with that. Can you tell me your address?"

Through mumbled words, Maria made out that Addie was from somewhere in Florida. "Do you live near a beach?"

"Pretty close."

"Do you know your mom or dad's phone number? Maria watched in her rearview mirror as Addie shook her head no. So many kids didn't know their parent's phone number. They were used to pushing a button on a cell phone.

It hadn't been too hard to get Addie out of the house. She had told one of Jackson's workers that she was going to spend the day at the spa and had to return some furniture. Could he please load the box in her car for her? Addie was small, so when Maria told her to stay in it, she did exactly that. Once the box was in the car, Maria, wearing a red baseball hat and big sunglasses, her black hair in a ponytail, got in her Mercedes and drove out as if nothing had ever happened.

And yet, everything had happened. Maria had known about Jackson's issue with girls for a few months. She hadn't noticed until they had been at one of their homes in Texas. It was a sprawling ranch with lots of outbuildings. Maria didn't venture to all of them. There was no need. One night when she was sitting on the porch, she saw a van drive in and thought she heard the voices of young girls for just a moment. She chalked it up to missing her family. Two days later, at almost the same time, the same van pulled in. She heard the voices again.

She knew better than to ask Jackson about it. She knew that he loved her, but very quickly after they got married, she felt owned by him, especially in the bedroom. He had no concern for her. He wanted what he wanted the way he wanted it.

The next day, Maria decided to go out for a ride on one of their horses. One of the wranglers, Luke, went with her. They passed the building where she had seen the van visit. "What's that building for, Luke?"

"That's a guest house, ma'am."

"Who stays there?" Maria hadn't known anything about the building until she asked. Many of their properties had outbuildings. Maria had assumed that they were for storage or for the staff that worked for Jackson.

"When Mr. Maifer has business associates come here, they sometimes stay there."

Maria caught that Luke looked away quickly, as though he didn't want to talk about it. "It's so pretty. Thanks!" Maria feigned a chipper tone to her voice, hoping that Luke would feel like she was satisfied with his answer. As they rode by, Luke in front of her, she saw a curtain move. She could have sworn she saw the face of a young girl in the window. She quickly turned back to Luke and nudged her horse forward into a trot. "Race ya! Whoever gets to the fence first wins!" She didn't want anyone to know her suspicions.

Later that night, she went into the kitchen and asked their housekeeper where Jackson was. "He's in his study and then has a meeting."

Maria nodded. "Would you mind letting him know that I'm not feeling well and that I'll be in our room? And, when you have a moment, could I have a cup of your famous tea, please?"

The housekeeper nodded and smiled. Maria did her best to be kind to each of them. They worked hard and although Jackson paid everyone well, the work they did was for the most part unrewarded.

Maria went upstairs and opened the doors to the terrace. A cool breeze pushed through the room and she grabbed a blanket and a book, finding a seat where she could see the guest house as she had the nights before. A quick knock on the door brought her the cup of tea she had asked for. "Thank you," she said as the housekeeper left the room. Maria waited, reading her book, occasionally looking over the top of the pages to see if there was any movement at the guest house.

About an hour passed and lights from one of the ranch's trucks drew a line down the driveway. It wasn't one of the worker's trucks, it was a lavish SUV that she and Jackson had ridden in many times. As the doors opened, she watched as three men got out of the truck. One was definitely Jackson. She could tell by the stretch of his shoulders and his walk. The others she didn't know. The front door to the guest house opened and Maria saw the silhouette of a girl. It wasn't a woman.

Maria waited for the door to close and then shut off all of the lights in their suite. She didn't want to talk. She couldn't talk. She crawled into their bed, which suddenly felt unsafe. She tried to settle down and tossed and turned for hours.

The next morning, Jackson wasn't in their bedroom. Maria got up and got ready to take her daily run. She went downstairs and found him, already dressed and showered in the kitchen, reading the paper and eating his breakfast. "Are you feeling better?"

"Yes, thank you. You didn't come in last night." Maria brushed against him, feeling her skin crawl, "I missed you..." Her words didn't match the repulsion she felt for him.

Since that day, Maria had been watching. When Jackson had said he'd like to go to Colorado, Maria secretly wondered if the girls she thought she saw would go with them. Then, when she was in the kitchen and saw the two girls walk across the foyer to Jackson's office, she knew her suspicions were real. She had gone back up to her room and vomited. To think that she had married a man who not only liked young girls but who kept them... it was unthinkable.

Only a couple of days had gone by when she saw one of Jackson's workers bring a tiny child into the house. Maria hadn't done anything about her suspicions yet. She hadn't been sure what to do. Jackson was a powerful man. He had every resource he needed in order to make someone's life amazing or miserable. Maria knew she would act. It was just a question of when. The little girl couldn't be much more than about five years old. Something in Maria broke. She looked the same size as Maria's youngest sister, Rosa. That's when she had decided it needed to end.

Maria noticed that Addie had fallen asleep in the back seat.

She reached over and touched her hand. The poor thing. It was probably the first time she'd had much of a meal in the last few days. Or however long it had been.

Maria's plan was simple. She would drive just over the line into Florida and find a police station or fire station or hospital and hand Addie off with a note in hand explaining that she needed to be returned to her parents. Maria would drive away and get on a plane back to Spain. Her life with Jackson was over. She knew she couldn't go back to him.

Ten hours into their drive, Maria decided they needed to stop. As much as she wanted to try to drive straight through, she knew that trying to drive for twenty hours wasn't smart. They stopped in Prichard, Alabama. It wasn't a big town, but there were just enough people that Maria felt like their presence wouldn't be noticed. They pulled into a little motel just off of the highway, Maria gassing up the SUV and then stopping for another sandwich for Addie and a salad for herself. They would hunker down in the motel for a few hours of rest and then get up early to make their way to the Florida line. Maria figured it would be easier for Addie to find her way home if she was at least in the right state.

The front of the motel was nothing to look at. Maria hadn't stayed in a one-floor establishment like this for years. The most recent time was years before when she was driving with friends outside of New York City after a fashion show to see some of the East Coast. That time brought back happy memories.

Maria pulled the Mercedes to the front of the motel and told Addie to stay in the car. She went into the office and paid for one night in cash. The clerk, who barely looked up from his phone, pushed a set of keys across the counter and took her one-hundred-dollar bill without a question. He didn't even ask her to sign in.

Maria got back in the car and pulled it around back. Addie

was awake and looking around. "Where are we? I want to go home!" The little girl started to cry.

"Honey, I'm so sorry for everything that has happened to you. We are just going to stop here for a few hours of rest and then we will get you back to Florida in the morning. Sound okay?"

Addie sniffled, "Do you promise?"

"Yes, sweetie. Let's go get some rest, okay?"

Addie nodded and hopped out of the car as soon as Maria put it in park. Maria took her hand and opened the door to room 103.

The room smelled dank and musty as if it hadn't been opened in months. Maria wasn't sure how much traffic the motel got. It certainly was possible no one had stayed in there for that long. She shook her head. It didn't matter how it smelled or what it looked like. She wanted to get Addie home and get on the plane back to her family.

Maria turned on the television to a channel with cartoons on it and put Addie on the bed that was closest to the bathroom. She opened the sandwich and set it in front of her. Addie looked suspiciously at her and then started to pick at the food. "It's okay. You can eat. Nothing bad will happen. Do you want to take your jacket off?"

Addie nodded. Maria helped her to pull her jacket off and laid it on the bed for her. Once Addie was settled, Maria sat down on the bed next to her. There was no telling how many people had slept on the bed or when it had been cleaned last. Jackson had been a freak about cleanliness. When they traveled, he insisted on a black light sweep of the room before he'd stay in it. If there were any stains to be found, he demanded a new room with brand new bedding.

Maria was leaving that all behind. She just hoped that he'd let her go. Jackson had a ruthless streak. Maria knew that. But she thought that when she married him on a beach in the Cayman Islands that streak would never apply to her. It hadn't yet, but she had seen him grow more distant over the last few months. She wondered if the girls had anything to do with it.

After Addie ate, she curled up on top of her bed and fell asleep. Maria did the same, but not before setting her alarm for four o'clock. She wanted to be up and out of Pritchard before anyone knew she was there.

MARIA HAD BEEN asleep for a few hours when the door banged open. Two men came into the room. "Close the door," one of the voices growled. "Honey, I'm home!" he said, quickly pinning her to the bed.

His hand clamped over her mouth and she struggled to breathe. She kicked but he didn't let go. "Oh, I'd forgotten how feisty you were, Maria." He pushed her down harder on the bed, his other hand wrapped around her neck. She couldn't breathe. "Where's the girl?"

The lack of oxygen to Maria's brain made it hard to answer. She shook her head no.

"What do you mean? You don't know? You just decided to take a road trip?" the man said. Maria heard him say, "Search the room and her car. That little slut has to be here somewhere!"

Maria started to blackout. The man on top of her let off the pressure on her neck long enough for her to suck in a deep breath, coughing and choking. "Let me go!" she shouted.

"Now, I can't have you shouting like that and waking up your neighbors, can I?"

Another male voice whispered in the darkness. "She's not here. The girl isn't in the car either. Maybe she already got dropped off?"

"Oh, Maria. You shouldn't have done that. Your husband,"

the word came out in a hiss, "told me that I should teach you a lesson."

Maria felt the pressure on her mouth increase as he lifted the hand off of her neck. She heard his zipper open.

"This is going to be fun."

Maria struggled with what air she had to breathe as the man pulled down her leggings and pushed up her shirt.

"So, this is what Jackson has had to play with for the last couple of years," he whispered in her ear. "Now it's my turn."

She tried to push away from him, but he had caught her wrists with a painful grip. While he was on top of her, he grabbed her throat, tightening it around her neck. Maria could not breathe. Her vision started to narrow and blackness covered her. All she could think about was Addie...

55

Lucy Williams pulled into work at the Prichard Motel and Inn twenty minutes late for her shift. She just hoped that the boss wasn't around to yell at her.

In her mind, it didn't really matter what time she got to work, though she did try to be on time. It wasn't like the hotel had that many guests. This morning, her daughter had woken up with a fever. She had to settle her in before she could get on to work. That was part of being a single mom.

She drove her old Chevy past the front of the hotel and parked in back, passing a fancy Mercedes as she came in. Must be someone interested in buying the place, she thought, locking her car and walking past a bank of motel rooms to get her house cleaning cart. As she passed between the Mercedes and the hotel, a door cracked open and a child ran out and grabbed her by the legs, crying.

"Well, dear me! Where are you coming from, little one?"

The little girl didn't speak. She just pointed at the room door that was open, tears streaming down her face.

"It's alright now. Let's just have you go back to your room."

The little girl shook her head no, her eyes wide.

"Alright then. Let me have a look and let your mom know you are okay." Lucy went over to the hotel room door and pushed it open, streams of sunlight pushing across the bed. "Dear God, almighty!" she said trying to stay calm. "Let's you and I go to the office and get us some help." Lucy grabbed the little girl's hand and took her to the office, whispering to the night clerk who had just woken up, "Call the Sheriff. There's a problem in room 103."

"What kinda...?"

"Just do as I say, boy. Do it now!" Lucy took hold of the little girl and sat her on her lap, "Now you are just fine. We are going to call the police and get some help. How about if you and I have a little sip of water while we are waiting?"

56

Kat and Van had stayed at the Morgan's house for another couple of hours as the agents worked to figure out where the video had come from. They needed a lead on Carlye Morgan, and they needed one fast. There was no telling what these people were going to do to her, or already had done, Kat thought.

"The encryption they use is top of the line, sir," one of the agents reported to Hollister. "I haven't seen anything like this since I was in the military."

Kat kept quiet as Hollister encouraged his team to keep digging, "We have to find something. These guys aren't perfect. It's their mistakes that get them. Keep looking."

"Sir, I don't know if..." the agent started to argue.

"Agent, do you see that family over there?" Hollister whispered, pointing to Tim and Alana Morgan. She nodded. "They need some hope. They need a solution. That's what we are here to give them."

"Yes, sir."

The agent started typing again, working feverishly on her

computer. Kat could tell by the look on her face that she didn't feel like she was making any progress.

"Van?" Kat whispered. "I feel like we need to do some more research on our own. I want to follow up on Maria Maifer while these guys work with the video. Maifer's first wife said the wives always travel with Jackson. He never leaves them behind. Maybe we can find her."

Van nodded, "Yeah, I think that's a good idea. Hollister and his team have this pretty much covered." Van looked at Hollister. "Mind if we head back to the station and work with Traldent on a couple of other leads?"

Hollister nodded and waved for an agent to escort them outside.

ON THE DRIVE back to the police department, both Kat and Van were quiet. Kat realized that the memory of seeing the girl branded would always stick with her. She couldn't imagine what Carlye was going through. It was almost too much to bear. But she knew they had to keep looking. She and Van would have to keep looking until they found her one way or another.

Back at the station Detective Traldent was waiting for them. "Hollister told me about the video. It's pretty bad."

Kat nodded, following him to the conference rooms where there were still agents and other detectives working. "Yeah. Not something I'm going to forget any time soon."

Kat saw Van plop down in a chair at the end of the table, rolling his head from side to side. Neither of them had slept much since the Morgan's had found them at the park. It had been nearly a week. "Anything in that video that would help us locate them?" Van asked.

Traldent shook his head, "I wish. The video was so dark that there was no way to see any of the features of the room. We've been doing an analysis. We know it was taken with a phone, but even the voice has been disguised. There's not much there. They did a good job covering their tracks."

Kat watched Traldent loosen his tie and sit down. It occurred to her that being in the police or the FBI was very different than being a journalist. She and Van weren't responsible for figuring anything out. They were only supposed to report what did happen. Guys like Traldent and Hollister -- if they couldn't figure it out, it was likely the Morgan family would lose their little girl and have to live with it for the rest of their lives. Kat couldn't imagine the pressure. Before she went too far down that rabbit hole, Kat decided to focus on what they could do. "Lance, what about the wife? Do we have a location on Maria Maifer?"

The main tech support agent had gone with Hollister, but there was another agent in her place. "Yeah, we've been tracking that lead," he said, looking up from his computer to point to an image he had just put up on the wall. "We don't show that she was on Maifer's airline anytime in the last three weeks." He typed a few more keystrokes. "So, I started looking into her credit card history. She's got one of those black cards that have basically no limit." He moved another image onto the screen. "What we see here is that she was in Texas for a time and then in L. A. She did a lot of shopping. Racked up twenty grand in clothes at one store."

"I should have her pay my alimony," Traldent muttered.

"Then we see her credit card active in Colorado over the last couple of weeks."

Kat squinted at the images across the screen. "Could someone else be using her card? I mean you guys were pretty sure that Maifer is in Texas or Florida..."

"Yes, ma'am, that's possible, but I don't think that's the case. The items that she bought are pretty consistent with what we see in her past purchase history. Private training, yoga classes, spa days and clothes. I guess she could have given the card to someone else, but that doesn't seem likely to me."

"Has there been any movement at the Texas or Florida homes?" Van asked.

"No, sir. Nothing out of the ordinary. We have a team of men at each house posing as gardeners or day laborers. They haven't seen any of the Maifer's there. One of the other workers at the Texas house said they had been there a few weeks back but had left."

"Did they find out where they were headed?"

"Naw, the agent tried, but the worker didn't know. Said they all know to keep their mouths shut."

Kat stood up and started chewing her lip. "So, the best information we have is that Maria Maifer is in Colorado? Is that right?"

"That's correct, ma'am," the agent said.

"If she didn't fly with Jackson, then how would she have gotten there? Did she fly commercial?"

The agent frowned. "I'm sorry, I hadn't gotten to that yet. I got a little distracted with the video. Give me a minute."

Kat stood behind one of the chairs in the conference room, while they waited for the agent to do a search on domestic flights.

"Ma'am, I think we have something..." the agent started. "I need time to verify this and see if she boarded the plane, but there is a commercial, first-class reservation for an M. Maifer about a week ago from LAX."

Kat felt a surge inside of her, "Where to, agent? Where did Maria go to?"

"Denver, ma'am. It looks like Denver was the final destination."

57

Sheriff Wallace Smith wasn't used to dealing with dead bodies. Pritchard, Alabama, was a sleepy town. The most excitement they usually dealt with was the local town drunk needing a ride home. The residents that lived in Pritchard had been there for a long time. They didn't even leave when a hurricane came screaming up through the Gulf.

When Sheriff Smith got the call that there was a dead body at the motel, he went lights and sirens. The noise was so loud he ended up turning it off. There wasn't any traffic anyway.

By the time he got to the scene, the only other patrol car they had was already there. Roger, his daytime patrolman, had sense enough to close the motel room door and put police tape over it. They had been at training the month before with other rural police departments to learn about investigations. The trainer, a man with a shaved head and pointed eyebrows said, "If you don't know what you are doing, stay away from the scene and let the professionals handle it."

That was exactly what they did.

Sheriff Smith pulled up to the front door of the motel and spotted Roger, the clerk and Lucy waiting for him. In the small town of Pritchard, he pretty much knew everyone. As he walked into the lobby, he saw Lucy sitting with a child on his lap. "What's going on here?"

Roger, the patrolman, said, "Sir, I think you'd best come with me."

The Sheriff grunted but followed.

The two walked past a few doors of the motel and stopped at room 103, where Roger had sealed the door closed. "I see you learned something at our training last month, son."

"Yes, sir."

As Roger used a passkey that Lucy had given him and opened the door, he saw the half-naked woman splayed on the bed, her eyes staring blankly up to the ceiling. Sheriff Wallace Smith sighed, "Let's get that door secured again patrolman, and let's give a call to Mobile and get the FBI out here. I think we are going to need some professional help."

"Yes, sir."

"And patrolman?"

Roger stopped as he was dialing his cell phone.

"Stay right here by the door. Give a call to Chickasaw and have them send some reinforcements. We need to secure that car, too, I'd imagine."

Roger nodded. Wallace walked back to the lobby. He took off his hat as he entered, "Who is this little young lady?" he said, kneeling down in front of Lucy, who was still holding Addie on her lap. Addie proceeded to bury her face in Lucy's neck.

"Now, now, Miss Addie, let me introduce you to a very fine man, Sheriff Wallace Smith. He's here to help us. Is that okay with you?" As Lucy said it, she gave Addie a little squeeze.

"Addie, I'm glad to meet your acquaintance. You can call me Wallace or Wally. Either one is fine with me."

He watched Addie closely. He might be a Sheriff in a small town, but he knew the signs of a child that was completely terrified. "Miss Addie, I have a very important job for you. Is that okay?" He noticed that she didn't move, but she stayed frozen in place. "Right now, I'd like you to just stay with Lucy. She's prone to cause trouble, you know. I need someone to keep an eye on her. That okay with you?" Wallace saw her nod. He stood up. "I'm going to have some medics come out to check her over for us, okay?" he said to Lucy.

"That sounds fine," Lucy said, hugging Addie closer to her.

"Did she tell you what happened to her mama?"

"Sheriff, the way she tells it, that's not her mama."

Wallace felt his stomach tighten. In a split second his very quiet town of Pritchard had become the scene of a major crime. That was a problem. A big problem. He knew from his training that all he could do was wait for the feds to arrive and keep the scene secured. He needed to stay calm so that Addie would do the same. "Well, isn't that interesting. Let me go check on Roger. You all just stay right here." Wallace saw Lucy nod. He knew that if anyone was going to soothe that poor terrified child, the right one was Lucy. She was wonderful with children.

Going outside, he noticed that even though the fall had come, the day would be a hot one. He walked over to Roger, who was just hanging up the phone. "Any news?" Wallace asked, wiping his brow with a handkerchief he kept in his pocket.

"There's an ambulance in route to check on the woman in the room..."

"I think we already know she's dead, son."

"Yes, sir, but they want to check. They will also take a look at the little girl."

"And the feds, son? Did you get ahold of anyone in Mobile or Chickasaw?"

Roger pulled out his notebook from a pocket in his shirt. "Yes, sir. I spoke to an agent at the Mobile FBI field office. They are on their way and should be here within the hour." Wallace turned as Roger was speaking, hearing tires on the gravel. "And, as you can see, sir, Chickasaw was more than happy to offer their assistance."

"Well, that was mighty nice of them, now wasn't it?"

THE NEXT HOUR crept by slowly. Wallace was eager for the FBI to show up. The ambulance arrived a few minutes after the deputy from Chickasaw and confirmed the body in the motel was deceased. They checked on Addie, at least as well as they could. Addie had glued herself to Lucy and wasn't willing to let go.

Just as the medics went back to their ambulance, a caravan of three black Suburbans pulled into the motel. Would be like the FBI to show up like that, Wallace thought. They couldn't drive normal cars, could they? Putting his irritation aside, he strode up to the first vehicle and introduced himself to the agent in charge. "Sheriff Wallace Smith. Glad you all could make it."

"Thanks for calling. I'm Dishon Honn. Mind if we take a look at what you have going?"

"Not at all, not at all. Right this way." Wallace called for Roger as the other agents fanned out. "Roger, come and take Agent Honn to the room if you don't mind."

Wallace went back into the motel lobby where two more agents were squatting down and looking at Addie. One of them was a woman. Addie seemed to be responding to her. "So, Miss Addie, I am so glad to meet you today. How are you doing?"

Wallace watched as the little girl peeked out from Lucy's neck. "I'm okay."

"I heard that you were very brave for the medics."

Addie nodded.

"Would it be okay if I asked you a few questions?"

From where he was standing, Wallace could see Addie grip Lucy's neck a little harder.

"You can stay with Miss Lucy the whole time, okay?"

From just beyond where they were talking, Wallace watched the agent work with the little girl. The agent sat on the floor, cross-legged, with a notebook in her hands. He heard her start with very basic questions.

"So, your name is Addie?" The little girl nodded, without ever moving from her position with her nose buried in Lucy's neck. "Your last name is Buckholtz?" Again, the little girl nodded. "Now, I have a very important question for you. What is your favorite flavor of ice cream?"

A smile spread over Wallace's face. The agent was smart. He watched as Addie whispered something in Lucy's ear. "Miss Addie said strawberry," Lucy said.

"Mine too!" the agent exclaimed. Wallace was sure she was just making it up, but whatever they needed to do to get the girl talking. "How about your favorite color?"

Wallace watched as the little girl turned to the agent. "I like purple."

"Me too!"

Wallace could see the agent write in big letters the word purple in her notebook so that Addie could see it.

"Just a couple more questions. Do you like to go to the beach?"

Addie nodded. "I have shells in my room."

"Who goes to the beach with you?"

"Mommy."

"What's her name?"

Wallace saw Addie stop for just a second. It looked like she was thinking. "Sandy."

"Does your dad go to the beach with you?"

Addie nodded.

"What's his name?"

"Dan."

"You did so good! Now, while I go talk to the Sheriff over there, this other lady is going to come over and scan your fingers with her special tool and she's going to take your picture. Is that okay? You can stay right where you are?"

Addie nodded. The agent got up off of the floor and walked to Wallace. "I suspect that she hasn't been taken for long. She established trust with me pretty quickly. We know that she at least has access to a beach community. With the information we have, we will find her family. It shouldn't take long if they filed a report."

As soon as the agent had walked away, Roger came back into the motel lobby. "They have an ID." He pulled out his notebook and read from the page. "Looks like it is one Maria Maifer from L. A. What would she be doing here in Pritchard with this little girl?"

"I don't know, but somebody got to her."

58

"Okay people," Hollister said. "Let's figure out where this Maria Maifer is right now."

"Sir," one of the agents interrupted him. "Sorry, sir, but you should see this."

Hollister went and stood behind the agent. "Holy crap."

Kat and Van went over to see what he was looking at. It was an alert from the agent's quick search on Maria Maifer. An update had just been posted by the Mobile, Alabama FBI field office. "She's dead?" Kat asked.

"Certainly looks that way." Hollister looked at the agent. "Get me the agent on duty at that office. Even better if they are still at the scene. Within a moment, the agent said, "Sir, you will have a call coming in from Agent Honn from Alabama. He's still at the scene." Before she could get the information out, Hollister's phone rang. Sean put it on speaker. "This is Hollister."

"Agent Hollister, this is DIshon Honn from the Mobile, Alabama field office."

"Heard you have a body there with you?"

"Yes. The ID reads one Maria Maifer. We are trying to confirm that now."

"What happened to her?"

"Looks like she was strangled and raped."

Kat drew in a sharp breath. Maria Maifer's death changed everything. How could she be in Alabama? She was supposed to be in Denver, or at least somewhere near there.

Sean's voice interrupted Kat's thoughts. "Listen, she's a person of interest in a kidnapping case. Will you keep me updated?"

"I can sir, but there's one other thing. There was a child with her."

Kat froze, waiting for Sean to ask for more information.

"A child? Can you give me more information?"

"Young girl. Blonde. About five. We've initially identified her as Addie Buckholtz. We just found the parents. She was taken from a daycare in Jupiter, Florida, about a week ago."

"Okay. Keep me posted."

Kat saw Sean rub his hand on his forehead. "Can you put up the map for me?" he asked one of the agents. "I need the one of Maifer's U.S. properties." A map appeared on the wall of all of the residential properties that Jackson Maifer owned in the continental United States. They were spread as far north as Montana and as far south as Florida.

Kat stepped to the back wall of the conference room and leaned against it. She felt the warmth of Van next to her. She was so tired that her bones ached. She wanted to see Jack and Woof and Laura, but she knew that they were safe with her cousin and the FBI agents. Most of all, she wanted Jackson Maifer, who looked more like a madman every day, to be stopped.

"Someone find me where Maria Maifer's body is." Within a few seconds, a star appeared on the map. It was at the base of Alabama, not far from Mobile. Kat watched as Sean walked closer to the map, trying not to get in the middle of the projection of it. She saw him tilt his head to the side and then turn around, clearly thinking. "Let's figure this out. If Maria Maifer was in Denver and she found this little girl, what was she doing in Alabama? Why not just fly her out on one of Jackson's jets?"

"Maybe she was doing more than trying to get the little girl back to her parents," Van took a step forward. "What if Maria knew that Jackson had girls and she found out about this little one? Maybe it's too much. Maybe Maria had enough of his antics. If that's the case, then maybe she gets the girl away from Jackson and decides to drive her back home."

Kat looked at Van. "And maybe someone caught up with her when she did..."

59

Sheriff Wallace Smith had spent the majority of the day hanging out with the FBI agents who had come to help with the dead body at the motel. He took off his hat in the sweltering Alabama heat and wiped his forehead. It didn't matter what month it was, it was always hot. When he retired, he might move somewhere colder for a while. South Dakota, maybe. Good hunting there.

As he put his hat back on, he wondered if the little girl was in the room when the woman was murdered? He walked back into the motel lobby, where it was a bit cooler, the window-mounted air conditioner pushing out as much cold air as it could through a persistent rattle that made it sound like it would die at any moment.

He found Agent Honn and another agent talking near the check-in counter. Addie was sitting at a small table with the female agent that had questioned her. She was eating a hamburger and french fries and was wearing a blue FBI t-shirt that hung almost halfway down her legs. "How are things going, Agent?" Wallace asked.

"We are in the middle of it, sir," Honn said, looking at his cell phone.

"Did you find Addie's parents?"

"Yes, sir. They are on their way. It will be a bit of a drive. I'm hoping we can move her over to your station until they get here?"

"Of course. That's not a problem. It's not fancy like the FBI, I'm sure." Wallace saw Honn smile.

"I'm sure it will be fine. Thanks for your hospitality."

"Uh-huh. One thing is bothering me. Wondering if you can clear it up?"

"What's that?"

"Where was Addie when that poor woman was getting choked?"

"We are still trying to figure that out. Let me show you."

The two men walked out of the cool lobby and back out into the heat. The door to the motel room was still secured with police tape and there were two forensics people working on the room. Maria's body had been moved by an FBI team after her hands were bagged and pictures were taken. Wallace had been more than happy to turn over the autopsy to the feds once he found out that little Addie had crossed state lines.

"We think that she fell asleep on the bed and then when she heard the noise of the men, she wedged her body in here." Honn pointed to a small spot between the headboard and the wall. "If the room was dark, they wouldn't have been able to see her even if they checked under the bed. This was a little girl that didn't want to be found. The team will do some testing to see if we can find fingerprints, fabric fibers or hair down there, even if we have to take the bed apart."

Wallace nodded. The space between the solid headboard and the wall was barely six inches deep, but he realized that Honn was right. If Addie had wedged herself in there, the intruders wouldn't have been able to find her even if they looked under the bed. She was a clever girl. It might just have saved her life.

The men walked out past the investigators, excusing themselves. That was one lucky girl, Wallace thought.

60

Dora's phone rang. It was Mr. Maifer. "Yes, sir?"

"Come to my office."

Dora got up from her desk and smoothed her skirt over her legs, checking in the mirror to make sure that her pink lipstick was still on after she had her morning coffee. Her heartbeat a little faster as she crossed over from the girl's side of the house to Jackson's. He rarely called her into his office and when he did, it generally wasn't good news.

She knocked lightly on his office door. "Come," she heard his voice, gravelly and low.

"Dora. Good. It has come to my attention that we've had a bit of a staffing problem."

Dora nodded. She knew that when he referred to staffing, he was talking about the girls that he kept with him wherever he went. Sometimes there were three, sometimes many more. One time they had twenty girls with them. He was currently on a bent where he wanted ten to fifteen girls ready for him and his friends at all times. He was showing preferences for younger ones as well.

Dora had been one of his first girls nearly ten years ago. She had been a college student looking for a way to make her tuition payments and had met Maifer while she was a cocktail waitress at a fancy bar in Las Vegas. Mitch had been the one that had talked to her about meeting up with Maifer and some of his friends after work. She had been told that the pay for a few hours would be ten thousand dollars.

Money like that was hard to resist when she had bills. She went to the party, taking a friend along with her from work. She figured they could split the money. When she got to the hotel room, Mitch pulled her in and sent her friend away. "We didn't invite her. Just you."

The first night had been scary. Jackson had a go at her, then two of her friends. They filled her with alcohol and something else. She had woken up in bed, feeling groggy, naked, but at least she was covered up. Her whole body ached. As she got up, she wrapped herself in a sheet and spotted an envelope on the dresser. In it was fifteen thousand dollars, plus a card that read, "If you'd like to make more money call this number."

A few weeks went by and Dora did just that. Over time, Jackson bored of her. She could tell by the way that he acted around her. Instead of being the first of the night, he'd watch or just hand her off to one of his friends. The pay was always the same. Unless someone got rough, of course. In that case, there was more to cover her medical expenses.

After a year of working for Jackson, she was sure he wouldn't call anymore. She got a text from Mitch to meet him on a corner of her college campus. "Mr. Maifer knows that you are going to be graduating soon. He'd like to offer you a job."

The job was to coordinate Mr. Maifer's girls. It started with Dora's friends and then moved onto other sources. Mr. Maifer didn't want to sleep with her anymore, but she had an eye for what he liked.

Standing in front of his desk, Dora realized that she had missed some of what Mr. Maifer had said to her, lost in her own thoughts. "I'm sorry, could you repeat the last sentence. I'm not feeling well today."

She saw Jackson squint at her. "There's a problem in the basement. I need you to fix it. My investment is declining in value."

With that quick comment, Maifer looked back down at his work. Dora knew that was her signal to leave.

61

Carlye woke up shivering. She had no idea how long she and Lily had been trapped in the basement. There was just a little light in the room coming from under the door as the bulb had been shut off when Mitch and Nathan left. As her eyes adjusted, she could see Lily, huddled in the corner. She was moaning, clearly in pain.

Carlye pushed the thoughts of what had happened out of her mind. Being dragged to the basement, seeing Lily beaten and bruised, chained to the wall. Naked. The glow of the white-hot branding iron that Mitch had used on Lily. A wave of vomit threatened to choke Carlye. Not that there was anything that would come out. Carlye couldn't remember when she had eaten last.

Before she could ask Lily if she was okay, the door slid open, the light from the hallway stinging Carlye's eyes. Every inch of her wanted to cry out for help, but she knew that would just land her in trouble. She kept her mouth closed, terrified that it was Mitch coming back.

The figure that walked into the room was clearly female. As her eyes cleared, Carlye realized it was Dora. Dora's heels clicked on the floor as she reached over and turned on the lights in the room. "Dear God," Carlye heard Dora whisper.

Both the girls instantly backed up against the wall. Carlye pulled her dress down over
her knees, trying to cover up. Lily didn't try to cover up. Neither girl said anything.

The jangle of keys helped Carlye to calm down. Dora leaned over and unlocked the cuff that was keeping her arm suspended in the air. She did the same for Lily. Dora walked out of the room, motioning for them to follow. Carlye tried to stand up. She looked over at Lily, who was clearly having an issue trying to stand. Carlye walked over to her and put her arm under her shoulder, trying to help the best that she could. She was a few inches shorter than Lily, but she tried to help her walk.

Neither of them said anything as they exited the room. Dora was standing just outside the door with a towel. "Here, cover yourself," she said to Lily, turning her head away. Carlye helped Lily wrap the towel around her body, trying to avoid touching the blistered area where she had been branded.

Dora didn't slow down for the girls. Carlye pushed at Lily to get her to move forward. She thought they might head back upstairs, but Dora took them another way. "We can't have you looking like this on the floor," she said, turning down a corridor that Carlye didn't recognize. Dora opened a door and the girls followed. There was a bed in the room. Not like a bed to sleep in, Carlye saw, but a bed like they have in the doctor's office. There was a woman in the room in scrubs.

Carlye saw the woman's face freeze when they limped into the room, both of them battered and bruised, Lily's arm swollen and blackened from the burn. She didn't say anything but got a curt nod from Dora, who said, "Once you are done with the nurse, go upstairs and shower."

Putting on a pair of gloves, the nurse pointed at Lily. Carlye helped her up on the table while she was examined. The nurse didn't say anything. She didn't take any notes. Carlye sat on a chair against the wall watching as the burn was dressed and covered in a salve. Carlye could finally see what it was. The initials JM. Carlye knew enough about burns to know that would leave a scar for the rest of Lily's life. She'd never be able to forget Mr. Maifer. The nurse asked Lily to lay down. She checked between her legs and then had her sit up. "You have a pretty severe infection." The nurse turned and pulled a vial of medication out of the cabinet. Carlye could see that there were rows and rows of bottles in there. She wondered how many girls ended up visiting the nurse. "Take this twice a day for the next week." She handed Lily some salve for the burn. "You can put this on whenever it hurts."

The nurse pointed and had Carlye sit up on the table. After being checked, Carlye got off the table and pulled her dress back down over her body. "You are okay."

With that, Carlye and Lily made their way to the door. As the nurse opened it, Carlye looked at her, searching her face for any recognition of what was happening to them. She whispered, "Please..." Without so much as a word, the door closed behind them. Carlye felt tears burning in her eyes. There had to be a way out. She knew if she didn't get away, she wouldn't survive.

Carlye followed Lily back upstairs where they each went to their respective rooms. As Carlye started to close her door, Lily stopped in the doorway, pale and weak. She whispered, "Don't complain. The girls that do, they don't come back."

62

Things were out of control. That much Jackson knew. What had started as a little weekend fun had turned into a nightmare. The core of the problem was that his appetites had grown. The other problem was that Mitch was out of control. Finding and maintaining the girls was expensive. They were an investment. He kept records on them just like any of his other businesses.

As Jackson walked from the bedroom to his office to begin his morning, he wondered where Maria was. Mitch hadn't called yet. When the Mercedes had left the estate, he assumed that Maria was doing exactly what he thought she was doing -- going for another expensive spa day. He'd never had trouble with her before. He knew that she was aware of the girls but had never asked him about it. The lifestyle he provided her should have been enough to keep her quiet. He thought it would be. Now he wasn't so sure.

There were transponders on all of Jackson's vehicles. Keeping track of things had been Jackson's path to success. Whether it was his investments, his business ventures, his vehicles or his stable of girls, he knew each and every one of them.

He didn't actually know their names. He didn't want to. He gave them all names. The newest one, the blonde who he had named Princess, had brought trouble with her. She was pliable enough, especially after a dose of ketamine, but he suspected that her family wasn't going to give up looking for her easily.

He sat back in his chair, twirling a Mont Blanc pen in his hands. He could just send her back. That was an option. He could have Mitch or the kid from the camp drive her somewhere and drop her off. Somewhere she'd be found. He could send her with a promise of a big payout if the family stopped looking for her. He had done it in the past and it had worked. Losing one girl was better than losing them all. Usually, a million dollars from one of his shell companies was good enough. It paid for college. That was all the parents were really worried about anyway.

There was a knock at his office door. "Come," he said, not happy to be interrupted before his day ever started.

Mitch came into the office. From the way he looked, he hadn't showered and he wasn't dressed properly. Jackson insisted that all of his workers -- even those working on the grounds -- wear collared shirts. There was something to being professional. Jackson's lip curled. There was something about Mitch that always bordered on the wild. More and more often, he was having issues with Mitch being reckless. That was an agenda item for another day. Right now, he wanted news on his wife and his latest investment.

"Where are they?" Jackson said, not inviting Mitch to sit down.

"Sir, there was an accident. We were chasing Maria in her car. She had the kid with her. She accelerated and got into a bad accident. She didn't make it, sir. I'm sorry."

Jackson waited for a moment to see if any feeling would come up. He was slightly sad, but not too much. "And my investment?"

"The police got there too fast. There were bystanders. I think they found the girl, but I can't be sure."

Jackson took a moment and studied his desk, straightening the papers until they were all at right angles. It was a habit he had picked up when he had started in business. The person that answered too quickly usually lost. Maria was dead. He'd have to find another wife. Or maybe not. That was a decision for another day. Her death would bring attention to him, especially if anyone figured out Maria had the little girl in the car with her. Getting angry at Mitch wouldn't solve the problem. "We will need to move the girls within the next twenty-four hours. We will move them after the next party."

"Where would you like to go?"

Jackson took a moment to think about which one of his properties to visit next. It needed to be somewhere out of the country. Far enough that he would escape from the media, but close enough in case he needed to come back to deal with the Maria issue. "Mexico. Let's use that property. Tell Dora to move all of my entertaining for the next month to Mexico. I will, of course, pick up any additional expenses for my guests."

63

Carlye showered, slept and ate some crackers that she had put in a drawer in her room. She felt sick to her stomach and her body ached. Whatever they gave her made her feel like she had the flu. She had put on the dress that had been left in her room, her hands shaking. This one was green.

Looking around, she realized that any evidence that Addie had been there with her was gone. The bed had been made. The sheets and comforter smelled like laundry. In some ways, it reminded her of home. Her stomach dropped. She knew that thinking about home wouldn't help. She wasn't sure if she would ever see her family again.

Before she had a chance to think too much, there was a knock at the door. She got up and walked over, waiting for the door to open. It was Myra. "It's time."

Carlye followed her, a knot of bile forming in her throat. She pulled back within herself and followed the older girl. They walked to the front door where Dora was waiting. Outside was a black SUV. The driver came around and opened the car door. "We are going to town. Mr. Maifer would like to see you there."

Carlye got in the car. There was nothing else that she could do. She sat in the back seat next to Myra, looking out the window, wishing she could jump out of the car. She could feel Dora's eyes on her. Although she was only eleven, Carlye knew that what Dora was doing was wrong. She wanted to cry, but the tears wouldn't come. They were locked away in a part of herself that she couldn't access anymore.

The drive took about an hour. She saw signs for Denver as they drove past the lights of the city. Her heart sank. She was a long way from Aldham. Fear crept up on her. How would her family ever find her? She realized they might not. She realized that she'd have to cooperate to stay alive. Lily had told her that the girls that misbehaved never came back.

Before Carlye had too much time to think about her family, they pulled up in front of the hotel. As the driver walked around to open the door, Dora hissed, "Don't embarrass me."

Carlye and Myra, the girl with the long dark hair and dark skin, followed Dora through the hotel lobby and to the elevators. Carlye had never seen a hotel like this one before. The staff was dressed in burgundy uniforms. There were fresh flowers on every table and the floor shone as if it had just been polished. There was even a man in the elevator to push the buttons for them. "Welcome," he said, holding the elevator door for them. "What floor are you going to?"

"The penthouse," Dora replied, handing him an access key.

"Excellent. Are you two ladies having a good time?" The operator looked at Carlye and Myra. Before they could answer, Dora interrupted, "My nieces are having a lovely time in Denver. They want to come back to ski."

"Oh yes, we have the best skiing here." The door buzzed. "And here you are. Enjoy your stay."

The doors opened directly into the room. The view was

expansive, walls of windows covering every inch of the suite. There was soft music playing and the lights were dimmed. "This way," Dora whispered, pushing the girls toward one of the bedrooms. She quickly closed the door. "Do what he says. I'll be downstairs when you are done." The door to the bedroom opened and closed before Carlye had a chance to think about what Dora said. Her stomach turned.

Carlye looked at Myra. The look on her face was resigned. She didn't ask any questions. She just opened the door and waved for Carlye to follow her out.

Mr. Maifer was there. He was sitting with another man who looked like he was Asian. They both had drinks in their hands. "I've brought us a little bit of entertainment tonight. You ready for some fun?"

Carlye looked at the man. He was wearing a suit, but the tie was loosened, like he had a long day at work. She remembered that her dad used to come through the door like that. The man with Maifer lifted his glass and drank the last of what was in his glass. "I'm ready when you are."

"Maybe we should get the girls some drinks first, don't you think?"

The man nodded. "They should party with us."

Myra didn't waste any time. Carlye saw her walk over to the bar and pour four new glasses of an amber liquid. Carlye's stomach turned watching her. When she took the first two drinks over to the men, the guest said to Jackson, "Don't you think she's a little overdressed?"

"I do."

Myra didn't need to be told what to do. She pulled off her dress. She wasn't wearing anything underneath. She had curves that Carlye's body hadn't developed yet. When she turned, Carlye could see a small black mark on her back. It read JM. She had been branded, just like Lily.

"Maybe we should put on some music?" Jackson said. He

pressed the screen on his phone and music came on. Carlye stood behind the couch, not sure what to do. Myra began to sway, raising her arms above her head, twisting her hips from side to side. Jackson got up as she danced. "I'll get you a drink," he said. Carlye saw him grab at her as he walked by. "Do you want some powder?"

"Sugar, you know I don't need no powder," she said, not missing a beat.

Carlye was frozen. "Look, the little one doesn't know what to do!" the Asian man laughed. Carlye caught Jackson staring at her from the bar. Myra came over and dropped her hips low, swinging them from side to side the whole way. On the way to standing up, she grabbed the hem of Carlye's dress and pulled it up over her head, turning her back to the men. "Come on," she whispered, "Just try. I don't want to get in trouble."

Carlye didn't know how to dance, at least not the way that Myra was. She just rocked back and forth. She didn't know what else to do. "That's so funny!" the Asian man yelled again, taking off his suit coat. "Jackson, I didn't know this one was so new. She has no idea what's going on, does she?"

"Well, maybe we can help her along with that." Jackson handed Carlye a drink. She could see some powder floating on the surface. "Drink this right now," he hissed in her ear. There was nothing kind about the way he said it.

Carlye stopped long enough to empty the glass. She felt sick, the liquid going down into her stomach that hadn't had much food in what felt like weeks. Nausea overtook her. She turned her head and almost threw up. She was able to hold it down as the room started to spin.

"So, which one do I get to play with?" the Asian man asked. Jackson had rejoined the Asian man sitting on a couch directly across from him.

"Which one do you want, Hiro?"

"Well, you are the host, Jackson. I think you should choose."

"When you put it that way, I guess maybe we should have both, don't you think?"

"That sounds like a great idea. I like the way you think!"

The whole time they were talking, Carlye saw that Myra hadn't stopped dancing. Carlye, her head spinning, felt like the only thing she was able to do was stand still. Otherwise, she might throw up. Whatever Jackson had given her wasn't the same as the last time. She could remember everything even though she didn't want to. She was seeing everything. She realized that it all seemed far away but was happening to her anyway. Was it a different powder? She didn't know. When Jackson took her hand and led her to the bedroom, Myra and Hiro right behind, she knew what was coming.

The bedroom was enormous, with a king-sized bed and a couch tastefully placed at the foot of it. The bedspread was still on it. The room had a view of the city and the mountains and the lights had already been dimmed. Myra ran around the bed, giggling, laying down on one side, pulling Hiro with her.

Jackson pulled Carlye to the other side of the bed and pushed her down. She turned her head to the side, feeling the warmth of Myra's body next to her. They were so close they were practically touching. She watched as Hiro pulled off his tie and unbuttoned his shirt, keeping a hand on Myra the whole time. Carlye heard her say, "Yes, baby, that's right."

Her attention turned when she felt Jackson's hands on her.

Jackson's hands didn't stop moving the whole time. He didn't try to kiss her. Carlye turned away, feeling his hands on her thighs and then between her legs. As she felt him enter her, she looked at Myra. Hiro was on top of her, her legs wrapped around his waist. He still had his pants on.

There was quiet in the room for a minute or so, just some moaning as the men finished. Carlye started to get up, but she felt Myra's hand on her arm. Before she realized what was happening, Hiro was on top of her, "Jackson, I've got to try this one out!" She felt Hiro's hand grab her and twist her half off of the bed, lying face down. Carlye felt Hiro push into her. Nausea swept over her. She looked away, trying to think about something else, but all she could see was Myra, standing up, holding onto her ankles, Jackson behind her.

Carlye closed her eyes and waited, going to a quiet place in her mind. She tried to tell herself that she was okay. She didn't want to feel anything. She didn't want to feel Hiro's hands on her body, rubbing against her or touching her. The drugs and alcohol just made her feel sick. Her body hurt. She went back into the quiet place and thought about nothing.

WHEN THE MEN WERE DONE, Carlye threw up all over the bed. Jackson stared at her without speaking and led Hiro out of the room, closing the door behind her. Myra stood up. "Get dressed. We have to go."

Carlye slipped the green dress back on over her head. She felt moisture between her legs. Myra went to the bathroom and wiped herself and then handed the towel to Carlye. "Clean up or you will leak all over the car on the way home."

They walked out of the bedroom closing the door behind them. Carlye caught a glance at the men, who were sitting outside on the balcony. It smelled like cigars.

"They have business to do. That's what Jackson always says," Myra whispered as they went out in the hallway. She walked to the elevator and pushed the button. Standing at the elevator, Myra looked at her, "No..." she said, looking at Carlye's legs. There was a trickle of blood running down the inside. "Wipe that up."

"I don't have anything." Carlye could barely walk let alone think about what Myra was asking her to do. She felt confused and dazed.

"Use the hem of your dress. Like this." Myra grabbed the

hem of her dress and pretended to wipe her legs. Carlye dabbed at the stains on her legs, getting blood on her dress. The only thing she could think about was whether Dora would be mad. She didn't want to have to go to the basement again.

The elevator operator wasn't on the elevator with them this time. Myra pushed the button and they glided down to the lobby, the elevator silently opening as it stopped. Carlye felt Myra grab her hand and pull her across the lobby, her own legs wobbly. She was glad that she did. Carlye didn't know where to go.

Outside, the doorman greeted them. Dora was waiting. Carlye saw the man look at both of them and then Dora. "You ladies okay?"

"Oh yes, of course," Myra answered, quickly getting into the car. Carlye paused and Dora hissed, "Get in. Now." As Carlye stepped into the car, she heard Dora say, "Oh yes, my nieces love this hotel. The younger one just woke up. She's a little confused."

Carlye was sitting in the seat that faced backward. She watched the doorman as they pulled away, knowing that she should have done something, anything, to let him know she was in trouble. Tears poured down her cheeks, but it was too late.

64

Kat was frustrated and angry. It felt like they had spent days looking for Carlye Morgan and were no closer. Now the one person they could use to find her was dead. Kat stepped out of the conference room. She needed a break. Detective Traldent followed her. "You okay?"

Kat pushed her hair out of her face, "No. I'm not. I can't figure out where we are with this. I mean, really, are we getting any closer to finding Carlye?"

"These cases can be frustrating. The way that these guys win is when we give up. We aren't going to do that. Sean isn't going to do that. We are going to find this girl."

"How can you be so sure?" Kat was trying to buy into Lance's version of how things would work out. If she needed hope, she couldn't imagine how Carlye might be feeling.

"Look at all of the resources the FBI has put into this. Now we have a body in another state. They are going to want to resolve this or it's a black eye for them. And, if they can grab a big fish like Jackson Maifer..." Lance paused and raised his eyebrows, "Can you imagine? That might be a career-maker for Hollister."

Kat furrowed her brows. "This isn't about Hollister's career. We have a girl whose life is in danger."

Lance nodded. "I know. I'm not trying to be callous, really. But when it gets personal for these agents..." he let the sentence stop. "All I know is that the more they have to gain by finding someone the harder they work."

Kat nodded. She knew it was basic human psychology. She didn't like it though.

Underneath it all, Kat was an idealist. She wanted Hollister and his team to look for Carlye like their lives depended on it because hers certainly did. She wanted them to spare no expense and find her. She also knew that if they didn't have something tangible soon on a location for her, they might move on to another case. Finding Addie Buckholtz might be enough. But, would it be enough for Kat and her family to be out of danger? She wasn't sure.

Lance interrupted her thinking, "Here's what I'm wondering... Maifer has to know that we've found his wife. He knows that you have been looking. That's what the threat to you was about. If we believe that, what's his next move?"

Kat stopped to think about his question. It was a good one. A very good one, in fact. It was pretty likely that Maifer had some idea that people were looking for Carlye. Now that Maria had been found, and they had to assume he knew that, what would a billionaire with a penchant for trafficking little girls do next? "That's the million-dollar question, isn't it?" She stopped for a second, thinking, her heart starting to beat hard in her chest. Kat grabbed Lance's elbow, "Get Van for me, will you?"

KAT MOTIONED at Van to follow her out of the police station. "I think we have been looking at this all wrong."

They stood in the darkness. "What do you mean?" Van asked.

"I think we have to start to think more like Maifer."

"More like a psychopath?" Van smiled. "I could be good at that."

"Don't joke. I'm serious."

"I know you are. Sorry. I'm just tired."

There was a pause. Kat said, "Here's what I think. If Maifer is as invested in these girls as you think he is he's going to be one step ahead of us. I mean, that's how billionaires become billionaires. They are master strategists."

"All right, I'll buy that. I think that fits with what we know of him."

"You bet it does." Kat started to feel more confident the more she talked through her ideas with Van. "We've got to look at this like a chess match. This guy has been steps ahead of us on every turn. How do we get ahead of him?" Kat started to pace in the parking lot, kicking at some gravel that was loose on the concrete.

"So, let's think this through. You are Maifer."

Kat grimaced. "Do I have to be?"

"This was your idea, right?"

Kat sighed. "Yeah, okay. Keep going."

"You know that Carlye's parents and a set of reporters are looking for her. You can assume the FBI has been called in. That's very different than a family who just uses local law enforcement."

"Correct. The other families might not have thought their daughters were crossing over state lines."

"You feel a bit more heat coming at you. But you are cool. High-pressure stakes are how you made your living. This doesn't scare you."

"That's it. That's the key that we have been missing. Maifer isn't looking at this with fear. He's not afraid of anyone!"

"I'd agree. I think that jives with the profile Hollister has been working from."

Kat stopped to look at him. "So, we know he makes logical decisions." She looked down the street. There was a car dealership on the corner. Looking at the new, shiny fancy cars clicked with her. "We need to go inside."

They went straight to the conference room where Kat's laptop was set up. She opened it and started scrolling back through a few articles that she had read on Maifer's background. "Here!" she said, pointing to an article. "Look at this, Van. This is something." Kat started to read, "The genius behind Maifer and his brands is that he treats everything as an investment. In one of his first, and boldest moves, he wanted to open a series of luxury car dealerships. When West Coast dealers wouldn't comply, he did something else. He bought the land their dealerships sat on. The time it took for them to relocate eliminated much of the competition. Many of the owners capitulated and sold their dealerships to Maifer, realizing there was no way to win."

"What are you saying?" Van had folded his arms across his chest.

"It's about his mindset. He is logical. Cold. He sees everything as an investment. I bet he sees the girls the same way." Kat stood up, a smile passing over her face. "What do you do when your investment is threatened?"

Van nodded, "You protect it."

KAT PULLED Hollister and Traldent away from their teams long enough to explain her theory.

"What you are telling me is that he isn't going to spend a lot of time mourning for his wife?" Sean asked, shoving his hands into his pockets.

Kat shook her head. "I don't think so. It doesn't fit. If he's as cold as we think he is, he could just have her buried and that would be it. He'd only make a show of it if it benefitted his business somehow."

Traldent looked at her, "But how does that help us find the girls?"

Kat chewed her lip. "What it helps us is to understand that the girls are an investment. He clearly can't connect with anyone the normal way. Love and affection aren't his thing. From everything I've read, he's as cold as they come." She saw Traldent raise his eyebrows. "That said," she continued, "If you had a precious asset what would you do if it was threatened?"

Kat saw the excitement grow in Sean's eyes. He said, "You either defend it or hide it."

"That's what I'm thinking. The question is, which one does he choose?"

A chime from Traldent's phone interrupted their discussion. Kat saw his face harden. "What is it?" she asked, leaning toward him.

"It's Alana Morgan. She just tried to commit suicide."

Kat and Van jumped in Van's truck, a team of FBI agents tailing them. Traldent followed in a unit from the department. Alana had been taken to Mercy Memorial, the same hospital where Kat's mother-in-law, Laura, had been treated for cancer. It was also the same hospital where the Apex story had originated. A chill went up Kat's spine as they drove past the sign for the entrance. This hospital, or any hospital for that matter, was the last place she wanted to be.

The memories started to flood back. Laura's diagnosis. The appointments. The treatments. The overnight stays at the hospital waiting for news. The night she was drugged. She pushed the memories back into a space in her head. She couldn't afford to get distracted.

Van pulled the truck into a parking space in front of the hospital. "Ready?"

"Yep." Kat tried to sound convincing as she opened the door to the truck. She stepped out into the night air. It was getting cool. Not cold yet. It didn't ever get too cold in Aldham. She wondered how Carlye was feeling right now. Was she cold? Was she hungry? Was Carlye being abused by some man as Kat and Van got ready to walk into the hospital to find Alana Morgan struggling to live? Again, more questions Kat had to put aside. She needed to take the next step, but it was getting harder and harder the deeper they got into the story.

Kat realized that Van was watching her. By the look on his face, he knew she was drowning in memories. "Come on." He extended his hand toward her. She took it.

As they walked across the lot to meet Lance, Van said, "You holding up okay?"

"Yeah. I miss Jack. I want him and Woof home."

"It's not safe, Kat. You know that."

"I know. I'm getting so angry. I can't imagine what Carlye is going through. She will never be the same." Kat felt Van squeeze her hand.

"None of us will be. But that's why we do what we do."

Their conversation stopped as the sliding glass doors to Mercy Memorial's emergency department opened. There was a guard at the door. Lance flashed his badge and said, "Morgan? Just brought in?"

The guard pointed down the hallway. "Try the information desk over there. They will be able to direct you."

Kat wondered how many times a day that guard had to direct a family whose day had been interrupted by a disaster. Another thought to shake off, she realized. Focus, Kat, focus, she told herself. She and Van followed Lance down the polished hallway past people reading magazines and playing on their phones. Some of them looked like they were waiting for treatment. Some of them looked like they were waiting for a friend or a loved one.

At the information desk, Lance took over. "I'm Detective Traldent. I'm here for Alana Morgan. Is she in the back?"

The woman at the desk pressed a button and the steel doors in front of them marked no admittance glided open. "I believe they are working on her now. Her family is back there with her. Bay three. Down the hall and to the right."

The emergency room seemed to be particularly busy. Kat had been there twice when Jack was a baby for an ear infection and once when Laura was first admitted to the hospital. Normally, there were at least a couple of bays open. Tonight, there were none. As they made their way down the hallway to find Alana's treatment room, Kat saw nurses moving in and out of a doorway like bees leaving a hive. They weren't running, but they were moving fast. Standing across the hall was Tim. He had Michael with him.

"Tim, what happened?" Kat went to him. She caught Lance's eye. He went toward the treatment room.

"I wasn't gone long... My office -- they have been so good about letting me work from home, but I needed a file. I wasn't gone for more than an hour. When I got back, I was looking for Alana. I found her in Carlye's room. She was on the floor." Kat saw a tear run down his face. He quickly wiped it away. "I shook her. She wouldn't wake up. She was all pale. I didn't know what else to do so I called for help."

There was nothing that Kat could say. She put her hand on Tim's arm, trying to steady him. "It's okay. We'll stay here with you."

Van knelt down. "Hey, there. How about if you and I go take a walk? I hear they have killer ice cream here."

Michael buried his head in Tim's leg. Kat saw Tim pat him on the back. "You remember Van, don't you? He's been to our house. Go on. Go get ice cream. You can get one for mom, too."

Kat saw Michael look up at his dad. He didn't say anything.

He just stared at Van and started walking. "This way, buddy," Van said.

As they walked away, Tim sighed. "He has barely spoken since Carlye was taken. I'm not sure he's old enough to know how to process this." Tim looked up at the ceiling. "I'm not sure any of us do."

"It's okay. We will get through it one step at a time." As Kat said it, she realized how stupid it sounded. The Morgan's were suffering. They wanted their daughter back. And now, Tim was going to have to do it alone, unless the doctors could save Alana.

Kat didn't have a chance to go down that road. Lance came out of the room, his face ashen. Kat watched Tim. She could tell that he wanted answers. Lance looked at him, sticking his phone back in his pocket. "They are working on Alana. The doctor said he will be out in a little bit to give you an update. Just give me a second with Kat, okay?"

Tim nodded and sat down in one of the chairs across the hallway from Alana's room. Kat followed Lance. "Where did Van go?"

"He took Michael to get ice cream. What's going on with Alana?"

Lance shook his head. "It's not good. They are doing what they can. She took a lot of pills. Painkillers mostly, from a back injury that Tim had about a year ago. He never touched the stuff, so she had a full prescription to take. Plus, her own doctor has been giving her antidepressants and anti-anxiety medication since Carlye was taken."

Kat tried to grasp the moment before Alana decided to take all the pills. She must have been feeling so desperate. Kat could picture her in Carlye's room, looking at her daughter's clothes and her books and wondering if things would ever be the same again. Kat knew the answer to that question, no matter whether they found her or not, would be no. No family was ever the same after a tragedy. "What are her chances?"

"The docs aren't sure. If they can get the pills out of her she might be okay. They aren't sure how long her brain was deprived of oxygen."

"Tim just said she was on the floor."

"Yeah, well when the paramedics got there, he was doing CPR on her. She had stopped breathing. They tried Narcan, but it didn't wake her up. Too much time had gone by. It's touch and go. We won't know anything for the next few hours." Lance looked at his watch. "I've got to get back. You and Van are welcome to stay if you'd like. I'll be back at the station with Hollister and his team." She saw him look towards the medical bay. "The best thing we can do for this family is to get their daughter back. I just hope we have enough time."

Kat nodded but didn't say anything. She walked back toward Tim, whose hollow face was nearly impossible to look at. How he was holding it together at all, she wasn't sure. She sat down on the chair next to him and put her arm around him. He sat up and she pulled her arm back.

"I'm sorry. I didn't mean to..."

"No. It's not you. I appreciate you guys coming. It's just this whole situation. First Carlye and now Alana. I just don't know what to do."

"There is nothing you can do. All you can do right now is be there for Alana and Michael. There are dozens of people looking for Carlye around the clock."

"We need her back. Alana needs her back. She's just lost all hope..."

"I know. It's okay." Kat could see Michael and Van coming down the hallway. Each of them had a giant vanilla ice cream cone. "Look, Michael's coming back."

She watched Tim turn to see his son. Kat knew that whether they found Carlye or not, the family was shattered. All of them would need help for a long time to put the pieces back together. Whatever pieces were left, that is. The Morgan's would never be the same.

Kat stood up. "Are there other people coming to help you?"

Tim nodded, "Yes. My sister is coming. She should be here any minute."

"I think the best way for Van and me to help is to keep looking for Carlye. Alana is in good hands." Tim nodded, but as Kat said it, her stomach dropped. Based on what Lance said, Alana's chances were slim at best. By the time this was over, the family could lose a mom and a daughter.

Kat saw Van ruffle Michael's hair. "Listen, buddy, when you are ready, let's go hiking. Okay?"

Michael nodded, still trying to finish his ice cream.

"I'm going to head out with Kat, but we will be back in a little bit."

Kat waved as they left Tim and Michael in the hospital.

BY THE TIME they made it out to Van's truck, Kat could barely breathe. All she could say was, "I can't..." The world around her began to spin. Tears were running down her face and her heart was racing. "I can't..."

She felt Van's strong arm come up around her back. He carried her the last few steps to the truck and lifted her inside. She crumpled over onto the seat, wheezing, hoping that she didn't pass out. Van stood by her side, the truck door open, pushing her hair off of her face. "Breathe, Kat. One breath at a time. You are okay."

She couldn't breathe. Her heart was pounding in her chest. She almost wished she'd just pass out, but she didn't. She hadn't had this strong of an episode for months. It was everything. The Middle East. The accident there. Her memories of it. Laura getting cancer. The man from Apex that she had to shoot to protect Jack. Carlye being taken. Jack being taken away...

The feeling of being overwhelmed was suffocating her. The memories were too much. Knowing that there was so little she could do to protect herself and her family was drowning her. Van's voice interrupted the rollercoaster that was going on in her head. "Do I need to take you back inside?"

Fury gripped Kat. She punched the dashboard. "No! Just give me a minute," she whispered. She leaned back in the seat. She was not going to let the circumstances win. She started taking deep breaths, counting her inhales and her exhales, just like her therapist had told her. In and out. Slowly, the world came back into focus again. Her breathing slowed. Her heart felt like it was moving at the correct pace again. She sighed.

"You okay now?" She realized that Van was still standing by her, the door to the truck open. "What happened?"

"It was all too much. Just... let's go, okay?"

With that, Van closed the door. Kat took a few more deep breaths, trying to steady herself.

The driver's side door opened and Van got in. "I've never seen you like that before. You sure you are okay?"

"Yeah."

"It's how my PTSD used to be. I was going to tell you it could happen, but then I was worried..."

"Worried about what?" Van started the truck and began to pull away from the hospital. "Worried that I wouldn't be interested anymore?"

"Kinda." Kat looked down at the side of the seat, trying to avoid looking at him.

"You are going to have to come up with something better than a little wheezing to scare me away."

"Really?"

"Well, not really. I only hang around 'cuz I like Jack."

Kat reached over and punched him in the arm. He smiled.

"Realistically, though, I've known a bunch of guys that have the same issue. We don't have to do this. Remember that. If it is too much, you can go up to Laura's cousin's house or wherever they are and just ride it out. We can let the FBI and Traldent's team handle this."

Kat knew that. She had known from the minute that she and Van had agreed to meet with Tim and Alana that they could walk away. Van had made that clear. There were other stories to chase. They could do the reporting at the back end. She didn't have to see this through. Or did she?

Kat took a deep breath and then another. She'd helped get Laura cured and taken down a major blackmail ring. As sorry as she was for what was happening to Carlye, did she really need to put herself and Jack at risk? She was all Jack had now that his dad was in prison.

"Pull the truck over," she said, leaning toward the door.

Van drove the truck to the side of the road, the gravel grinding under the tires. Kat leaned out of the door and threw up. She crawled out as more waves of nausea came over her. The waves came again and again until there was nothing else that could come up. Somewhere in the middle of her retching, Van had come to her side of the truck. "You okay? What can I do?"

"Nothing," she said. "I'm okay now. We can go."

When she got back in the truck she swallowed hard a couple of times and then took a sip of water from a bottle that Van had handed to her. "I know that we don't have to keep going, but we have to."

"That didn't make a lot of sense," Van said, turning on the blinker.

"You know what I mean. I can't give up. What if it had been Jack?" Kat saw the muscles in Van's jaw ripple. She knew that he had become attached to Jack ever since Steve had been arrested.

"This would never happen to Jack," he said stonily. Van softened a bit, "It really is okay if you don't want to do this. You are having panic attacks and throwing up on the side of the road..."

"It's probably nothing compared to what Carlye is going through. That's why I can't stop. I'd never forgive myself." She saw him nod, soaking in the idea. "It's like a mission. No matter how hard it gets, you keep going."

"That I understand. What do you want to do now, boss?"

"Maybe brush my teeth and lay down for a little bit..." Kat smiled. "And then regroup."

65

Once she got in the door of the house, Kat decided that she needed a shower. She took off the pistol she had been wearing at her side all day long and went upstairs. By the time that she had come back downstairs, she could smell eggs cooking. She picked up the mail that had been dropped through the slot and walked into the kitchen, thumbing through as she did.

There wasn't much there. A bill from the cable company and one for the electric. There was a manilla envelope addressed to her. She set the rest of the mail down on the kitchen table, saying to Van, "That smells good," as she opened it. As she pulled the papers out, she realized there were pictures inside. "Oh my God," she whispered.

Van came over and looked at the papers. Inside the envelope were images of Jack and Woof. Jack was outside. She could see Laura in the background. There was no note. It didn't need one. Kat collapsed on a kitchen chair. She handed the envelope to Van. Tears streamed down her face. She couldn't face something happening to Jack.

She could hear Van on the phone. She was sure he was

talking to Traldent or Hollister or both of them. The call only took a minute. "They are on their way. Just try to relax."

Kat couldn't speak. She just sat on the chair and stared at the floor. She didn't want to look at the images. She couldn't. It was too much to bear. She felt numb. She didn't want to fight. She just wanted things to go back the way they were. She wanted to play outside in the sandbox with Jack and pick up his toys and make him hot dogs for lunch. She wanted to go to the park and have Van bring them breakfast sandwiches. She wanted her old life back.

Kat didn't know how much time passed, but it wasn't long before there was a knock on the door. She heard male voices talking quietly and saw flashes of agents passing by her, doors opening and closing. They were searching her house and securing it. She knew that.

Traldent was the first in the kitchen, "Kat, I'm sorry. We should have kept the detail on your house."

"It wouldn't have done any good. These came through the mail, I think."

She saw Traldent pull a pair of gloves out of his pocket. She suddenly wondered if Lance found pairs of gloves in his clothes when he was out. It seemed detectives always had them handy. He thumbed through the pages but didn't say anything.

Hollister and Van joined them in the kitchen. "What happened here?" Sean asked, kneeling down in front of Kat.

"We were coming back from the hospital…"

"Because of Alana Morgan?"

"Yeah. We were there with Lance." She saw Lance nod. "When we got home, we found these in with the mail." She pointed to the envelope that was on the kitchen table.

Sean nodded and looked at her. "Are you okay?"

The circles under her eyes must have given her away. "I'm okay. It's been a long day for all of us."

Sean nodded. He stood up and pushed the pages around with the end of a pen. "Do we know where these were taken?"

Kat turned back to the pictures. She had been so shocked that she hadn't even bothered to look that closely at them. "I don't know..." Kat reached for one of the pictures. Sean pulled her hands back. "Hold on. Let's get you some gloves." Another agent quickly pulled gloves out of her jacket and handed them to Kat.

Kat looked closely at the images. They were clearly of Jack and Woof. There were two that had Laura in them, but something had been done to the pictures. She couldn't tell when or where they had been taken. "I'm not sure. I can't see the background well enough."

Van leaned over her shoulder. "Could these have been altered? It looks like they've used a blurring effect to prevent us from seeing the background."

Hollister raised his eyebrows, "With this case, anything is possible. Realistically, we are seeing criminals that are highly sophisticated with their use of technology." He leaned over and tried to get a better look. "I'm going to have our lab take a look. They may have better luck. There was no note with this? Any chance it was just someone getting you some pictures of your son?"

Kat was instantly angry, "What do you think, Sean? Does this look like just a friendly neighbor based on what is going on?"

Sean held up his hands in surrender. "You are right. I'm sorry. Just gotta ask the question."

"No, I'm sorry. I shouldn't have barked at you like that. It's just..."

"Yeah, I know. It's a lot. There is nothing saying you and Van have to keep at it with us."

Kat felt her anger rise again. She pushed it back down. "We do." Kat must have said it more strongly than she thought. Van,

Sean and Lance all looked at her as though they didn't know what to make of her.

"Well, you heard the lady. Let's get this bagged and tagged. I want the lab on this right now." Sean walked away to answer his phone.

Van and Lance stayed in the kitchen with her. A tech came over and took her fingerprints and Van's so they would have them for exclusion as they ran tests on the envelope. "Sean said they are going to double the detail on Jack and Laura. They are also going to leave agents here again until this is over."

Kat took a deep breath and nodded. She was starting to feel like herself again. "Make sure they know to keep an eye on Woof. The last thing we need is to have something happen to him. He's been Jack's rock. These people are crazy enough they would hurt him." For a moment, Kat was sure that the agents thought she was out of her mind. Protect Woof, too?

"We've got this. We have seen perps do stuff to animals before. We will watch all of them. Don't worry." Sean nodded. "Let's just get this resolved so you can go back to your life and I can go back to my boring cases. Gotta go make a couple of calls. I'll meet you back at the station, okay?" He grinned at them.

As soon as the agents left, Kat called Laura. She didn't give her any of the details about the envelope. "I just wanted you to know that there will be more agents around than usual."

"You are getting close?"

"It seems that way," Kat sighed. "Shouldn't be too much longer."

"Don't worry. We've got it covered."

"Thanks, Gramma. By the way, keep an eye on Woof, too."

"Will do."

Kat looked around the kitchen and wondered if they would ever get their life back. She had just been feeling better after the incident with Apex and now they were facing another enemy.

Hollister had left four agents at the house. Two inside and two outside. If the threat wasn't so real to her, she might feel important. She wasn't sure she ever wanted to be that important again. "Have you seen Van?" she asked the one that was positioned in the kitchen with her.

He pointed down the hallway. "Family room."

"Thanks." Kat wandered down the hallway to see what Van was doing. He was sound asleep on the chair, the television on to a football game, his pistol next to him on the table. How he could sleep with all of this going on, she wasn't sure. She looked toward the stairs and wondered if she should go upstairs to try to get some sleep. Being alone upstairs didn't sound appealing, so she put a blanket over Van's legs and sat down on the matching chair to the one that Van was sleeping on, kicking off her shoes and socks on the floor.

She took the remote, thinking she'd like to change the channel, but she didn't. She stared at the game, watching the players break into a fight over who had the ball. Everything seemed so inconsequential to her at that moment. Everything but her family and Carlye.

KAT HAD SLEPT FITFULLY on the chair next to Van in the family room. At least she had slept a little. Knowing that the agents were in the house and Van was right next to her gave her comfort.

She woke up to one of the agents touching her on the shoulder, "Ma'am? Special Agent Hollister would like the two of you to come to the station as soon as it is convenient. There's been a breakthrough overnight."

The news that there had been progress pulled Kat out of what sleep she had. "Breakthrough? Did they get her back?"

"No ma'am, but just the same you are wanted at the station."

Even with the conversation practically in Van's ear, he hadn't heard a thing. The man could sleep, Kat thought, a smile coming to her face. "Van?" she said, touching him on his shoulder. "We've got to get ready. Hollister has something."

"Yeah, okay. Gimme a sec."

Kat stood up, picking up her shoes and socks. "You've got a few minutes. I'm going to run up and take another shower."

"I'll make coffee. Okay for me to use Jack's shower?"

"You have clothes with you?"

"My go bag is in the truck."

"Sure. There's shampoo and soap in there already." Kat smiled. Military guys were funny. Who else would have a go-bag in their truck just in case? That would be someone like Van. She really liked his quirkiness. The best part of it was that he didn't think it was quirky.

Kat took the steps two at a time, an agent following her. "Ma'am, let me just give a quick check before you go in, please." The agents Hollister had left behind were thorough if nothing else. Kat started the shower and was grateful for the hot water and the smell of the soap. She dried off with a towel and put on a fresh pair of jeans, a tank top, a flannel shirt over that and a fleece vest. She dabbed some lipstick on and clipped the top sections of her hair back, leaving the bottom hair loose. It would dry as they went, she knew.

By the time she got down to the kitchen, Van had showered and had a fresh set of clothes on. He had poured coffee into two travel mugs. "Should we stop on the way for some bagels?" he asked.

The agent following them leaned in, "Special Agent Hollister thought you might be hungry. He's already sent out for food. We are ready to take you as soon as you are good to go."

Getting them food must have been Hollister's way of hurrying up the process. Either way, it worked. Kat and Van got in the Suburban with the agents and they left the house. Two agents were with them and two agents were keeping an eye on things while they were gone.

Once they got to the station, one of the agents accompanied them into the building while the other parked the car. Kat wished the protection wasn't necessary, but after Maifer's people had been able to get to them more than one time, she knew Hollister didn't want to take any chances. He didn't need more than he had on his hands at the moment with Carlye missing, Maria Maifer's body and Alana Morgan in the hospital.

"Morning!" Hollister greeted them enthusiastically with a toothy grin. "Did you get some sleep?"

"Some," Van said. "Did you?"

"Some... The good news is that things are moving. There's food over there." He pointed to the end of the table where there was a tray of bagels and breakfast sandwiches wrapped in foil. "While you are eating, here's what has happened. While you were resting, we got authorization to send a drone over Maifer's Colorado estate." Hollister pointed to an agent, who put the footage up on the wall. "While it was dark, we did see this vehicle come in and out. Let's zoom in on that for them, okay?"

"I had no idea you were going to use drones," Kat said.

"Yeah, we put in the request yesterday. Didn't know if it would come through, but it did." Hollister smiled. "Can't let you know all of my secrets, can I?"

Kat took a step forward as she took a bite of her sandwich. Out of a black vehicle came a woman and two girls. One of the girls looked to be older and the other one was small with blonde hair.

"Show them the stills, please."

The image changed on the wall. The woman looked up at something and so did the blonde girl. The video had been distilled down to frames. "Is that...?"

Hollister nodded, "We think it is Carlye Morgan. Who the woman is, we aren't sure. The images are grainy, but we are fairly certain that is her."

Kat saw Van tilt his head to the side, "Out of curiosity, how did you get that image?"

Hollister smiled, "This one is something you can't report on, okay?"

They both nodded.

"We have new drones that are really small, small as a bird in flight. From the ground, especially at night, that's what they look like. They were developed for urban settings where the buildings are really close together. This particular model came with nature sounds to cover the hum of the propellers. The pilot told me that when he got close, he had the drone make a bird noise. He just wanted to cover his tracks, but we got this great image of the girls looking up."

Kat wrapped the rest of her sandwich back in the foil. She was too excited to eat. "So, what does this mean? What do we do now?"

"Easy now. Remember this is an investigation. We have to be deliberate. We are starting to position assets and people in place. I've got a call with the federal prosecutor in a half hour. With any luck, we will have a search warrant by nightfall."

That just didn't seem good enough to Kat. "By nightfall? Why can't we go now? What if they try to move her?" She started to pace. "You know as well as I do that if Maifer gets her on a plane she could end up anywhere!"

"I get it. I really do. But we want to be careful. Maifer is a powerful man. I want him as badly as you do. I want Carlye home, but I have to do it the right way." He pointed to the wall, where there were more images of the estate. "Look, we've gotten the go-ahead to keep the drone on them. I've got agents in the woods watching the house. Unless they try to leave through underground tunnels, we will see them. I promise you..." Sean looked at this phone. "I gotta go make this call. Be patient. We are almost there."

Kat was frustrated, but she knew he was right. The problem was that Maifer was just smart enough to have underground tunnels or some other way to move the girls. They just couldn't lose Carlye. Kat knew if they got away she and Jack would never be safe.

66

Carlye woke up feeling lightheaded and groggy, not much different than the night before. The mixture of drugs from the night before had been potent. Her body wanted more. She sat up on the side of the bed, realizing that it wasn't morning anymore. On the bed next to hers was a red dress and a new pair of shoes. This time, there was a sweater on top of the pile. It was open in the front. She thought that her mom had called those "cardigan style" sweaters. She didn't like them.

Carlye got into the shower, letting the hot water wake her up. She was tired. As she washed, she could feel the bones of her ribs sticking out. She knew she hadn't eaten much in the weeks since she had been taken. Had it been weeks? How long exactly, she didn't know. What she did know is that the longer she was at the house, the less hope she had. There seemed to be no way to escape.

She remembered the doorman from the night before. She knew, even though she had been drugged, that he saw her. She tried to give him a pleading look but wondered if he noticed. She was sure that with so many people coming in and out of the hotel, he might not know why people were there or if they were in trouble.

Having finished her shower, she toweled off and put the dress on and pulled the sweater over her shoulders. She looked in the mirror realizing that she looked much younger than eleven. The dress and sweater, with the matching patent leather red shoes, made her look like she was seven or eight years old. Maybe that was what Mr. Maifer liked. She straightened the edges of the sweater and started to comb her hair. Long strands were falling out. Fear balled up in her throat. She didn't know why her hair was falling out. Or why she had to wear this stupid dress. Where were the clothes that she came in?

Carlye walked out into the bedroom and started looking in the drawers. There was nothing in them. Nothing that was hers from before they had brought her here. Nothing that tied her to home. After she opened the last drawer and found it empty, she slid down onto the floor, tears streaming down her cheeks. As much as she had tried to not think about her family, all she wanted was to hear her mom tell her to do her homework. If she could go home, she'd never get angry at her family again...

67

While Hollister was waiting for the federal prosecutor to get the search warrant drafted and approved by a judge, he sent Kat and Van over to Mercy Memorial to check on Alana Morgan. "Do you want us to show Tim the image of Carlye?"

"That's a hard no," Sean said. "Listen, as excited as I am that we think we've found her, can you imagine what would happen if either it's not her or she's been moved? They would be devastated. They don't need any more bad news."

Kat nodded. There was some logic to what he was saying, although every part of her wanted to go outside and scream the news that they were going to get Carlye and bring her home. The anticipation was killing her. They agreed and let the agents take them to the hospital.

By the time they left, Detective Traldent had joined them. They all rode in the SUV together, not saying much. Kat figured they were all wondering how the rest of the day would go. She was too. If it was Carlye, the day could have a real happy ending. Jack could be home within hours with Laura and Woof. Or, if it wasn't Carlye, then twenty-four hours from now, they would be doing the same thing they were doing right now. Hoping and waiting.

It was early enough that the hospital wasn't too full of people. Kat knew from Laura's stays there that the majority of the people in the building would be nursing staff. The doctors didn't start rounds until about eight o'clock and they weren't there yet. Lance went to the information desk and got information on Alana. "We need to head up to the second floor. She's in ICU."

Kat was just happy that she had made it through the night. They took the elevators that
were halfway down the hall up to the second floor and were faced with a call box and metal doors. Lance pushed the button and held up his badge. "Here to see Alana Morgan."

The doors opened without a word. Kat, Van and Lance went through, the smell of the hospital stronger than on the first floor. It was quiet and dark. The ICU was arranged with individual bays encircling a large monitoring station. There were three nurses at the station, as well as what looked to be several doctors. Screens on the walls poured out colorful EKG patterns, blood pressures and blood oxygen levels by bed number. High tech medicine at its best, Kat thought.

She watched Lance approach the desk, nodding his head. He came back, his brow furrowed, "She's in bed eight. Tim is there too. She's not doing well."

"What does that mean?"

"From what her nurse said, she's on a ventilator. She hasn't woken up yet and they don't know why. She took such a cocktail they aren't sure how it interacted with her body. It's a waiting game."

They walked past the nursing station and to Alana's room. Kat glanced into each bay as they walked. She was surprised that some of the patients didn't look that bad. One of them was even sitting in a chair next to his bed. The man next to Alana had an enormous dressing on his left leg. It looked like he'd just had it amputated. By choice or in an accident, Kat couldn't tell. It reminded her of the time she spent in the Middle East. She shook off the thought. She couldn't afford to go down that path today. She needed all of her energy and all of her focus. They were close to getting Carlye back. She just knew it.

The door to Alana's ICU bed was closed. There were signs on the door about oxygen use and psychiatric hold. Kat imagined that if Alana woke up, she'd have a long road to recovery ahead of her, both mentally and physically. Alana was tipped slightly upright, by just a few inches so they could see her face from the hallway. Her color was better than it had been the day before. She was wearing a hospital gown and had a full bank of IV's connected to a line in her arm. Kat counted and realized there were five different bags of medicine going into Alana to help her heal. A tube was coming out of her mouth, her chest rising and falling in a steady rhythm.

Tim was sitting next to Alana's bed, holding her hand. As soon as he saw them, he got up and came out, closing the door behind him. Lance was the first to speak, "We wanted to come and see how Alana is doing."

Tim sighed. Kat noticed that he looked rumpled. She doubted that he had left the hospital all night. "She's doing okay from what they've told me. They are worried that she hasn't woken up yet."

"Is there anything we can do?" Seeing Alana in the bed reminded her of when Laura was so sick. Kat wanted to be able to do something for them.

"No. I'm okay. My sister came in. She's got Michael at home. She brought her kids so it's keeping him busy." Tim looked at them searchingly. "Any news on Carlye?"

Kat drew in a breath, ready to speak, but Lance's hand on her arm stopped her. "Nothing firm. We have more leads that we are following up on. Believe me, this case has the attention of everyone. We will let you know as soon as anything happens." Lance reached into his pocket and pulled out his phone. "Sorry, I've gotta take this."

As he walked away, Kat and Van stayed with Tim. "There's something going on, isn't there?"

Kat glanced at Van, whose expression didn't change. Van answered, "Like Lance said, as soon as we know anything, we will tell you. I promise. Our goal isn't to keep anything from you. You just keep an eye on your girl, okay?" Van started to move away from Tim, back toward the entrance where Lance was on the phone. Lance waved at them that it was time to go. Kat didn't move, even though Van was already halfway to where Lance was standing.

Tim looked at her, "You know something, don't you?" He leaned toward her, "Please tell me. I need something. Something to think about other than this." He motioned to Alana's room.

Kat bit her lip. She knew that she wasn't supposed to talk about what they had found. "I can't say anything, but we are close. Just hang in there with us a little longer." She tried to tell him with her facial expression. She was hoping that told him what he needed to know.

"Please, just tell me..." Tim pleaded as Kat backed up.

"I can't say more. We will be in touch, okay?" Kat turned and walked to Van and Lance.

"Did you tell him anything?" Lance asked.

"No, just said what you said..." She hoped that Tim could read between the lines.

"I certainly hope so. We have to keep this under wraps so that the investigation isn't compromised."

"I know, I know. I didn't tell him anything, I promise!" Kat felt like she had been scolded by a teacher.

They started to walk back toward the parking lot, Lance

leading the way, Van and Kat lagging behind. "What did you tell him, Kat?" Van whispered.

"Nothing. Really. I told him we were close. That's all."

Van rolled his eyes at her. "You are something else."

"That's why you like me."

She felt him smack her backside. She started to laugh.

68

Finding Maria and the little girl hadn't gone the way that he expected it to, Mitch thought, pulling into the garage at the Colorado house. At least he had done part of his job right. He shut up that wife of Jackson's. She had been nothing but a pain since the day that he married her. She just walked around and watched everything. It was creepy.

He pulled the Lexus back into the spot where it was kept and handed the keys to one of Jackson's porters. The car had been pulled out for a full wash and detailing before Mitch even made it into the house.

The point of the whole trip had been to find the little girl and bring her back with Maria. That much had been a failure. He and Nathan had searched that room but couldn't find her. They didn't want to risk turning on the lights for fear of someone seeing them moving around in the room.

Mitch was sure that it was Nathan's fault. He was the one that was in charge of the search part. Mitch's job had been to subdue Maria and get her back in the car. What Maria didn't realize when she stole the little girl from them was that Jackson had transponders on all of the cars. They always knew where she was. The whole time she was running away, he was sitting in his office watching her little blip on his computer.

Nathan was useless. It was bad enough that Maria died, but to not come back with the little girl would require explaining. Even though the original plan was to bring Nathan into the business, Mitch would be cutting Nathan loose soon. He'd have to find work elsewhere. He couldn't be trusted. One simple job and he'd failed.

To top it off, Nathan didn't have the same appetites that Mitch had. When he was done with Maria, he had even offered to let Nathan have a go. Nathan looked at him like he was crazy and said, "No thanks, man. I'm good," before he walked out of the room. It was like he was judging Mitch. That was something Mitch didn't need. The girls were part of the benefits package the way that Mitch looked at it. There had to be something wrong, seriously wrong, with Nathan if he didn't want to enjoy Jackson's girls once in a while.

Mitch walked to the kitchen and started to make himself a sandwich. As he pulled a plate out of the cabinet, he caught a whiff of what smelled like Maria's perfume. He was sure it was just left over from her being in the house. The smell reminded him of the night before. When he pinned her down on the bed, she thought she was all strong and tough and could push him off and get away. He showed her. The more she struggled, the more he liked it. He put two slices of bread on the plate, added some roast beef and cheese and grabbed a bag of chips from the cabinet. The whole time, he kept thinking about Maria.

Jackson had it good, he realized. Maria was built. And, the look on her face when she realized what was going to happen — it was priceless. She had no idea what he was planning on doing to her. Not that he did a lot of planning, he realized, opening the door to his office. Either way, the princess had fallen off her perch.

Mitch set the sandwich down on his desk and turned on the

monitor mounted on the wall. He usually used it for watching the girls in their rooms and the stable. Jackson had outfitted the place with surveillance in pretty much every room of the house. There were few places you could go where you wouldn't be seen. Instead of seeing the girls, he flipped on the sports news. He was ready for a break. All the traveling he did was exhausting. As he put his feet up on the desk and took a bite of his sandwich, his cell phone chirped. It was Jackson. He wanted Mitch to come to his office.

Mitch grabbed another bite of sandwich and wiped his hands on his jeans. He got up and closed the door to his office as he headed to Jackson's. The winding hallways led him over to Jackson's side of the house. He crossed the foyer and knocked on Jackson's door.

"Come."

Mitch opened the door to the office and sat down in one of the leather chairs that were in front of Jackson's desk. He said nothing. He learned a long time ago that it was better to wait for Jackson to start the meeting. It went smoother that way. Mitch glanced around the office. There was a fire going in the fireplace that was along the back wall. To Mitch's right, he could see the sitting area. There was a red dress crumpled on the couch, two empty glasses on the table with just a little bit of what Mitch guessed was scotch in them. Looks like Jackson had gotten some action last night, Mitch thought.

After a few minutes had passed of Jackson reading something in front of him and shuffling some papers, he looked up at Mitch. "We are going to have to move the girls."

"Of course."

"Do you know why?"

"I'm not sure, sir."

"Because you are getting sloppy."

Mitch's breath caught in his throat. No man scared him except for Jackson. "I'm sorry, sir."

Jackson looked back at the papers on his desk. "The situation with Maria was unfortunate. I'm sure she ran from you."

"She did, sir." Mitch stared at his boots, wondering how upset Jackson was. Maria had been his wife, after all.

"And the girl..."

"We weren't able to find her, sir. Maria must have had her stashed somewhere or she ran off after the accident."

"That's not the case."

Jackson slid a file folder over to Mitch. Mitch opened it and saw a copy of FBI reports. Glancing over it quickly, he saw that one Addie Buckholtz had been recovered from the scene at the hotel. Jackson had to know there was no car accident. Addie had been hiding between the headboard and the wall. There were pictures of Maria's naked body there as well. Mitch swallowed hard, not because he was upset by what he saw, but because he wasn't sure what Jackson would say next. He was pretty sure that Jackson couldn't tell what he'd done to Maria, but if he ever got the autopsy report, he would. Mitch stammered, "I had Nathan look, sir. Again, I'm sorry."

Jackson looked up from the paperwork on his desk. "Because of all of this," he motioned to the file that Mitch had set back on his desk, "we need to move the girls. Somewhere quiet. Somewhere safe so I can entertain."

"Of course. Where and when, sir?"

"Twenty-four hours. Please have the house in Mexico ready."

Mitch stood up without saying anything.

"And Mitch..."

"Sir?"

"Don't lie to me again. And, make sure that there are no distractions this time. The feds are on us pretty hard. I don't need that kind of publicity. Take care of ending that, please."

Mitch nodded. "Sir, I've been working on that. The reporter -- that Kat Beckman -- I think I've got her on the ropes." Mitch pulled out his phone and showed Jackson the photos that he had his guys take. "That's her son. The FBI has them in protective custody. See, now they know that we can get to them. I think they will back off."

Jackson exploded. "Do you know anything about her? Have you bothered to do any research? Do you realize she took down an entire blackmailing operation and killed a man on her own?"

Mitch leaned back in his chair, silent.

"This is why you work for me. This is why I'm the boss and you aren't. You are too busy enjoying the side benefits of my entertaining, including with my wife, to pay attention to the larger issues."

Mitch watched as Jackson leaned back in his chair. There was a moment of quiet.

"Threatening them is not going to make them go away. That's why we need to move the girls. You..." Jackson pointed directly at Mitch, "need to learn from this. The FBI is not going to give up because Beckman won't. You need to deal with her directly. Do you understand?"

Mitch nodded. Having Jackson angry at you was a way to get fired, at a minimum. There were other workers that Jackson had a problem with that left one day and didn't return. Mitch started to wonder how many bodies were buried at the back of the property in the same place they stuck the girl from the stables. "I'm sorry. I'll take care of it."

Jackson didn't say anything more. Mitch took that as his sign to get up and leave.

As Mitch closed the door, he knew that more words wouldn't fix the problem. He also knew that the next time he had to have a conversation about this Beckman woman and the FBI, it would be his last. He had to take care of this, and fast. On the way back to his office, he sent a text to Dora letting her know that they would be moving the girls tomorrow. That's all she needed to know. Mitch also texted the pilot they used to move the girls and told him to be ready to fly.

Opening the door to his office, the channel was still tuned to sports. Mitch sat back down to finish his sandwich and chips. He needed time to think.

69

Hollister was still on the phone when Kat, Van and Lance had returned to the police station from the hospital.

Kat sat down in one of the conference room chairs and leaned back, wondering what would happen next and how quickly. She didn't have to wait long for an answer.

Hollister came into the conference room. "Listen up. I've just gotten the search and arrest warrants approved. We have a judge who is eager to put Jackson Maifer away if he has done what we think he has done." Kat saw him pause. "This guy isn't your common criminal. He's much more along the lines of a cartel guy. Lots of money, lots of options. We can't take anything for granted. Everybody hear me?"

The other agents in the room muttered their agreement.

"Good. Here's what is going to happen. We will be here for one more hour. At that point, we will head to the airport. I've got a jet coming in to take us to Denver. Denver's field office is spinning up an assault team. They will meet us at the airport. What I need from all of you is to coordinate with each other and get your information into one package and get it over to Denver so they have it while we are in the air. Got it?"

There were more murmurs of agreement. Kat could hear fingers moving rapidly over keyboards and two agents were on their phone before Sean ever stopped talking. "Now, you three..." Sean nodded Kat's direction, assuming he meant Van and Lance, too. "Do you want to go along? We've got room on the plane."

Kat nodded. She felt a pit in her stomach as memories started to flood back after their Apex experience. "Yes, I want to go." She tried to sound as firm as she could.

Sean looked at her, squinting. "Are you sure? I know what happened to you a couple of months ago. You good to go?"

"Yes, I'm fine."

She saw Van and Lance nod. She knew that the easy thing would be to stay back. To stay by her phone or watch a feed of the assault. But she wanted to be there if Carlye was at that house. She wanted to be there to hold her and to tell her it is okay and that her mom and dad were waiting for her to come home. She wanted to tell Carlye that no one had given up on her. Kat hoped she'd have that chance.

"All right. Get your stuff together and let's meet back here in an hour."

Van motioned to her. "Let's run out and get our stuff. I need to refill my go bag." They headed out of the station and got back in the SUV with two agents. "Just run us back to Kat's," Van said, leaning between the two front seats. The agents nodded. With lights and sirens running, they made it through the morning traffic in Aldham in just minutes. Van's truck was still outside of Kat's house. "I'm just gonna go back to the apartment and get my stuff. He looked at his watch. I'll be back in thirty minutes, okay?" He gave her a quick peck on the cheek as she went into the house.

70

Van left Kat at the house with the agents. The drive to his apartment took just seven minutes. He had driven it so many times in the last few months that he didn't even have to think while he drove. As he passed the park, he remembered that he needed to grab an extra charger for his cell phone. It was at the office.

Driving past the local post office, he tried to call Alyssa, his assistant. She didn't answer. It struck him as strange. She was always at the office. Early or late, she was always there. He left a message, but it occurred to him that if she wasn't there, he still needed it. Turning the wheel hard to the right, he took a side street that would take him on a quick detour to get the charger. He left the truck in the first spot he could find, locked it up and headed up the stairs, taking them two at a time. He didn't want to keep Kat waiting. He was sure that Sean Hollister had the engines fired up on the jet, ready to take them to Denver.

When he got to the landing, he noticed that the door to the office was open. He started to push the door open when he noticed that the frame was splintered. Someone had broken in. Van's right hand moved reflexively to his hip and his chest tightened. Like Kat, since this whole ordeal started, he had been wearing his H & K pistol pretty much everywhere. Just in case. His military training took over. He pushed the door open with his left hand while his right hand gripped the gun in front of his face.

The morning sun was shining in the windows. That was about the only thing that was normal in the office. There was paper strewn everywhere. Computers were knocked on the floor and furniture was toppled over and shredded, as though someone was looking for something. As Van made his way further in the suite, he saw that drawers had been pulled open and dumped.

Stepping carefully, he tried to move as quietly as he could through the offices. He prayed that Alyssa hadn't been here when whoever did this broke in. As he stepped past Alyssa's desk and into his own office, he stopped in his tracks.

Alyssa was sitting in his desk chair, her head lolled over to the side. She had been shot in the head. Van's heart started pounding in his chest. It was obvious that there was nothing he could do for her. Her lips were already blue. He finished clearing the office, making sure that no one else was there. It was then that he noticed the spray-painted heart on the wall behind his desk where Alyssa's body was sprawled in his desk chair. KB plus VP, it read, in dripping red paint with a heart around it. His initials plus Kat's. It was a clear threat.

Van swallowed hard. He turned around and walked out of the office, reholstering his gun. He pulled his phone out of his back pocket and dialed Lance Traldent. The detective picked up on the first ring. "You on your way?"

"Nope."

"Where are you?"

"At my office. I need you over here."

"Why?"

"They've been here. Send the coroner."

Van sat down on the step outside his office to wait.

DETECTIVE LANCE TRALDENT drove lights and sirens over to Van's office, escorted by two other cruisers. An ambulance would meet them there.

On the way, he called Sean Hollister and told him what he knew. "We're going ahead."

"I know. I'll stay with Van. Take Kat with you?"

"Will do. Want me to tell her?"

"Probably. Van's going to be with us for a while."

As they hung up, Lance pulled up to the office building with the other officers. They fanned out, some of them checking the perimeter and two others following Lance up the steps.

They found Van sitting on the top step. "He's armed!" one of the officers said, reaching for his own gun.

"Stand down. He's with me." Lance waited for Van to stand up. "Okay, walk me through it."

Lance followed Van into the office. Lance whistled through his teeth. "They made a mess." He noticed that Van didn't reply. As soon as they got into Van's office, Lance saw the body. "I'm sorry about this, man."

"I am too. She didn't deserve this." Van pointed to the wall behind the desk. "They smashed the picture I had up there, and spray painted my initials."

"And Kat's..." Lance added.

"Yes, and Kat's."

"Doesn't look like this is about anything but the work you are doing on the Maifer case, does it?"

"It doesn't. Kinda looks like a threat to me."

"Kinda feels like one too."

71

One of the agents handed Kat a cell phone while she was putting some things in the bag that was sitting on the bed. "Hollister would like to speak to you, ma'am."

Kat took the phone and wedged it between her shoulder and her ear, trying to find space for her sweatshirt. "Hey, Sean. I'm ready. Just waiting on Van."

"He's not coming."

"What do you mean?"

"Kat, I don't know how to say this other than just saying it. He stopped at the office and found his assistant. She's been murdered."

Kat sat down on the bed, letting the information soak in. "Oh my God, is he okay?"

"Yes, he's fine. Lance is with him."

"What happened?"

Sean told her again that Van had stopped at the office and found Alyssa's body. "The place was trashed. It was like they were looking for something."

"That might not have anything to do with the Maifer case,

right? I mean, we are journalists. We make enemies. That's part of the job."

"The thing is that his initials and yours were spray-painted on the back wall above the body. It's a pretty clear case."

Kat felt her body go numb. "I don't know what to say... How did she die? Alyssa, I mean?"

"One shot to the head."

Kat felt her heart start to beat fast in her chest. This was getting out of control. First, the video of her, then the pictures of Jack and now they had killed someone? "That poor girl," Kat said. Words started to form on her tongue, but she didn't know what to say.

"Kat? Are you still there?"

"Yes. Sorry." She sighed, feeling the weight of the situation drop like darkness over her. "I don't know what to do. What do I do now?"

"I already talked to Lance. He and Van are staying put. They have to do the investigation here. You can stay or you are still welcome to come with us. Take five minutes to decide. We can't hold the operation any longer than that. Tell the agents what you want to do. They will communicate with me."

"Okay. Thanks." Kat handed the phone back to the agent, who stayed just outside the doorway to her room. A tear slid down her face. Alyssa's death was clearly retribution for the investigation they were doing. The poor girl, she thought. She probably had no idea what happened. At least Kat hoped she didn't.

The agent leaned into the doorway, "Ma'am, not to rush you -- I'm sorry about this -- but we need to know in two minutes if you are staying or going on the operation."

Kat wiped the tears from her face. "Yes. Sure. Just give me a minute."

Conflict raged in her. Should she go? Did Van need her?

She grabbed her cell phone and dialed Van's number? "Are you okay?"

"Yeah, but they killed Alyssa."

"I heard. I'm so sorry. Sean said they trashed your office."

"They did."

The agent motioned to Kat that she only had one-minute left. "Listen, I have to make this quick. Do you need me to come? Do you want me to stay? I'm not sure what to do..."

There was a brief pause. Kat wasn't sure what to make of the silence. As soon as she was about to ask Van again, he said, "You need to go, Kat. Bring Carlye home."

Kat was about to reply, but she realized that Van had hung up. He knew that she'd argue. He took that option away from her. The agent looked in the room expectantly. Kat nodded, "I'm going," she said, slinging her bag over her shoulder.

The agent led Kat down the stairs and another one walked behind as they put her back in the black SUV.

Kat didn't feel anything. She wondered if she should. She leaned back in the seat and watched as they hit the city limits of Aldham and turned onto the freeway. "Where are we going?" she asked the agents.

"To the airstrip, ma'am."

Just outside of Aldham was a small airport. There were a couple in the area, but this one was the closest to the city. "Ma'am, while we are driving, could you please unload and clear your weapon? Hollister said you can have it with you once you are on the ground in Denver, just not while we are in the air."

Kat nodded and reached over to pull the Sig out of her holster. She ejected the magazine and cleared the chamber, locking it open. She handed it to the agent riding in front. The agent simply nodded and held it for her.

The ride to the airstrip didn't take any time at all. Kat didn't know if it was because the ride was actually short or if it was because she was preoccupied. Flashes of Jack and Laura passed through her mind. Woof carrying a ball and following Jack. Seeing Alana Morgan weeping over Carlye and then hooked up to a mass of machines in the ICU. The image of Carlye from the drone, looking vacant and scared. She felt numb. It was like pictures of people she didn't know and yet they felt like family. Maybe they were.

Her thoughts were interrupted as they passed through a cyclone fence with barbed wire on top of it. Kat had never flown out of a private airstrip before. There was no TSA, no baggage check, just a bright white polished jet with steps extended onto the ground. The black SUV pulled up next to the plane, joining two others that were already there. The agents got out with her and followed her to the steps where Hollister was waiting.

"You okay?"

She felt his hand on her shoulder. "Yeah. I'm okay. We've got to get this guy. It's getting out of control."

The agent with Kat handed Sean the pistol she had been wearing ever since the whole mess with Maifer had started. "I'll take care of this until we get on the ground. I'll clear you with the Denver guys. Let's get going."

Kat nodded and headed up the steps into the jet. Once she was inside, she saw that the plane was nicely furnished. Probably nothing like what Maifer used, she thought, but nice enough. There were wide seats, two next to each other on one side and a single row on the other side that extended from front to back. All in all, they could probably seat about twenty people on the plane. The team they were taking was about half of that. Kat walked about halfway back and took a seat. A flight attendant walked by, "How long is the flight?" Kat asked.

"About two and a half hours. Did you need anything else?"

"No, thanks. I'm good."

"I'll be back once we are in the air."

Kat nodded and the flight attendant moved toward the front of the plane. Kat pulled a set of earbuds out of her bag and a phone charger and started to listen to some music. By the time Kat looked up, the jet's door had closed and the front of the plane was nearly full. The agents were all quietly adjusting to their seats, checking seat belts and putting their bags away. There was a solemn quality to the team. There was little talking, little chit chat.

It didn't take any time at all for the plane to get in the air. Kat realized that traveling privately was a much different experience than the ones she had flying commercial. The long lines, the hassle just to get a bottle of water, the herd of people trying to get on and off the plane -- private air travel certainly had its benefits. That was probably why Maifer had bought his own jet company. It gave him freedom well above what he could ever get just being a first-class member. She imagined that most billionaires flew privately but wondered how many owned their own company. It was also a perfect cover for his location and the location of the girls. He could literally move around the world and no one would be the wiser.

The clouds were surrounding the plane now. Their ascent had been steep and quick. Being in a private jet was a lot more like a darting racehorse than the draft horse of a commercial liner. The agents had started to move around the cabin. A few were sleeping, but several of them had huddled up over laptops, discussing what the files in front of them. Kat watched them group and regroup for a few minutes, fascinated by the way they worked together. She should write a story on how law enforcement teams work some time, she thought.

Hollister came back to where she was sitting and took the chair across the aisle. "How are you doing?"

"I'm fine. Just glad we can get on with this part of the mission. Any word on Van or Alana Morgan?" Kat had been wondering how the investigation was going into Van's assistant's murder. She also wondered if Alana Morgan had woken up. She prayed that she had, or Carlye might not have a mom to come home to.

"No word from Lance. I'm sure they are just working the scene right now. That can take some time. I sent a team over there since it looks like it is linked to this case. Hopefully, we can tie all of this together."

"And Alana?" Kat held her breath a little as she waited for him to answer. She both wanted to know and didn't want to know how Alana was doing. Her heart broke for her. Kat understood the desperation that she must have felt. She had felt the same when she was going through the roughest episodes of her PTSD after coming home from the Middle East. The anxiety had been suffocating. Kat imagined that Alana had felt the same way.

"No change. Tim is still there. I've got an agent with them and at their house. If these jokers got to Van's assistant, it would make sense that they'd target the Morgan's." Sean raised his eyebrows, "If there are no Morgan's to press the search for Carlye, they might think they could get away with it. They'd be wrong, of course."

"Of course."

Sean sighed. Kat sensed that he was going to change the topic. He did. "I just got an update from the Denver team. We'll meet the team leaders at the airport when we land. There's a conference room at the hangar they have all set up already. They have the drone overhead at Maifer's house keeping watch. We've also set up a loose observational perimeter around his house using the parkland that surrounds it. We've looped in the Park Service."

"Aren't those guys a bunch of naturalists?"

"You'd be surprised. Most of those guys have as much or more training than we do. They do a lot of drug interdiction and are really good on rough terrain."

"Good to know."

"What I'd like you to do is to stay with me unless I send you elsewhere. I'm responsible for delivering you back to Van in one piece. I don't want to disappoint him..." Sean gave her a toothy grin. I know you want to be in it and we will let you go as far as we can. You just gotta listen to me, okay?"

"Yes, sir," Kat said with a little sarcasm.

Sean smiled but didn't say any more. He got up and went back to the front of the plane. Kat put her earbuds back in, the strains of gentle music still playing. She rested her head and closed her eyes trying to get some sleep. There was no telling when she'd get to sleep again.

72

Carlye could hear voices in the hallway. She couldn't figure out why or what they were saying. She went over to the door and tried it. Someone had left it unlocked. She cracked the door, just enough to see three girls in white dresses walk down the hallway. Her stomach turned as she wondered where they were going.

Carlye hadn't seen Lily in a couple of days. She couldn't risk going out of her room to find her. She didn't want to end up in the stables again. Bile crawled up her throat as she thought about it. She closed the door with a quiet click and crawled back into bed, curling up in a fetal position under the covers. Her head ached all the time. She wondered if it was because of the powder that they gave her with the drinks they forced her to take. She felt groggy and nauseous too. She didn't want to eat. Even the crackers they offered her sounded awful. As she laid in the bed, she realized that the bones in her knees were pressing together. She didn't care. She just wanted to close her eyes.

But closing her eyes brought another kind of pain. She tried not to remember home, but she did. The smell of her bedroom.

The feel of her soft blankets. The sound of her mom making dinner, pots and pans clanking. The way her dad always sat with his leg crossed while he watched football. Even Michael and how he broke into her room when she wanted to be left alone.

Carlye rolled over in the bed, facing the window, her eyes closed. Her head hurt less with her eyes closed, she decided. There was nothing to do. There were no magazines in the room, no television. Carlye had no idea what day it was. When she first arrived at the house, she cared. She didn't anymore. Her head hurt so much that nothing else mattered. Even if there was a magazine or television, she wouldn't watch it. She could feel the sun come through the locked window, the warm rays covering her blanket. That, at least, was some comfort.

By the time she woke up again, it was dinner time. A quiet knock on her door told her it was time to eat. She went into the dining room and sat down with two other girls. They didn't speak. They each had a half of a peanut butter sandwich and some juice. The room was totally quiet. The girls that Carlye had seen disappear down the hallway weren't there. Lily wasn't either. Carlye wondered if she would ever see her again or if she had been taken away.

Lily had talked about girls that had been taken away while they were sitting in the dark in the stable. She hadn't said much. Through her headache, Carlye tried to remember. Lily had only said that girls that were a problem didn't stay. But Carlye didn't think they went home either. Thinking about what happened to them made her afraid.

She finished as much of her food as she could and gave the rest to the girl next to her. She wiped her table and chair down with an antibacterial wipe and left. Dora had other girls doing the clean up now. She went back to her room and closed the door, laying back down on the bed. Her headache hadn't budged.

Time had passed and a knock came on her door. It was Dora. "Get up, it's time to go."

Startled, Carlye shot up out of bed and put her shoes on. White patent leather was the color of the day. She quickly followed Dora downstairs and across the main foyer where she had seen the woman with the black hair in the kitchen the last time she had been in this part of the house. They were at Mr. Maifer's office door. Carlye recognized at least that much. Dora knocked quietly.

"Come," the voice inside said.

Dora opened the wooden door and walked in. Carlye didn't know why they were there. Her stomach started to hurt and she tried not to cry. She was afraid. She was sure that Mr. Maifer was the one that had ordered Lily to be burned. She knew that everyone seemed afraid of him. She was no different.

"Take her in the back room. I'll be in soon."

Dora didn't say a word. She just started to walk toward a tall wooden door that was in the back corner of Maifer's office. Carlye didn't know what else to do other than to follow. Dora opened the door. Inside, the furnishings were sparse. There was a bed, a chair and a door that led off of the room. It looked like a bathroom. Carlye vaguely remembered the room from the first days she was at the house. She couldn't remember why. To anyone else, it would look like a regular bedroom, maybe even a guest room, like the one they had at home.

The nurse that had taken care of her and Lily was in the room when they walked in. Carlye felt surprised and unsure. Why was she there? Dora looked at her, her face like stone. "Lay down on the bed. Leave your shoes on."

Carlye did as she was told, not wanting to get slapped. Without a word, the nurse came over to her, pulled up her sleeve and gave her an injection, wiping it with something that smelled like alcohol when she was done. There was a burning in her arm. The nurse looked at her, "This will wear off. I promise," she whispered. Carlye wondered why she looked so sad.

Carlye watched as Dora and the nurse left and closed the door. She didn't move. The burning in her arm was terrible. It felt like she was on fire. She tried to get up and realized that she couldn't. Her arms and legs felt heavy and asleep. She had no feeling in them. Terror gripped her throat. What had they done to her? She wanted to scream for help, but she knew that none would come. She could still roll her head to the side. As she looked away, tears rolling down her face, she heard the door open and close. She rolled her face toward the door and saw Mr. Maifer. He looked angry.

"You have caused me a lot of problems, Princess," he growled, walking toward the bed. "Problems that are distracting and causing me money." She felt his hand run down the side of her face, "So, I had the nurse prepare a little something for you." He moved away from the bed for a moment. She felt the bed move as he climbed up onto the other side. "Don't worry, it will wear off soon. Did she tell you that?"

Carlye didn't say anything.

"That family of yours won't give up. Usually, they do by now. They will all pay. I will make sure of it."

The tears were rolling down her face now. All she could think of was her family. "Wipe your face," she heard him say. "And stop with the crying." Then she heard him laugh, "Oh, that's right! You can't... Oh well."

He was laying on the bed next to her. She had turned her head away from him. She was waiting for him to touch her. The roaring from the terror in her mind was more than she could take. There was no safe space anymore. She couldn't feel anything. Her vision started to get blurry, so she closed her eyes. She didn't want to know what was going to happen to her.

The bed moving made her open her eyes. She knew Maifer was off the bed. He walked around to the side where she was looking. "You know what? I'm done with you. I don't even want to be around you. I have no idea why they brought you here." She saw him texting someone on his phone. "I'd tell you to wait, but you aren't going anywhere, are you?"

Carlye watched, wide-eyed as Maifer left the room. He hadn't touched her, except her face. She was petrified. What did he mean that he was done with her? Was he going to kill her? Carlye tried to struggle to a sitting position. She couldn't. The drugs in her system wouldn't let her move. She couldn't turn on her side or even move her arms. She was paralyzed.

A few minutes went by and the door opened again. Carlye had closed her eyes and tried to calm down in the quiet while she was waiting. There was nothing else she could do. Into the room came the nurse, Mitch and Nathan. No one said anything. Mitch grabbed her arms and Nathan took her legs. The nurse followed as they carried her out of Jackson's office. Carlye caught a glimpse of him while they carried her out. His head was down, only the top of his graying hair was visible. He was staring at paperwork and didn't bother to look up.

As they entered the hallway, the nurse closed the door to his office. "Let's take her to my office."

"No. Jackson wants her in the stables. He's done with her."

Carlye heard the nurse argue, "She needs medical attention. She needs to be observed."

Carlye felt her body keep bumping along. They weren't stopping. She heard Mitch's voice. "Then you'll have to do it from downstairs. Jackson wants her down there. He's done with her."

The nurse didn't say any more than that. Carlye saw them pass through the pine tree door and past the dining room hallway. When they got to the top of the steps, they stopped. "I'm just going to take her down myself. She's light enough."

Carlye felt her body get thrown up over Mitch's shoulder. He smelled like grease and dirt. The area around them got darker and darker. If Carlye's body could have stiffened, she would have fought him, but she couldn't. When they got to the bottom of the stairs, she heard Mitch say, "Yeah, open that one. Let's put her in there."

It was the same corner stall that she had been in when she tried to escape. The stall next to the girl that Mitch had beaten to death. She felt ground underneath her as Mitch set her down in the corner. She started to slide to the side, unable to hold herself up. The nurse caught her as she laid down. "Can you hear me?"

Carlye tried to nod.

"I want you to take a nap. When you wake up, drink this water. It will make you feel better. The drugs will wear off in about an hour or so. Don't worry."

"Let's go, Florence Nightingale!" Mitch shouted at her. "I gotta lock this one up so I can get back to work."

Carlye felt the nurse's hand on her cheek. It was the first kind touch she'd had in weeks.

73

The plane made a rapid descent into a small airstrip outside of Denver. Kat could see the downtown area as they landed, but they were miles from it. The jet taxied for a minute and then pulled up close to a hangar. From her window, Kat could see more black SUVs parked nearby. She wondered exactly how many of them the FBI owned. There were people milling around. Some of them had on the blue FBI jackets with the bright yellow lettering on the back. Some of them were dressed in tactical gear.

The door opened to the plane a moment after they had stopped and powered down the engines. Kat followed at the end of the trail of agents and gear, slipping her backpack up over one of her shoulders and pulling her sunglasses down over her eyes to shield them from the sun. She had been to Colorado once before and had forgotten how bright it was.

"Over here, people," Sean yelled and waved at the team. "Let's get this started. I want to be on the road in ten minutes."

The group quickly massed at a table that had been hastily set up in the hangar. The agents that had arrived before them had sandwiches and bottles of water ready as they started their presentation. Kat grabbed a bottle of water and made her way to the back of the group. She was, technically, only supposed to be an observer.

"For those of you that don't know me, I'm Special Agent Sean Hollister. We've been tracking Jackson Maifer," he pointed to an image that was being projected on the wall, "in connection with multiple kidnappings of young girls. In addition, the body of his wife, Maria, was found strangled to death in Alabama. There was a young child with her that had been kidnapped out of Florida. I'm happy to say that she's back with her family today." Sean nodded at the tech team. "Maifer is fifty-two years old, a billionaire and we believe sex trafficking little girls for his pleasure and the pleasure of his cronies. This is one sick dude."

Pictures of Carlye were on the screen next. "We have a search and arrest warrant for Maifer and persons of interest in this young girl's kidnapping. Carlye Morgan. Eleven years old. Taken fourteen days ago from a camp about an hour from her house. This image," Sean pointed to the one from the drone, "shows a girl that we think is Carlye entering the house last night. This was a drone shot. We have no reason to believe that she isn't still in the house."

The images disappeared off the screen. "This is a complex event. We don't have a layout of the house or any idea how many girls or employees may be in there. I can tell you that Maifer is a chess player. He's been two steps ahead of us this entire time until we got a little outside help."

Kat saw Sean point at her. She felt her cheeks flush.

"Team, this is Kat Beckman. If you don't know her, you should. She's a journalist who was embedded with our military in Afghanistan. She is the one that helped us find Carlye. Please treat her as one of our own. Are we clear?"

"Yes, sir."

"These people are dangerous. Kat's editor, Van Peck, was

supposed to be with us on this trip, but he's stuck in Aldham dealing with the murder of his assistant. We believe it is tied to the Maifer mess." An image of the crime scene appeared on the wall. Kat was shocked by how violent it was. She had only met Alyssa a few times -- they mostly interacted via email and as she and Van got closer, Kat didn't talk to her at all. Reaching back into her memory, Kat realized that she hadn't talked to Alyssa in months. There would be time for her to help Van through Alyssa's murder. The time just wasn't now.

Kat refocused on what Sean was saying. He went over the basics. How they would get to Maifer's house, what they should be prepared for, transit times. "Some of the breech team members are here with us right now." Kat saw a few of the guys wave or nod to the rest of the team. "The rest of the team is positioned about a mile out from the house. I've sent scout teams ahead of them. They are positioned on each side of the house just beyond the property line, keeping an eye on movement. Questions?" The group was quiet. Everything inside of Kat was screaming that they needed to go. They were so close to getting Carlye back. She just hoped it wasn't too late.

74

"Where are we with the girls?" Mitch poked his head into Dora's office.

"With moving them? Is that what you mean?" He saw Dora look up from her computer. She was always pecking away at the keyboard. Mitch couldn't figure out what kind of paperwork would take all day for her to do. Her job was pretty simple. Acquire the girls, get the girls to dress up for Jackson and his friends. Deal with scrapes and boo-boos. That was it. "Yes, that's what I mean. I'd like to get the first batch out of here soon and then move the rest in the morning."

"Is Jackson flying out this afternoon?"

"Yeah. He decided he wants to go on the first plane with them. Mile high club and all that, I guess." Mitch shrugged his shoulders. "The flight is scheduled for six. Can you have the first batch of girls ready for me by four-thirty?"

Dora nodded. "How many do you have room for on the first plane?"

"I can take six with Jackson's bodyguard and him. How many does that leave us?"

Dora pulled up a file on her computer, "Eight, plus me and anyone else."

"That's fine. You can hold down the fort here, right?"

"Sure. I'll have the girls ready for you."

"Good." Mitch closed the door to her office. Sometimes he liked Dora and sometimes he didn't. Today, she was tolerable. Mitch realized that it was nearly lunchtime and his stomach was rumbling. He went to the kitchen and opened the refrigerator, taking two pieces of fried chicken and a couple of cookies from a plate that had been left on the counter. There still was some time before he had to start moving people to the airstrip, so he could relax for a while.

As Mitch walked back to his office, he realized he was pretty lucky. He had a relatively easy job with great perks and made lots of money. He didn't get much time off, but he didn't need much. He didn't have a family. They had disowned him years before when he lost his temper and kicked their cat so hard it died. It wasn't the first time one of his outbursts had caused harm, but it was the last for his family. He sat down behind his desk and resumed watching the replay of a football game that had been on a couple of days before. He decided that he was looking forward to going to Mexico. It would be warmer than Colorado. He could wear shorts again and go into town for his favorite tacos and tequila. Mexico was always a good time.

Mitch started mentally thinking about the girls that would be traveling. He remembered that he had a few stashed in the stables, including the one that Jackson called Princess. He picked up his phone and texted Dora, "Remember, I've got a few in the stables."

In a moment, his phone chirped, a thumbs up emoji back from her. Let Dora deal with them, he thought.

75

Carlye had tried to fall asleep, leaning against the wall of the stall. Her body felt so heavy and uncomfortable from the paralytic drugs that all she could manage was to close her eyes. She could feel the scratchy texture of the wood on her back. She couldn't move her arms or legs. She tried not to cry. If she did, there was no way to wipe the tears from her face. Fear was all around her. It was in the darkness of the stall, the rough ground beneath her and the murky dampness that was soaking into her dress.

She thought of home and wondered what her family was doing. She knew they were looking for her, but she worried if they had given up. She knew she was far away from home. How would they find her? A voice inside her head told her that it was hopeless. Even if they still cared about her, how would they ever find her? She was in the mountains, locked in a stall in the basement of a man who terrified her. She closed her eyes again, fighting away the fear.

Carlye had never known fear like she had felt over the last few weeks. Being taken, being trucked all across the United States, drugged, not to mention what the men had done to her.

It was just too much to think about. She tried to reach back into her mind, into a place that was quiet. Even her quiet space was covered with the trappings of fear.

If I could just move a little, she thought. Had enough time gone by, she wondered. Was the nurse lying to her like everyone else? What happened to Lily? Was she down here? Carlye tried to move her right hand. She could start to squeeze her fist together. Her fingers barely moved, but they did move a little bit. Her left hand, too, was starting to wake up. Her legs were not.

"I heard what they said to you. It takes longer than an hour." A voice cut through the darkness, coming from the stall next to her. "You can't believe anything they say. All they do is lie."

"Who are you?" Carlye's voice was scarcely above a whisper. She was terrified that Mitch would hear her talking and she'd get punished. Being locked in the stalls was bad enough.

"I'm Becca. I didn't want you to think you were here alone. We'd better be quiet now."

Carlye had questions but tried not to talk until one slipped out. "Are we alone down here?"

Becca whispered back. "No, there are a bunch of us. I'm not sure how many, but at least five."

Carlye didn't answer. Knowing that there were other girls in the basement with her made her feel just a little better. Using her hands, she was able to lay over on her side in the dirt. She curled up in the corner and stared at the ceiling. There was nothing else to be done.

The transit time to Jackson Maifer's Colorado estate only took about thirty minutes from the airstrip where the team had landed. At least that is what Kat had been told. After the briefing, she followed Sean out to one of the SUV's where he handed her back her pistol. "We normally don't extend carry rights to outsiders, but I'll make an exception this time." He smiled his toothy grin at her. Kat was amazed at how relaxed he seemed. She'd be interested to see if he stayed so relaxed once the mission started.

As they closed the doors to the SUV and it started pulling away, Kat leaned forward in her seat, "Any updates from the house? Do you think Carlye is still there?"

Sean didn't look back at her, keeping his eyes on the road. "We don't have any reason to think she's not there. No one has left the property since the team got into position this morning."

Kat leaned back, her stomach in a knot. She couldn't tell if she was excited or scared or both. In Afghanistan, she had to fight to get to leave the base. Here, they invited her willingly. It was a big difference. She just hoped that she didn't let them, or herself down.

77

Mitch got a call on his cell phone that sent him scrambling out of his office. He ran down the hall, his boots making a thumping noise with every step. He barged into Jackson's office without knocking. "Boss, we've got a problem."

Jackson barely looked up, his shock of gray hair hovering over paperwork on his desk. "What could be so urgent that you'd come in without knocking?"

"We are being watched."

Mitch watched as Jackson immediately got up from his desk and went to the window. He stood to the side and looked up at the ridge above the house. "What do you mean?"

"One of the guys in the yard just texted me. He saw a glint off of what he thought was a binocular lens."

"A binocular lens..."

Mitch was surprised how slowly Jackson spoke. It was almost like he was digesting the words instead of reacting. "What do you want me to do?"

"Do you think it could be a hunter? Someone else?"

"The guy outside said they are on your land. They were too

close to be on the park's side of the line." Mitch knew where the property lines were. He and his team were up there regularly getting rid of hunters and nature freaks.

"Go check it out."

"Yes, sir." Mitch walked out of Jackson's office and sent a text. He'd send a couple of his guys up to go check on them. Jackson was right, it was probably just a hunter. "I want to hear back from you in 15." He got a reply back agreeing.

Mitch spent the next fifteen minutes pacing in his office. He couldn't figure out why this incident was rattling him. They had hunters lurking around every single week that they were here. One time, they had even found a shotgun hole in one of the outbuildings. Hunters were all over the place.

Ten minutes went by, then twelve. There was nothing back from his team. When a half-hour had passed, he finally called. There was nothing. Not only did his guys not pick up, but the call wouldn't even go through. He fought with himself about whether he should panic. Service was sketchy at the house at times. They all knew that. It was especially the case when you were out in the woods. That's why so many hunters carried satellite phones. He walked back down to Jackson's office, "Still no word, sir," Mitch said, walking in.

Jackson sat at his desk, not moving. Mitch saw him turn his head, as if he thought someone was watching him through the windows. Someone he couldn't see. "Let's give it a few more minutes. They might be out of cell range. Any other sightings?"

"No, sir."

Jackson turned back to his work. "You worry too much, Mitch. You should have one of the girls give you a massage. It always helps me."

78

Kat saw four other vehicles at the staging site. They were a mile out from Jackson Maifer's house. She jumped out of the car and walked behind Sean as he joined the team.

"Report," Sean said as the team gathered up, looking at a laptop computer perched on the hood of one of the cars.

"Ready, sir."

Kat didn't know the name of the man talking, but he was clearly a tactical officer. He was dressed in the same level of body armor and weapons that she had seen worn by the SEALs in Afghanistan.

"Good. The plan is to maintain the perimeter and then breach the front door. We will knock nicely once, but after that, it's full go. The priority here is to grab Maifer and any girls we can find. This is a big estate. We are going to have to crawl all over it. Are we clear?"

"Yes," the group said at the same time.

Kat saw Sean nod. "Let's go get this done."

Kat got back in the SUV with Sean and two other agents.

They were second in line behind the tactical team. He turned toward her, "Doing okay?"

"Yes." Kat tried to be convincing even though she felt like she was going to throw up. Nerves were getting to her.

"Good. When we get there, stay with me. We need to let the tactical guys do their job, okay?"

"Of course." Kat tried to relax against the back of the seat. Her heart was pounding. Her hands were shaking. She wasn't sure she could shoot her gun if she had to. She had no idea how the teams stayed calm.

Although they were only a mile out it could have easily been ten miles. There were hills and trees and boulders bigger than any Kat had ever seen. Twists in the road and the heavy foliage made it impossible to see the house that they were approaching.

All of a sudden, the caravan of vehicles made a sharp left turn onto something that seemed more like a driveway. Kat leaned between the seats to get a look at where they were. There was a manicured lawn on either side of them and up ahead was a metal gate, flanked by fencing that went as far as she could see.

Kat saw Sean reach for his radio. "We are a go. Repeat, go!" The tactical team pulled up close to the gate and waited. "Here we go," Sean said. No one else in the car said anything at all. Kat's breath caught in her throat. Was Carlye still there?

79

Mitch watched the whole thing from his office. As soon as he saw the black vehicles turn down the driveway, he started running for Jackson's office. "It's the FBI, we've got to go!"

Jackson stood up, momentarily stunned, and then grabbed for a sheaf of papers. Mitch realized that he looked confused.

"Sir, we will take you out the back. I don't think they have that driveway covered."

"The girls, what about the girls?" Jackson stared at Mitch as they started for the back of the house.

"I'll get them. You just go."

They stopped in the hallway after running from Jackson's office, just outside the steps that led down to the back entrance. "Mitch, don't leave any of this behind. Nothing. No record we were here. You know what to do."

Mitch sucked in his breath and then nodded. "We will keep them at the gate for a couple of minutes so you can get away. I'll get the girls." With that, he pushed Jackson through the door where a white SUV was waiting for him. There was a second one behind it ready to take whoever else could go.

They had practiced this monthly. Jackson was sure that a day would come when they would have to leave quickly, either because of a blizzard or because of law enforcement. Today was the day. He ran back toward his office, yelling for Dora. "Dora! It's the FBI! Get the girls. I already called for the car. They are waiting."

He saw her eyes go wide. All she did was nod and run out of her office and up the steps. He knew what she would do. She would go upstairs, open all of the doors and have the girls follow her down to where Jackson was waiting. Some would go with him and some with Dora in the next vehicle. Mitch sent a quick text to Jackson's pilot. All it said was, "Code red." The pilot would be ready when they got there.

Mitch stood in the hallway and took a breath. The buzzer for the gate sounded again. It was the second one. Mitch knew that if he didn't answer, they would breach. "Yes?" he said, opening a closet door.

"This is the FBI. We have a search warrant. Open the gates."

"Sure..." Mitch fumbled for something in the closet. "Just give me a minute. I'll send someone up to open them. Our remote isn't working."

Mitch pulled the jug out of the closet and shoved the lighter in his back pocket. He took the steps two at a time upstairs, knowing he didn't wouldn't have a lot of time. He ran to the end of the hall and opened the canister. The acrid smell of gasoline filled the air. Mitch quickly spilled it all over the floor, dumped some into the girls' rooms, which were now empty and as he got to the stairs, tossed a match on it. The fire started immediately. Mitch ran down the steps, dumping more gasoline as he went, leaving a gap so the flames wouldn't catch up with him.

His phone buzzed again. "This is the FBI. You have thirty seconds to open this gate or we will breach."

Mitch threw his phone down and kept on spilling gasoline down the hallway, the flames licking at his boots as he went.

His next stop was the front doors. He spilled gasoline all over the carpet and into Jackson's office, covering his papers with the flammable liquid. Another match and the first floor was engulfed in flames.

Mitch knew he had only seconds to get out of the house. He poured more gasoline as he went the flames eating up the expensive carpets, upholstery and bedding eagerly. The smoke was intense. He ran to the back door and spilled the rest of the gasoline down one of the sets of steps to the stables. He threw a final match and the can down the steps and pushed the door open, the flames nearly following him out the door.

80

Carlye was awoken to the thump of a container hitting the floor near her stall. As she sat up, she could smell smoke. Her heart started to beat in her chest. She tried to back away, seeing a trickle of flames start to grow on the steps, but her legs were still asleep. She used her arms to push herself back towards Becca's wall. "Wake up!" she screamed. "Fire!"

"Oh my God, what are we going to do?" Becca screamed.

Carlye started to cough. "I don't know…"

81

The breach team had lost their patience. Kat saw them ease their reinforced truck forward and then push the gates inward until they gave in. There was a crunch of metal and the gates snapped back on their hinges and allowed for the caravan to move through.

Kat heard a crackle of a radio, "Two white SUVs leaving the back of the property!"

"Son of a..." Sean yelled. "Get them!" he said over the radio. "Who didn't plan for a rear exit?"

"I don't know, sir," the driver said.

Kat held on as the SUV raced toward the house. The house loomed larger the closer they got to it. At least three floors, made of stone and rough-hewn beams, it had to be ten thousand square feet, Kat thought.

The SUVs raced to the front doors, while Sean yelled into the radio, "Who has Maifer?"

The radio replied that there were units moving to intercept the white vehicles. They were already on the highway. No one knew if Maifer was in them or not.

There wasn't time for Kat to ask Sean what he was going to

do. The SUV she was in screeched to a stop. Kat jumped out of the vehicle and ran behind it, staying next to Sean while the breech team ran to the front door. They got into position quickly, two columns of agents, one following the next, the leader ready to aim the battering ram at the door. Out of the corner of her eye, Kat caught something moving. She screamed, "No!" just as the leader hit the door with the ram.

The explosion from oxygen hitting the growing fire so quickly knocked everyone off their feet, raining burning debris down on the team that was at the door. Kat was flat on her back, Sean next to her. They both scrambled up running around the front of the SUV.

The breach team was down. Of the eight agents, three were unconscious including the guy that had swung the battering ram. The others were dazed. Sean and Kat helped them behind the SUV while Sean called for the medics.

By this time, the house was fully engulfed in flames. Glass shattered above them as the heat from the fire burst out through the windows. Smoke was pouring out of the hole where the front doors had been.

"Carlye!" Kat screamed, running from window to window, looking to see if anyone was moving inside the house. She started running around the side of the house, down a hill and toward the back. No one was moving. She ran back to the front of the house. "I didn't see anyone," she said to Sean, out of breath. "There's no one moving in the house."

"I don't know how anyone could survive this fire..."

82

The smoke was getting thicker and thicker. Carlye and the other girls were starting to cough. Carlye laid down on the ground, trying to find some cool air. It was getting hot. She started to cry. She was going to die. She knew it. She knew that the end of her life was in front of her.

Becca rattled the door at the front of her stall. "Let us out! We are here! Help!"

Carlye wasn't sure it would matter. No one cared. No one was coming. She closed her eyes and waited.

83

Kat had to do something. She had to get into the house. "Sean, we've got to get in there. Do you have a fire extinguisher?"

"Kat, it's not going to help you! That place is an inferno. I've called for help. They are on their way. We can't go in until the firefighters do. It's not safe!"

"What if Carlye is still in there? She's gonna die!"

Kat looked at Sean and then she looked at the house. She ran to the back of the SUV and pulled a door open, seeing a fire extinguisher. She pulled it off the mounting and ran towards the front door, jumping over debris that had fallen. She made it just inside the front doors, enough to see the smoke and flames rising on the second floor. "Carlye!" Kat screamed at the top of her lungs. The fire was roaring. She wasn't sure anyone could hear her. A woman came staggering toward her, coughing and barely able to stand up. Kat dropped the fire extinguisher and put her arm under her, pulling her as quickly as she could to the opening where the front door had been.

"Are you crazy?" Sean yelled at Kat as soon as she handed off the woman to a couple of the agents.

Kat was bent over, her hands on her knees, trying to catch her breath. "She's got to be in there, Sean. We have to find her." Kat didn't wait. She didn't have the energy to argue. She took off down the side of the estate.

Around the back of the house, there was a rolling door, the kind that you'd see on a farm. It was chained closed, smoke leaking out from around the edges. She tried to slide it enough to see in, but as soon as there was a gap, smoke poured out. The fire had clearly gotten to the bottom level of the house. Knowing that she couldn't get inside on her own, she ran for help. If Carlye was in there, she hoped there was enough time.

84

"Faster!" yelled Jackson Maifer from the backseat of the white SUV. "We have to get in the air now!"

The SUV took the corners with a screech. The half-hour drive to the airstrip where Jackson kept his jet ready and waiting seemed like it was taking forever. "Do we know who made it out?"

The passenger in the front seat, one of Jackson's security guys, looked at his phone. "We don't. I'm sorry sir."

Jackson was angry and frustrated. This whole thing had gotten out of control. As soon as Princess arrived it all went to hell. When her parents wouldn't stop looking and got the FBI involved, he should have just had Mitch drop her off somewhere. This wasn't worth it. Not a good use of his time or his energy. He pushed his hair back off of his face, trying to find some composure. If they could just make it to the airstrip and get on the plane, they would be fine. They'd be in Mexico in a few hours. He could regroup. He could begin entertaining again. Things would go back to normal.

They rounded the last corner to the airstrip. Jackson folded the papers that he had in his hands in half, trying to make them more presentable. He hadn't had time to get his laptop or his briefcase. He hoped that Mitch had doused his desk the way he'd been told. Mitch had been trained to pour gasoline all over his desk if the Feds showed up and got into the house. Jackson didn't need the Feds prying into his work, that was for sure. It wasn't their business. It was his. What he did with his investments was his prerogative.

The gate to the airstrip was open when they got there. The two white SUVs rolled up on a jet that was fueled and ready to go. The flight attendant and crew were on board. There was a man standing by the ladder, ready to help them get on board. Just a few minutes, Jackson thought, sliding out of the SUV. Just a few minutes...

85

Based on the chatter on the radio, it seemed like half of Denver was racing to stop Jackson Maifer. Agent Jeff Adams was new to the Denver team. This was the most excitement he'd seen since he was out of the academy. He pressed the accelerator on their black SUV down, hearing the engine roar. "We should be just a minute out now, sir." He yelled into his coms, connecting him directly with Sean Hollister. "Do not let him get away," was all Jeff heard in his earpiece.

The SUV pushed through the last intersection before the airstrip. The drone that had been overhead at the Colorado house had been moved by the pilot to follow the two white SUVs that escaped right before their raid. Hollister had stayed behind with the team to deal with the fire and the injuries. Adams wondered if there would be bodies, too.

They rounded the corner to the airstrip and saw the gate was open. They didn't bother to stop. "So much for airport security," one of the other agents said. The jet was up ahead. A woman and a girl were boarding. Adams saw them react when they saw the lights and heard the sirens. The girl paused, staring at them, the hem of her dress blowing in the wind. The woman behind her pushed her up the steps. Adams just hoped they weren't too late.

86

Kat could hear the roar of a helicopter overhead and sirens approaching the house. It was deafening. As she ran back up from the side of the house a caravan of firetrucks approached. Three ambulances brought up the rear. The helicopter landed right on the front lawn of the house, uniformed and helmeted firefighters jumping out and running toward the group of SUVs. Kat ran to them. "There's a door. It's chained. I've got to get in there!" She pleaded with the firefighters.

"Where? Show me!" One of the firefighters took off at a run with Kat before Sean could argue. He followed her down the hill and around to the back of the house.

"There," Kat pointed at the sliding door with the chain on it. The firefighter, his nametag said Alvarez, used his halagan to jimmy open the door within seconds. The chain fell in a clank down on the ground.

Kat was about to charge in when she felt a gloved hand on her arm. "Let some of the smoke clear. Stay here. I'm going in."

"I've gotta go! Carlye might be in there!"

Alvarez looked at her, pulling his oxygen mask over his face. "You won't last thirty

seconds in this smoke. Stay here!" He queued up his radio, "Southwest corner of the house. Lower level. I need help with the search. Over." The radio squawked to life as Alvarez wandered into the smoke-filled area.

All Kat could do was wait.

87

Jackson's plane was just about ready to go when he spotted the lights and sirens coming at them. "We've got to go now! Get this thing in the air!"

"Sir, not everyone is on board..." the flight attendant said.

Jackson, who had seen the SUVs coming in fast ran to the front of the plane. "Get on board now!"

Dora and a young girl ran up on the plane just as the SUVs surrounded the plane. They passed Jackson, who was standing in the doorway. "Get this thing in the air!" he yelled to the pilots. Jackson saw them look at each other, waiting. "I said now!"

"Sir, we can't. They have us surrounded."

Jackson reached into his waistband and pulled out a gun. "Now," he said, suddenly very calm. "I'm your boss. I'm telling you to get the plane off the ground."

88

Jeff Adams and the team had surrounded Maifer's plane. They weren't going anywhere. It was just a question of how quickly they could get him apprehended. "Gun, gun!" he heard over his radio. He immediately ducked down behind the SUV. While he did so, he saw two agents, out of the view of the plane, lay tack strips down in front of the wheels. Even if they tried to go, the tires on the landing gear would immediately go flat. Maifer had lost. He just didn't know it yet.

What they hadn't anticipated was Maifer having a gun. Adams saw him come to the door and yell, "I'm leaving. You can't stop me."

"Sir, we are ordering you to shut down the engines and come off of the plane. We have you surrounded." Adams was on the loudspeaker now, repeating what Hollister told him to say.

Jackson disappeared for a minute. Just as Adams started to wonder what he was up to,

he reappeared with a young girl in front of him, gun to her head. She was wearing a white dress and matching white shoes.

Adams realized that she couldn't be more than about twelve years old. He had a niece that age.

Rifles came up without being ordered. Adams knew that if ordered, they would take Maifer out. But now he had hostages. Things had gone from bad to worse.

"Sir," Adams called Hollister. "He's got a gun to a girl's head. Your order?"

"I can see what is happening. We have the drone, remember?"

"Sorry, sir."

Adams waited for what seemed like an hour. He was sure it was only a minute or so. "I don't think he's gonna shoot anyone. Let's go for breech."

"Affirmative. Going for breach."

The plane's steps were still fully on the ground so getting up into the aircraft wasn't a big deal. The problem was managing the distance between the SUVs and the top of the steps. Adams knew that once the team was on the plane it would be settled in seconds. He gave the signal to go.

Two teams of agents approached the plane from underneath and started up the steps. Maifer stared at them, his face blank. In an instant, he let the girl go, firing his gun at the agents that were coming up the steps.

It all seemed to happen in slow motion for Adams, who had stayed behind the SUV to relay information to Hollister. He saw the girl twist away from Maifer and go back into the plane, as Maifer raised his gun, his finger on the trigger. The first shot hit an agent in the arm. He didn't get a second shot off. The lead agents tackled him within seconds.

"Suspect in custody. One injury," he reported to Hollister.

Adams ran out from behind the SUV, gun raised as they finished securing the plane. He saw Maifer, suddenly silent, handcuffed and dragged down the steps of the plane. "Clear," he heard over his radio. He reholstered his weapon and waited at the steps. Behind him, a van and three ambulances arrived.

People started coming out of the plane. Maifer was already in the back of one of their SUVs and had been read his rights. The flight attendant, pilot, co-pilot, a bodyguard and a woman were all brought out in handcuffs. After them were five young girls all wearing matching dresses and matching shoes. None of them said a word, their wild eyes searching.

"We've recovered five girls," Adams said over the radio to Hollister.

"I see them. Get their names back to me ASAP," was the only reply.

89

The house was fully engulfed in flames by the time two more black helmeted firefighters joined the one that had already gone into the lower level. There was so much smoke that Kat had to back up and away from the house. She could hear the structure creaking and crackling, the wood splintering like a big bonfire.

As best she could, she peered into the blackness. There was no movement. She didn't have a radio, so she couldn't hear what was going on. She felt panic rise in her throat. She just hoped they could find Carlye and that it wasn't too late.

Kat wracked her brain. If Carlye wasn't here, where else could she be? Kat ran around the back of the house. She could see flames licking through the windows and the roof. There were firefighters everywhere, trying to control the blaze. She knew that fires in Colorado were a serious business because of the mountains, but she was taken aback by how many had come to help. As she ran, she kept yelling for Carlye, hoping to see her come to a window or out a door. The house didn't look like it could last much longer. Kat wasn't sure if anyone who was left inside would be able to survive.

Kat ran back to the barn door that Alvarez had pried open. A firefighter in a white helmet,

Kat realized it was probably the fire chief, was waiting. "How many men did you see go in?" he asked.

"Three. One named Alvarez I think and two more. Why?"

"The floor is about to collapse. I gotta get my men out."

Kat's heart sunk. If they had to leave the house, they would never find Carlye. If she was in there, the only way they would find her is after the fire had been doused. There was no hope.

The fire chief's radio beeped and then transmitted. "I've got one. Coming out."

Within a few seconds, a firefighter emerged through the smoke, a girl with long black hair over his shoulders. He placed her gently on the ground and took his oxygen mask off, setting it on top of her face. "They were locked in there like animals. Stevens and Alvarez are still in there."

Kat saw the fire chief turn away and speak into his radio. "Medical support on the east side of the building."

They all turned back to the smoke pouring out of the building. A moment later, another black helmeted firefighter came running out of the smoke, carrying another girl. Another one was trailing behind, holding onto his jacket. He dropped to his knees as soon as they got out of the building. Kat ran to the girls to help them get away from the fire. "Have you seen a girl named Carlye? Are you Carlye?" The girls had soot smudged on their faces and under their noses, but both of them shook their heads. Before Kat could ask them anything more, the fire chief yelled, "Back! Everyone back! The structure is about to collapse."

Paramedics had come down the hill with stretchers and equipment. The first girl had already been loaded and taken up the hill. Even with all the soot on her, Kat could tell she was emaciated and dirty.

The fire chief yelling on the radio broke Kat's concentration on the girls, "Alvarez! Alvarez! Get out of there now!"

There was no response.

Kat waited with the fire chief, the paramedics and the firefighters. The creaking and groaning of the structure was deafening. A house that size coming down would kill anyone who was still inside if the fire didn't already do it. All they could do was wait.

"Alvarez! Now!"

There was still no response.

"Alvarez, if you can hear me, sound your alarm." The fire chief's voice had softened. All Kat could do was watch.

"What's going on?" Hollister asked, coming up behind Kat.

"There's a firefighter still in there. The chief thinks the house is going to come down."

Sean's eyes widened. "Oh my God. Any sign of Carlye?"

"None."

Another thirty seconds went by with no word from Alvarez. Kat watched the door, her throat clutching in her chest. The fire chief didn't move, the two other firefighters took a knee behind him.

An alarm sounding broke the silence. "Go!" the fire chief bellowed to the two firefighters behind him. "Bring him in!"

The edge of the smoke broke. Kat saw the lost firefighter break through, dropping to his knees, a young girl in his arms. The chief and paramedics were on the pair immediately, dragging Alvarez and the girl away from the entrance to the house. "Get back!" the chief yelled. "It's going down!"

The splintering of joists and the collapse of the main area of the house sounded like the crack of thunder. A cloud of dust added to the smoke that was already billowing out of the house. By the time Kat turned around, the young girl was being attended to by the paramedics, Alvarez standing beside her, an oxygen mask on his face.

"She couldn't get up. I had to carry her out. She was locked in," he said breathlessly.

Kat nodded and looked at the girl who was laying on a stretcher, a mask over her face, streaks of soot and dirt all over her and her clothes. Her legs were twisted unnaturally, but she looked up at Kat, her big eyes terrified. "Are you Carlye? Are you Carlye?"

The girl nodded.

Kat dropped to her knees, next to the stretcher. "We've been looking for you…"

90

The FBI had Carlye on a medical flight back to Aldham two hours after they had found her. Sean Hollister and Kat joined her. An ambulance met them at the private airfield where Kat and Sean had left just hours before. Their time in Denver had been short.

Kat spent the entire flight sitting next to Carlye, holding her hand. Carlye didn't say much. Neither did Kat.

At the airfield, there was an ambulance waiting, an FBI SUV and an unmarked police car. As Carlye was transferred to the ambulance, Kat and Sean walked down the steps. Van and Lance were waiting. Kat ran to Van, throwing her arms around him.

"You smell awful. What did you do, go to a barbeque?" Van asked, wrapping his arms back around her.

Kat didn't answer. She just cried and buried her head in his shoulder.

She and Van rode in the ambulance with Carlye on the way to Mercy Memorial. The FBI SUV led the way, lights and sirens blaring. Lance followed the ambulance in his unmarked car, his own lights spinning.

They pulled up to the emergency entrance of Mercy Memorial, a trauma team waiting. "It's not often we get the FBI bringing us a case," the head of emergency medicine said, her black hair piled on top of her head.

"This is a special one," Sean said.

The paramedics pulled Carlye off of the ambulance, an oxygen mask still on her face, two IVs pumping into her body. The medical team quickly took over, listening to the paramedic's notes and moving her down the hallway. There were doctors and nurses as well as two people Kat was sure were from the psychiatry department.

Before they could get Carlye to treatment, she passed a small group of people.

Tim Morgan, Alana in a wheelchair, Michael holding her hand. Jo Bennett from the Blue Water Center. They were all there.

Kat watched as Tim Morgan ran to his daughter's side.

"Carlye?"

Kat saw Carlye look up at her father from the stretcher and then closed her eyes. "Daddy? You didn't forget about me…"

EPILOGUE

Jack, Laura and Woof came home later that night to two large pizzas with everything on it. They celebrated Carlye coming home and the arrest of Jackson Maifer. From what Sean Hollister and Detective Lance said, both agencies would have months, if not years, of work ahead of them in dealing with the investigation and prosecution. While they were celebrating, Maifer was in federal custody, spending his first night in chains.

Kat got a call from Sean when she was on her third piece of pizza. After the fire had been put out at the Colorado house, three other bodies had been found in the same area as Carlye. Three girls had made it out. Three hadn't. A man's body was found just inside the back door of the house. He was nearly unrecognizable, but a gas can was found near him. The authorities assumed that he was the one that set the blaze.

Sean also said the doctors told him that both Alana and Carlye would make a full recovery physically. Jo Bennett and the psychiatrists working with the family were cautiously optimistic, cautious being the keyword. There was a long road ahead for all of the Morgan family, from Carlye and Alana to

Michael and Tim. Kat suspected they would be spending a lot of time in therapy, individually and as a group. Their life would never be the same, but it would be a life, nonetheless.

After pizza, Kat and Van sat on the chairs outside, watching Woof, Jack and Laura play in the sandbox. "We have it pretty good, don't we?" Kat said, squeezing his hand.

"Yes, we do," Van said, squeezing her hand back. There was a pause. "It's even better now that you don't smell like a human bonfire…"

A NOTE FROM THE AUTHOR…

Writing about sex trafficking was a sad pursuit in many ways. Though I love to craft stories that I hope will engage and entertain, I believe my readers also have the opportunity to learn from me and from other authors.

This book was not in any way meant to glorify what happens to children around the world each and every day. No matter what country you live in, children are being put into slavery and trafficked. It is an evil of historic proportions.

If you have been moved by the story of Carlye, then I'd encourage you to take action. Support great organizations that are doing the work to save lives every day. Though there are many groups working to end sex trafficking – and you should do your own research – one I can suggest is Rapha International. Look them up and let them know I sent you.

ABOUT THE AUTHOR

K. J. Kalis is an author who specializes in thrillers and Christian non-fiction. Currently living in the Midwest, when she's not writing, K. J. spends her time chasing her two dogs, traveling and trying to get her husband to pick up his socks.

For more information on books written by K. J. Kalis and upcoming releases, visit www.karenkalis.com.

CPSIA information can be obtained
at www.ICGtesting.com
Printed in the USA
BVHW041733060220
571663BV00012B/195